MADMAN WALKING

Also available from L.F. Robertson and Titan Books

Two Lost Boys

MADMAN WALKING

L.F. ROBERTSON

TITAN BOOKS

Madman Walking
Print edition ISBN: 9781785652837
E-book edition ISBN: 9781785652844

Published by Titan Books
A division of Titan Publishing Group Ltd
144 Southwark Street, London SE1 0UP

First edition: May 2018
1 2 3 4 5 6 7 8 9 10

"Futility" by Wilfred Owen is from *Wilfred Owen: The War Poems*
(Chatto & Windus, 1994), ed. Jon Stallworthy

A CIP catalogue record for this title is available from the British Library.

Printed and bound in the United States

To Richard Robertson

AUTHOR'S NOTE

Truth really is stranger than fiction. The story that follows is inspired by something that happened, in California, late in the twentieth century. The characters and a lot of the details of the story are invented, but the basic premise—that a man with serious mental illness was charged with murder, allowed to represent himself at his trial, and ended up on death row, even though everyone involved knew that the actual killer had confessed to the crime and exonerated him—is fact.

For a DREAM is a good thing from GOD.

For there is a dream from the adversary which is terror.

For the phenomenon of dreaming is not of one solution, but many.

For Eternity is like a grain of mustard as a growing body and improving spirit.

For the malignancy of fire is oweing to the Devil's hiding of light, till it became visible darkness.

For the Circle may be SQUARED by swelling and flattening.

For the Life of God is in the body of man and his spirit in the Soul.

For there was no rain in Paradise because of the delicate construction of the spiritual herbs and flowers.

For the Planet Mercury is the WORD DISCERNMENT.

For the Scotchman seeks for truth at the bottom of a well, the Englishman in the Heaven of Heavens.

CHRISTOPHER SMART (1722–71), *Jubilate Agno*
(WRITTEN IN ST. LUKE'S HOSPITAL FOR LUNATICS,
BETHNAL GREEN, LONDON)

Still I sing bonnie boys, bonnie mad boys,

Bedlam boys are bonnie

For they all go bare and they live by the air,

And they want no drink nor money.

TOM OF BEDLAM (ENGLISH FOLK SONG)

1

"You have to help me."

The man's voice on the phone both pleaded and commanded. "You have to help me, Ms. Moodie, as an officer of the court. A terrible fraud has been committed against me by the court and the police. I'm the victim of an unconstitutional conspiracy by the district attorney of Taft County and the court and the County of Ventura. Sandra Blaine and Judge Redd must be exposed. God will judge them, the betrayers, he will judge them on the final day—" The voice was rising now, the tone more urgent, the words clattering out in a jumble of legal language and fragments of biblical-sounding passages.

"Dammit, Ms. Moodie, they framed me because they knew they cheated me in my legal settlement," he went on. "They knew I was in jail when the man was killed. I have the proof, all the paperwork. You have to write to the director of the FBI. No, you have to go see him in his office, tell him to come talk to me, they have trampled on my constitutional rights, Ms. Moodie, they have my blood on their hands. And every day you let this happen, you are as guilty as they are. Call my lawyer, Brian Morris, tell him to come see me right away, tell him he needs to petition the Supreme Court to hear my case now—"

He continued talking, stopping only for breath, for the entire fifteen minutes before the prison phone system automatically cuts off inmate calls. Once in a while I managed to utter a syllable or two when it seemed I should respond to something, but I don't think I'd managed ten words by the time the phone went dead in the middle of one of his sentences.

I shook my head a couple of times to clear the clattering from my ears and looked up Brian Morris's phone number on the State Bar's website. He answered on the second ring.

"Mr. Morris," I said, "this is Janet Moodie from the state defender. I just had a call from a client of yours, Howard Henley?"

"Oh, yes, Howard." I could hear a sigh in his voice.

"He seemed pretty agitated," I said. "He wanted me to call you." I left out the part about petitioning the Supreme Court.

"Did he want you to call the heads of the FBI and the CIA and both senators and representatives from his district, and—oh, God, I can't remember all the people he's told me to contact," Morris said, with weary humor.

"Most of them. He wants you to come see him, too," I

said. "He seemed pretty delusional, but really desperate. Is he all right?"

"It depends on what you mean by all right," Morris said. "He's always delusional and desperate; that never changes. I've had his case for two years, and I don't know how many lawyers he's called, not to mention judges, the governor's office—anyone who happens to take his calls. Did he talk about the colonies on Mars?"

"No, not that."

"Poor guy, he's his own worst enemy."

"I can see that," I said.

"Yeah. Thanks for letting me know he called. You may hear from him again, now that he has your phone number."

"Lucky me."

"Yeah, I'm sorry."

That was the first Howard call, something over ten years ago. He did call again; in fact he called me a half-dozen times before apparently giving up and moving on to someone else. By the last call, I flinched when the receptionist said his name. But for some reason I couldn't refuse him. It seemed important, somehow, to hear him out and let him run headlong through his pleas, his patchwork of Old Testament fulminations, and his speculations on outer space.

After me, Howard called almost all the other attorneys in the office. Eventually his name became a rueful joke, a trigger for rolled eyes and guilty laughter among those of us who had been treated to his breathless monologues. And when one of us complained about a difficult client, someone would inevitably say, "Hey, at least you don't have Howard Henley."

And then one late-winter morning a few years later, my husband drove to a lonely park road in the Oakland hills and shot himself.

Terry's death shattered my little family, sending me and our son, Gavin, reeling apart like fragments from an explosion. But it wasn't just a private family tragedy. Terry Moran was famous in the small community of attorneys who defend capital cases—a trial lawyer with a string of miraculous wins; an expert at identifying and litigating the legal and factual issues that can save a client from the death penalty; a speaker at criminal law conferences all over the United States. I was also in that community, but much lower in the pecking order. Along with the genuine sympathy I received from people who stayed close to me in the dark, numb months after Terry died, I learned some uncomfortable lessons about who had befriended me only because of him. And I felt, from some colleagues, particularly those who had been close to Terry, but not me, a hurtful undercurrent of judgment, a conviction that I was somehow negligent in not preventing Terry's death, that I Should Have Seen It Coming.

The next year, I left the state defender's office, everyone I knew, and all of it—the damned sympathy, unspoken blame, and unanswered questions—and moved with my shock, anger, and miscellaneous emotional baggage to an old cabin up the California coast, in a scatter of old farmhouses and vacation cabins called Corbin's Landing. I made a cottage industry of doing what I knew and worked on court-appointed appeals out of my spare bedroom. For a long time I stopped having anything to do with death-penalty cases, except to take phone calls from, and write holiday and birthday cards to, former clients in San Quentin, some of whom had become like extended family over the years in which I'd worked on their cases. I didn't hear from Howard Henley, and I almost forgot about him.

Once, when I was at San Quentin paying a birthday visit to a former client, I heard Howard Henley's voice again, raised in a harangue hardly different from the one he had repeated in each of his phone calls to me. From my spot in one of the facing rows of attorney visiting-cages, I looked around for the source of the voice. It was projecting from one of the cages directly across the passageway. Howard, in his prison blues, was leaning forward, almost rising from his chair, his hands clutching the edges of the small table, his body trembling with tension. He was thin, almost ascetic, with a high forehead, eyes set deep in their sockets, and uncombed salt-and-pepper hair. Across from him, his visitor was sitting back in his chair as if pushed there by the force of Howard's tirade, his eyes on the notepad in front of him and his shoulders hunched as if trying to ward off blows. I felt sorry for him.

2

When Mike Barry called me, I was temporarily incommunicado—out in my yard on a not-too-cold February day, cleft-grafting a dozen apple, pear, and plum saplings at my picnic table. Grafting involves whittling twigs with a very sharp knife, and I'm no expert at it, so I was doing my best to work in undisturbed concentration. I was oh-so-carefully slicing into a rootstock when the knife slipped and sliced into the base of my thumb instead. Blood welled up from the cut, dripping onto the table and the pot with the baby apple tree. Cursing, I joined the twigs together and wrapped up the graft, leaving red smears on the tape, and stormed into the bathroom, holding a paper towel around my thumb to keep from dripping more blood onto my shirt and the floor. The phone in my office rang, and I threw a tube of toothpaste in its general direction as I rummaged through the medicine cabinet in search of bandages.

I was still cursing as, my hand swathed in gauze, I stomped across the room and punched the button to listen to the voicemail. "This is Mike Barry calling for Janet Moodie. Would you please give me a call at—" and a number— not that of the state defender, where he and I had worked together. I called him back, furiously punching keys on his answering-machine menu, until his line rang.

"Michael Barry," Mike's voice said on the other end of the line.

"Walt Klum," I said.

"Janny! Thanks for calling back so fast. No, Walt's fine."

In the state defender's office, Mike and I had been Walter Klum's attorneys for his appeal. Walt had shot his ex-wife, her sister, and her parents, and then tried to kill himself, but the bullet circled inside his skull around his brain, and he had survived, only to be tried for three murders (his wife's sister had survived to testify against him) and sentenced to death. Mike and I had then spent five years putting together what we thought was a compelling case, in a four-hundred-page appellate brief, that Walt wasn't competent to stand trial or fully responsible for his actions at the time of the crimes. He had suffered a traumatic brain injury caused by a truck accident two years before the murders. Medical records presented at Walt's trial showed that he had been in a coma for two months after the accident and that about an eighth of his brain was simply missing, atrophied as the result of trauma and loss of blood supply. His family and friends said his personality had changed after the truck accident. He had gone from being a quiet, easygoing guy to a man who was gloomy, unpredictable, depressed, and prone to sudden attacks of anger and paranoia. In the county jail, tormented by hallucinations and flashbacks and remorse at what he had done, he tried again to commit suicide; and he spent his trial half-asleep from sedatives and psychotropic medications.

The state Supreme Court had given short shrift to our arguments, affirming Walt's conviction and death sentence in a unanimous opinion.

About a year later, the court had appointed Walt a new lawyer to investigate and file a habeas corpus petition, a separate proceeding to present additional evidence that hadn't come out, for whatever reason, in Walt's trial. Mike and I did what we could to help Walt's new attorney, but by the time the habeas petition was filed I'd left the office. Unlike some of my former clients, Walt wasn't inclined to write or call anyone; except for the brief thank-you notes he sometimes sent in response to the Christmas and birthday cards I sent him, I hadn't heard about him in years.

Walt really didn't care much if he lived or died, and he suffered from bouts of black depression and terror, becoming convinced from time to time that his food was being poisoned or that guards were planning to plant some contraband item in his cell as an excuse to search it and then kill him. No regimen of medications tried by the prison doctors seemed to keep him stable for very long. That's why my first thought on hearing Mike's voice after such a long time was that something terrible had finally happened to Walt.

"No, Walt's as well as he ever was, as far as I know. How are you these days?"

It occurred to me that how I was at the moment would probably not interest most of the people I knew from my previous lives, Mike included. So I refrained from mentioning that I was no longer bleeding out from a grafting wound, and said, "Pretty good. How are you?"

"Okay. Enjoying private practice. And you?"

"Same, I guess. How long have you been out of the state defender?"

"Four years—a little less than you. Sue retired from the school district, and we moved north to Sonoma County. We have two grandkids nearby we get to spend more time with; Hannah just had her second. And Adam graduates from law school this year. And my commute is now fifteen minutes, instead of an hour."

"God, how time flies," I said. "You're ahead of me. No grandkids yet. Gavin's in Australia doing a post-doc, and he has a girlfriend, but he isn't married yet. Got you beat about the commute, though. Mine is about thirty seconds."

After a little more small talk, Mike got down to business. "Are you busy at the moment?" he asked.

"I'm just finishing up a habeas petition, but I'll be free in a few weeks."

"Are you interested in another capital case?"

Oh, shit, I thought, but then my curiosity got ahead of my better judgment. "Maybe," I said, doubtfully. "Tell me about it."

"Do you remember Howard Henley?"

"Oh no," I said. "Not Henley. No way."

"Really?" Mike sounded a little downcast. "I took his case, and I could use someone to work with me on it."

"Henley? Really? What were you thinking?"

"Oh, God," Mike sighed. "I let myself be sweet-talked into it by Evelyn Turner at the court."

I chuckled. Evelyn Turner, the state Supreme Court's appointments attorney, had a reputation for being, one might say, persuasive. Her magic was mysterious, but faced with her blandishments, otherwise rational attorneys accepted impossible cases at the court's miserly pay rate, and ended up thanking her for thinking of them.

"You pushover," I said.

Mike laughed. "Yeah. But seriously—would you work with me?"

"Why me?"

"I thought of you because of Walt Klum, actually. And another case or three—you were kind of known in the state defender for your crazy clients."

That was actually news to me; I'd never felt particularly known there for anything except being a constant minor irritant to the little clique of bureaucrats who ran the office.

"Maybe," I said. "Just because it's you and you're flattering me. But… Howard? Is he any better than he was?"

"Not better, no. But he's calmed down some. He's been on medication for a while. He's still crazy, but actually bearable."

"Lovely. So tell me about the case."

"Howard has a habeas corpus petition pending. His lawyer on it was Gordon Marshall."

"Wow."

Gordon Marshall had ascended into the ranks of the elite among death-penalty lawyers by winning a couple of high-profile appeals early in his career. Terry, my late husband, had also occupied that rarified professional space, but he didn't think much of Marshall; in Terry's opinion he was too much about publicity and personal fame, and lazy about working on his cases. Marshall claimed to be a distant descendant of John Marshall, the first Chief Justice of the Supreme Court. Judges loved him.

"How did you get Howard's case from Marshall?" I asked.

"You didn't know?"

"Know what?"

"Marshall had to retire a while ago—had a stroke, apparently. All his court-appointed cases had to be reassigned."

"I'm sorry to hear about Gordon," I said. Whatever I thought about him, the news was sobering. "Jeez, we're all getting old."

"I don't like to think about it," Mike said. "All the old guard are retiring or dying. I don't know half the people at seminars anymore."

"But here we still are until it's our turn."

"Yeah. I don't know if I'll ever be able to afford to retire. But back to Howard—all the briefs were filed, and I thought I'd just be babysitting the case until the petition was denied. I'd had it for about three months when the court issued an order to show cause."

"That's unusual—good news for Howard, though." I couldn't help thinking that having Marshall as his lawyer had a lot to do with an ordinarily merciless court granting Howard a hearing. Marshall had a gift for getting good results for his clients. "What issues is the court interested in?"

"The questions are about innocence: what evidence there was at the time of the trial and what new evidence there might be that Howard wasn't involved in the murder."

"Even better news."

"Yeah. After I read it, I called Evelyn and whined until she agreed to ask the court to pay for a second attorney. I just got the court's okay yesterday."

Call it diminished capacity. Or maybe I was addled by shock and blood loss. But somehow, I found myself agreeing to at least consider working with Mike on Howard's case. "Terrific. I'll send you some of the briefs and the habeas petition, for a little background, and then we can set up a day to meet."

Damn, I thought, as I headed back into the bathroom to replace the blood-soaked bandage on my cut finger, *I should call him back and say no way*. But I didn't. Instead, I printed out the state Supreme Court's opinion affirming Howard's conviction in his appeal and began reading.

3

Confucius supposedly said, "Virtue is never left to stand alone." Like a lot of philosophers, he had no experience with the criminal justice system.

According to the court's opinion, Henley had been charged with capital murder for allegedly hiring another man, Steve Scanlon, to kill a competitor, one Jared Lindahl, in a dispute between small-time drug dealers.

Before Henley's trial his lawyer told the judge he was concerned that Henley wasn't mentally competent to stand trial. The judge appointed two psychologists to evaluate Henley and write reports for the court.

For a criminal defendant to be mentally competent to stand trial, the law requires two things of him. First he has to show he understands the legal proceedings, meaning he has to know basically what he's been charged with, what could happen to him, and which people in the courtroom are the judge, the prosecutor and his own attorney. Second, he has to be able to assist his attorney "in a rational manner."

A defendant can be mentally ill, even psychotic, but if he can manage both those things, he's fit to be tried for his alleged crimes.

Both psychologists decided that Henley was competent. They agreed he understood why he was being prosecuted, but wasn't getting along with his lawyer. One doctor said it wasn't clear whether he was mentally ill or just an eccentric with some strange beliefs. The other concluded that Henley could cooperate with his lawyer, but was choosing not to.

Henley was entitled to a hearing on the question of his competence, but after seeing the reports, his lawyer, perhaps seeing where things were going and trying to salvage what might be left of his relationship with Henley, decided not to pursue the issue. The judge ruled that Henley was mentally competent. Henley promptly fired his lawyer and represented himself from then on.

At his murder trial, Henley didn't cross-examine any of the prosecution witnesses, but he tried to call witnesses of his own: his father, who testified that he had had to give Henley money for his rent the month Lindahl was killed, and two men who had told the police Scanlon confessed the murder to them. Both men said Scanlon had told them more or less the same thing: that Lindahl was killed on orders from the Aryan Brotherhood prison gang and that the guy the police had arrested had had nothing to do with the crime. The district attorney objected, arguing that the two witnesses could testify that Scanlon told them he'd killed Lindahl, but that everything else in their statements was inadmissible hearsay. The judge agreed and excluded the testimony.

The judge's ruling left the prosecutor free to argue to the jury, "You have not heard any evidence—anything—that contradicted our evidence that Howard Henley hired Steve Scanlon to kill Jared Lindahl."

The jury convicted Henley of conspiracy to commit murder and murder for financial gain, a death-penalty offense.

The shock of getting convicted must have jolted Henley briefly into lucidity, because he asked the judge to appoint him an attorney for his penalty phase, saying he thought he was in over his head. The judge refused, and Henley continued to act as his own lawyer. The district attorney presented evidence of a long string of prior convictions and uncharged, mostly minor, crimes—assaults, drug possession, disturbing the peace, resisting arrest, and brandishing a kitchen knife during a confrontation with a police officer.

Henley didn't present any evidence on his own behalf and gave a closing argument which even the state Supreme Court described as "rambling and incoherent." But it affirmed his death sentence nonetheless. The court noted that both the psychologists appointed by the court had said that Henley was competent, and that because Henley was mentally fit to stand trial, he was fit to make the decision to represent himself. He wasn't entitled to a lawyer for his penalty trial because he'd waited too long to ask for one. The court also held that the trial judge had been right when he ruled that the men to whom Scanlon confessed could testify that Scanlon told them he committed the murder but not that Henley wasn't involved. And because that ruling was correct there was nothing wrong with the district attorney arguing to the jury that Henley hadn't produced any evidence that he wasn't guilty. The prosecutor was simply stating the truth, even though she knew of the evidence and had been responsible for keeping it from the jury.

4

Mike emailed me the briefs in Howard's appeal, along with the habeas corpus petition filed after his conviction was affirmed and a packet of police reports about the crime. The facts related in those papers told a story a bit different from the state Supreme Court's opinion.

Jared Lindahl had been killed in Wheaton, a small city in the Central Valley. His body had been found behind the seedy trailer park where Howard was living. When the police asked people in the park if they'd seen anything, two or three said Lindahl had recently started living in a cabin behind the park. Lindahl had recently been released from prison, and he was trouble, stealing from denizens of the trailer park and strong-arming them for the meager amounts of money and valuables they owned. Howard had been selling small quantities of marijuana and pills, they said, and Lindahl had gone to his trailer one night, beaten him up, and taken his money and stash.

Howard had spent the days after the beating in a rage

and had asked a couple of acquaintances in the park if he could borrow a gun to kill Lindahl. The police had arrested Howard for Lindahl's murder, but had been forced to release him when they learned he was in jail on the day Jared Lindahl was shot, serving a weekend for failing to pay a fine for a speeding ticket.

Convinced that Howard must have had something to do with Lindahl's death, the detectives investigating the case kept hunting for evidence that Howard was somehow behind the killing, and they found Freddy Gomez. Freddy, who lived in the trailer park, told them that after the beating, Howard had asked him where he could buy a gun, and Gomez had given him the name of a guy he knew. Gomez had been in Howard's cabin buying weed one day soon after that; Steve Scanlon, a guy who sometimes visited the park, was there, too. Freddy claimed he had heard Howard offer to pay Scanlon to kill Lindahl and had seen him give Scanlon a handgun.

Freddy Gomez wasn't just a good citizen. As he was forced to admit under cross-examination at the preliminary hearing, he was a heroin addict who had just been arrested for trying to kill his girlfriend and possession of heroin for sale. He was desperate to get out of custody, so he wouldn't have to endure the agony of withdrawal from the drug. So he called a jail guard over to his cell and told him he might have some information about the Lindahl killing.

On the basis of Freddy's information, the detectives

arrested Howard for hiring Scanlon to kill Lindahl. Gomez
was released from jail the next day.

Acting on Gomez's information, the detectives went
looking for Scanlon. At first they couldn't find him, but
then they received a tip from a parole officer in El Dorado,
near the Nevada border. A client of his had reported that
Steve Scanlon had visited him and confessed to a murder
in Wheaton. By the time they drove to El Dorado and
interviewed Scanlon's friend, Scanlon was gone. But his
friend said Scanlon had told him he'd killed a man in
Wheaton on orders from the Aryan Brotherhood, and that
the police had arrested another guy who had nothing to do
with the hit. Scanlon was picked up a few days later.

Howard's family hired an attorney for him. The lawyer
declared his doubts about his client's mental competence
after a couple of court hearings in which Howard repeatedly
interrupted the proceedings with rambling rants accusing
the prosecutor of framing him for Lindahl's murder because
he knew the sheriff's son bought cocaine in the trailer park,
and insisting his attorney was working with the prosecution
by refusing to present his alibi defense.

After Howard fired his attorney to represent himself, a
local defense attorney was appointed to be what they call
advisory counsel, someone to be available to help him with
legal questions he might have and to do legwork, like legal
research and interviewing and subpoenaing witnesses, that
a defendant can't easily do from jail. But Howard called

the shots. And he had his own ideas about how to try his case. He exercised his right to a speedy trial and refused to ask for extra time to do any work on the case, so he was picking a jury two months after his motion to represent himself was granted.

Howard's voir dire of the trial jurors consisted of asking a half-dozen jurors whether they had heard that he was in jail on the day of the murder and whether they accepted the truth of the Book of Revelation. He randomly asked a couple whether they knew about the secret colonies NASA had established on Mars. He ignored their answers and challenged no one.

Freddy Gomez had disappeared after testifying at the preliminary hearing in Howard's case, and by the time the case was tried, no one could find him. The prosecutor and a deputy were allowed to read his prior testimony to the jury.

In addition to Gomez's testimony that he had given Howard the name of a gun dealer after the robbery and had later seen Howard give a revolver to Steve Scanlon, the prosecutor presented several witnesses from the trailer park to establish that Howard had been beaten and robbed of drugs and money by Lindahl and that Howard had threatened to kill Lindahl after the robbery. Howard tried to cross-examine the first of them, asking if he knew about a lawsuit Howard had once filed against the County of Ventura and if he was aware that Howard had been in jail on the day of the murder. The prosecutor objected that the evidence wasn't relevant, and the judge agreed. After that, Howard asked no more questions.

The one rational thing he did, presumably on the advice of his advisory attorney, was to try to call the two men to whom Scanlon had confessed—the friend who had reported him to his parole officer, and another man who had reported that Scanlon had told him essentially the same thing when he was in jail waiting for his own trial. After the judge ruled they couldn't testify about anything Scanlon told them beyond the fact that he had killed Lindahl, Howard said, in a rare moment of insight, "I have no way to prove my innocence," and rested.

Howard tried to argue to the jury that he was innocent of the murder. "I had nothing against the man," he said. In her closing argument, the prosecutor hammered at the lack of any evidence presented that Howard was anything but guilty of a murder for hire. "Did you hear any evidence," she asked rhetorically, "that anyone—*anyone*—but Howard Henley had a motive to kill Jared Lindahl?"

At the penalty phase of the trial, the prosecutor presented evidence of violence and criminality in Howard's background, to convince the jury he deserved to die. Howard's record wasn't long, but it wasn't going to make him any friends among the jurors. He had spent a year in a state mental hospital in Florida after being arrested for attacking another man at a homeless shelter. Howard told the police the man had been trying to poison him by putting drain cleaner in his coffee. A psychiatrist from the hospital testified that he believed Howard had faked mental illness in order to avoid going to jail for the attack. A former neighbor testified that Howard had once come to his house with a shotgun and threatened to kill him and his dog because the dog was barking too much. A supermarket clerk said Howard had thrown a cantaloupe at him after an argument over whether he had been shortchanged for some groceries. It seemed that Howard had spent most of his adult life alienating people.

Howard's closing argument—the one which the state Supreme Court had described as "rambling and incoherent" —returned again and again to his insistence that he had been framed for the murder as revenge by the sheriff, interspersed with comparing himself to the early Christian martyrs who were tortured and killed for their faith. Somehow he also managed to work in a prediction that men like Steve Scanlon would someday colonize outer space.

It took the jury just over an hour to come back with a death verdict.

Gordon Marshall, Howard's appointed lawyer for his habeas corpus proceeding, had asked him to agree to see a psychiatrist for an evaluation of his mental health. Howard had filed a motion with the court insisting on having Marshall replaced as his lawyer—a request the court denied in a one-sentence order.

Even without the benefit of a psychologist's opinion, Marshall had no trouble finding evidence, including psychiatric records and declarations from relatives, that Howard had been mentally ill for a long time. In the habeas petition, he asked the court to overturn Howard's murder conviction because Howard was mentally incompetent and should never have been allowed to go to trial, let alone represent himself. Howard responded by filing a complaint against him with the State Bar.

For most of the clients I'd worked with, the path that led them to prison had begun with a traumatizing childhood of abuse, neglect, and family disintegration. Howard's background and upbringing had been surprisingly stable.

He had grown up in Wheaton, where his father had started out managing an auto repair shop and then become a partner in a car dealership; his mother had worked as a teacher and then the company's bookkeeper. Howard was their first child. After him there had been another baby boy who had been born with a fatal brain anomaly and died soon after birth, and then two more sons, Robert and Kevin, and a daughter, Corinne.

Neither Bob nor Corinne had any use for Howard. In his declaration, Bob said that even as a child Howard had been overbearing and weird. "When we were small we lived in a house where the boys all shared a bedroom," Bob had written, "and Howard drew a line around his area with masking tape. If he saw me or Kevin cross the line he'd throw a temper tantrum."

Howard did well enough in high school to get admitted

to Cal Poly, the state university in San Luis Obispo, but he never finished his first year. Early in his third quarter he tried to commit suicide by swallowing a bottle of aspirin. He spent the next year in a mental hospital and never returned to school.

When he was in his early twenties Howard had held a few jobs, but he never lasted long, because he'd either be fired or leave. After the last one and a fight with his father that ended in another mental hospital commitment, he bought an old motorcycle and disappeared for a couple of years. From time to time he would call his mother and ask her to send him some money; she remembered that once he called from Texas and another time from Florida. Eventually he returned home, sunburnt and rail-thin, without the motorcycle.

For a while he lived in a small apartment over his parents' garage, but when he threatened to kill them and burn down the garage during an argument over his housekeeping, his father called the police. Howard spent a couple of weeks in the locked ward of the county mental hospital, and after he was released he left again, for southern California. When he came back again, his parents gave him rent for an apartment in another part of town, and then another after he was evicted from the first one. His history of mental disability made him eligible for a small monthly welfare payment, which covered most of his expenses, since Howard, whatever his other problems might be, was frugal.

He became something of a local character to the police in

Wheaton because he was constantly in trouble with the law for minor crimes like disturbing the peace and shoplifting. Once he was charged with burglary for breaking into a church, after a group of volunteers found him asleep on the floor of the multipurpose room, surrounded by an odd collection of trophies, candles, and crucifixes retrieved from offices and closets in the building. He pled guilty to breaking and entering and spent thirty days in jail.

A few years before Lindahl was murdered, Howard was hit by a bus in the city of Ventura while walking across a street. He broke his ankle, but was otherwise unhurt. The Henleys' family lawyer filed a claim with the county and got him a small settlement. Although Howard had agreed to the settlement, he soon grew angry that he had been paid too little. He filed pro se lawsuits trying to reopen the case until he was barred from court as a vexatious litigant. He wrote long, incoherent letters, citing strings of legal decisions and statutes, to the mayor, the controller, and every other city official whose name he could find. He invaded city council meetings and harangued the supervisors until he was permanently barred, which resulted in his filing yet another lawsuit against the county.

When he was arrested for Lindahl's murder, he was convinced that the murder charges were brought in retaliation for his attempts to re-litigate his personal injury case and that the charges were part of a conspiracy to silence him.

Oh, what fun, I thought, as I finished reading the last of the briefs. Still not sure whether I wanted to get involved again with Howard, I called Mike Barry and made a date to see him to talk about the case.

5

"So Howard's actually innocent; now what?"

I felt old and cynical saying it. Not that Mike is that much younger than I am, but he was—he'd always been—enthusiastic about his cases, his clients and his life in general. Walt Klum, who lived in his depression like a tortoise in its shell, couldn't stand seeing Mike; and while we worked on his case, visiting Walt had defaulted to me, I guess because my energy was low enough to keep him fairly comfortable.

Mike hadn't changed much since I'd last seen him. His light brown hair was a little more interspersed with gray, but he was still good-looking, and the energy that had been too much for Walt Klum when we were at the state defender's still showed in his quick smile and his upbeat attitude about Howard's case.

"Hey," Mike said, "we're getting an evidentiary hearing to prove it."

"Not quite," I told him. The state Supreme Court had issued an order to the referee—the judge who would be appointed to preside over Howard's hearing—to take evidence and make recommendations on a specific set of questions. One was whether evidence was available at the time of the trial that Lindahl's killing had been ordered by the Aryan Brotherhood and not Howard, and what that evidence was, and whether a jury might have reached a different verdict had they heard it. The other was whether there was evidence not available at the time of Howard's trial that warranted setting aside his conviction.

"If we win, he'll get another trial, that's all."

"Close enough," Mike said. "If we win, I don't think they'll want to try him again. There's a lot of evidence out there supporting Scanlon's story. I've hired an investigator, Dan Connelly, and we went to see Scanlon right after the order to show cause came down."

"You found Scanlon?" I asked. "Is he still in prison?"

"In a prison in Utah."

That surprised me. "How did that happen?"

"Kind of a long story. I guess while he was on the run after killing Lindahl he did some robberies in Salt Lake City. A few years ago he was nailed for one of them by a DNA cold hit and extradited to Utah. He pled guilty after California and Utah agreed that he could serve out his sentence in Utah. The move probably saved his life."

"How was that?"

"He was in the AB, but he dropped out after they sent someone after him and almost killed him. He was stabbed pretty badly—almost died from loss of blood. After that he debriefed."

"Debriefed?"

"Means he sat down with some state prison gang investigators and told them everything he knew about the AB. Named names. Wrote an essay for the prison about all of it."

"And now he's permanently on the AB's hit list," I said.

"Definitely."

"And that's how the prison system is protecting him?"

Mike shrugged. "Yeah. He was lucky, as these things go."

"So he's willing to talk with you? He kind of blew Gordon Marshall off, as I recall."

"Yeah. But back then he was still in the AB. Now he doesn't have much to lose by talking. And he seems to feel genuinely bad that Henley's facing death because of him. Wants to set things straight."

"So what now?"

"I have Dan Connelly looking for the two guys Scanlon confessed to. There's Sunderland, the guy Scanlon hid out with, who told his parole officer what Scanlon told him, and another fellow, Niedermeier, the one he talked to in the jail. He's also trying to locate some of the people from the trailer park named in the police reports."

"Has he had any luck tracking down Freddy Gomez? He seems pretty pivotal."

"Yeah. Unfortunately, Gomez is dead."

"Damn. What happened, an overdose?"

"No, prison stabbing. He got arrested again not long after Howard's trial and sent to the joint. I'll never be able to prove it, but I wouldn't be surprised if the police had a pretty good idea where Gomez was before Howard's trial but decided it was better if the jury didn't see and hear him. That said, after he'd snitched on Scanlon the Aryan Brotherhood had him on their list."

"Oh."

"Yeah. Dan's trying to find out whether he talked to anyone about the case before he was killed. I'm going to see if I can get Scanlon's debriefing report, and we need to file a discovery motion, to get access to the prosecution's files and witness interviews. I was hoping you'd do that."

"Sure. Was there a previous one?"

"No. For some reason Marshall never filed one. He sent an informal request to the DA, but she just wrote back she'd see him in court, and he left it there."

"Huh." Not filing a motion was an unusual move; I wondered what Marshall had been thinking.

Mike looked at a clock half buried under papers on his desk. "You want to grab an early lunch? I have a court appearance at one thirty."

"Sure."

"Oops, before we go—" Mike rummaged around the surface of his desk and produced an envelope. "My paralegal made this for you—it's the rest of the files we got from

Marshall. I had all the paper materials scanned."

I folded the envelope around the thumb drive I could feel inside it, and tucked it into an inner pocket of my jacket.

6

We walked through the rain to a Mexican restaurant near Mike's office. Over burritos and chiles rellenos, we caught up a bit on each other's lives.

"You seem to have a good office setup," I said.

"Yes," he answered. "It's a suite with four attorneys. Mary does secretarial work for all of us. Annie, our paralegal, is a freelancer; she's been working for me and one of the other lawyers. Saves money over having to pay the whole cost of an office and staff."

"Nice," I said.

"Sue and I sold our place in Oakland; now we have an acre just outside Petaluma. It's just us, now that the kids are grown, so it's pretty quiet. Sue volunteers at the food bank and sings in a community chorus; she's having a great time being retired. What are you up to these days?"

"I have a little house in the redwoods off Highway One, above Fort Ross. I do court-appointed appeals, mostly; I work out of my spare bedroom."

"Are you in touch with any of the old guard at the state defender?"

"Not really."

"I don't think it's changed much since you left. A couple of people retired, a couple of new hires." Mike paused for a second or two. "You know, I forgot to even ask you if you've decided you want to work on Howard's case."

"Will he call me more than once a week?"

"I'm sure he'll try. But feel free not to take his calls, if you don't want to. I think he's used to it."

"I must be crazy."

"Yeah, that's what I thought when Evelyn called me."

"Yet here we are."

"Yep." Mike smiled. He had a great smile. Years ago, when we were both a lot younger and better-looking, I had sometimes found him almost dangerously attractive, to the point that I occasionally wondered what might have happened if we hadn't both been married to other people. Even now, he still had a good deal of his old charm. "So, I take it you're in?"

"Oh, hell, I guess," I said.

He exhaled. "Okay, then." I realized as he did that he'd actually not been sure I'd be interested—but then, neither had I. "Great. I'll call Evelyn and get the paperwork going to ask for your appointment."

After we separated I did some shopping, since I was temporarily back in civilization—a hardware store, a plant nursery, the supermarket—before starting for home.

The drive took me through miles of bright green hills, wet with winter rains and dotted with the long barns and little white houses of old dairy farms, and then up Highway One, with the hills rising steeply to one side and the Pacific Ocean, blue-gray and seemingly infinite, on the other. I navigated the rain-slick road, thankful that there were almost no other cars on it with me. The ghosts of bad memories raised by talking about the past faded with every mile of highway, and I felt tired, but more myself again, as I pulled in to the space near my door.

7

"Congratulations," Mike said, when he called a week later. "You're now second counsel for Howard Henley."

"I've changed my mind."

"Too late!" he said brightly. "We should probably go see Howard. When are you free to visit?"

"Oh, any old time."

"Week from Wednesday okay?"

"You have too much energy. But yes."

It takes three hours or more, depending on traffic, to drive from Corbin's Landing to San Quentin, where the state keeps its death row. On the Wednesday in question I woke up, as I generally do before prison visits, in a state of free-floating anxiety an hour before my alarm went off.

A March rainstorm swept sheets of mist and rain across the coast highway, and I inched around the tight turns and switchbacks, acutely conscious of the cliffs beside me plunging to the invisible Pacific far below, and the fact that a cup of tar-colored Italian roast hadn't completely blasted the mists of sleep out of my brain. For that first half-hour, I longed for the second cup of coffee in the cupholder in my car, but didn't dare take a hand off the steering wheel to grab it or lower my guard away long enough to drink.

On the freeway in Marin, someone far ahead of me had inconsiderately skidded into the rear of another car, and I inched for half an hour in a stop-and-go backup, cursing the accident, the driver who caused it, the commuters in their cars ahead of me, and my worn windshield wipers, which smeared the glass with streaks of oily water.

I reached San Quentin a half-hour late to our appointment. Mike wasn't in the parking lot or the long, drafty shed outside the gatehouse where visitors waited for their turn to be processed—a bureaucratic word that suggested we would emerge from the shed as some sort of lunch meat. I rang the electric bell at the gatehouse door, and the lock clicked open with a buzz, letting me into the relative warmth of the visitor processing area.

The guard at the desk started to tell me I couldn't keep my umbrella, but before I started to plead for a dispensation, a second guard at the X-ray machine told him umbrellas were okay. As I put my raincoat back on after walking through the metal detector, I thanked him. "No problem," he answered. "You look like you haven't been having a good day."

San Quentin State Prison is a bleak sandstone fortress built on a peninsula on the bay north of San Francisco. When the state put its first lockup there, soon after the

Gold Rush, the place was a muddy sandbar in the middle of nowhere, with the breadth of San Francisco Bay between it and the relative civilization of the city. Times change, and the prison now looms over water views for which people down the road in Tiburon and Sausalito pay tens of millions of dollars.

On this unlovely spring morning, the bay was choppy and dirty gray, half obscured by rain and fog. The wind threatened to turn my umbrella inside out, and rain blew in under it. By the time I had made the trek to the visiting building I was cold, damp, and full of self-pity; and my papers and legal pad, wrapped in a plastic supermarket bag because briefcases are prohibited, were starting to go limp.

As I came out of the rain into a small vestibule and waited for a barred gate behind me to close and another gate into the visiting area to open, I saw Mike and Howard in one of the cages that pass there as attorney-client meeting rooms. Howard was talking, pointing, and gesturing, a stack of papers and envelopes on the table in front of him. Mike was writing something down on a legal pad. As the inner gate rolled back, he looked up, saw me, and rolled his eyes. Howard went on talking.

Inside the visiting area, I left my ID with a guard seated behind a window in the small foyer and put my umbrella in a wastebasket with a sign taped on it that said, "Visitors Leave Umbrellas Here." I walked over to the little cage containing Howard and Mike. Howard fell silent and turned, unsmiling, toward the door and me.

"Sorry I'm late," I said. Another guard appeared nearby, waiting to let me into the cage, and I felt introductions could wait. "Can I get you anything from the machines?" I asked.

"No," Howard said, as though I'd proposed bringing pizza to a church service. Mike shook his head. "Nothing to eat for me," he said. "Maybe a coffee, sugar, no cream."

The guard moved aside as I turned, with an apologetic smile, to walk toward the vending machines. When I reappeared at the cage, with two coffees and a package of cookies on a plastic tray, she let me into the cell and locked it behind me with a clash of keys and metal bars.

It has puzzled me, over the years, why schizophrenia seems to bring out the worst detritus from the sufferers' subconscious minds. The negativity and nastiness that sane people brick up inside walls of denial seem, much too often, to spew like venom from people whose inhibitions have been freed by psychosis. Howard wasn't walking down the middle of some city sidewalk shouting Bible verses and calling the women he passed whores, but it appeared to me, from the dark expression on his face, that anger and hostility were percolating inside his splintered mind.

He had aged, but he was recognizably the man I'd seen briefly all those years ago. His hair, now receding and completely gray, was brushed back from his forehead, which seemed even higher, his sunken eyes larger. He was gaunt; his prison blue shirt hung in folds from his shoulders. The cuffs of a worn thermal undershirt, more yellow than white, showed beyond the ends of his shirtsleeves. He was holding a pair of dark-framed prison-issue eyeglasses in one hand and tapping them, lightly but impatiently, on the table in front of him.

I smiled a greeting, moved the coffees and cookies from the tray to the small table and stood the tray on the floor against the bars of the cell. "I'm Janet Moodie," I said then, holding out a hand. I wondered if Howard would remember me from the phone calls when I was at the state defender, but he didn't seem to recognize my name. Reflexively, his hand came up from the table, clasped mine for a fraction of a second, and then returned to where it had been, next to his stack of papers. Mike, I noticed, had a similar pile about half as high next to his legal pad. I moved past Mike to the only remaining chair at the small table and sat down, setting my folder on the table in front of me.

"Howard and I were talking about the issues for the evidentiary hearing," Mike said.

"There's only one issue," Howard broke in, impatiently. "The conspiracy between Sandra Blaine, Judge Redd, and Ventura County to frame me for this man's murder. Expose that conspiracy, that's what you need to do, and they will have to let me go."

"Howard tells me," Mike said, and I could tell he was choosing his words carefully, "that Lindahl was killed as part of a conspiracy to get Howard convicted of capital murder so that the county could stop him from reopening his accident case."

"But didn't Steve Scanlon confess that he'd killed him for the Aryan Brotherhood?" I asked.

"No, no, no," Howard broke in, shaking his head emphatically. "Steve was tricked into killing Lindahl. Freddy Gomez told him that Lindahl had drugs and money and the AB wanted him dead. Freddy was part of the conspiracy. He was supposed to find someone to kill Lindahl and then pin the crime on me, so he tricked Steve into doing it. I wanted Steve to testify at my trial and tell the truth about what happened, but they wouldn't let him. He took the Fifth."

"But that was because he was charged, too," I said. "He wouldn't want to confess to the crime with his own trial coming up, would he?"

Howard looked at me as though I'd just said something truly idiotic. "He didn't need to take the Fifth. It was too late; he'd already confessed. And the man he confessed to, Sunderland, he was afraid of them, too. I had to subpoena him, and he tried to avoid my investigator. Sandra Blaine threatened to have his parole revoked if he testified. The judge covered up for her by refusing to let him testify."

"Oh," I said.

"Lindahl's father wanted him dead. He was a bigwig in the Taft County Transportation Department; Lindahl's mother is his ex-wife. He wanted to get his son out of the way because he was an embarrassment to him. And if he could get me convicted for the crime, he'd get the restitution money, too."

"What restitution money?" Mike asked. Restitution is money the court can order a convicted criminal to pay his victims for economic losses resulting from the crime. "The court didn't order you to pay any restitution."

Howard looked intently into Mike's eyes. "That's what I thought," he said. "But money is being taken from my books."

"That's not good," Mike said.

"No, it isn't," Howard announced in a tone that suggested Mike was a bit slow not to have grasped the seriousness of the situation.

"Do you have proof?" Mike asked. "A statement of your trust account?"

"My counselor gave me one," he said, "a couple of months ago. He said the only deductions were for canteen and routine things like a doctor appointment and eyeglasses. But there was too little money left."

"You know they charge five dollars for a medical appointment," Mike said.

"Yeah," Howard said, almost reluctantly.

"And did you actually get new glasses?"

"The doctor told me I needed them for reading. But I don't believe the glasses cost as much as I was charged. And the canteen I bought, I'm sure it wasn't as much as they deducted. I think they're skimming money and sending it to old Lindahl. I want you to investigate it and make them stop."

"I'll see what I can do," Mike said, "but it'll be hard to prove."

"Huh," Howard said. "But they need to be stopped. They're committing a crime."

"Yeah, but it may be easier if I just send you a bit more when I put money on your books." *The gentle art of bribery,* I thought. Sending a client some money they can use at the prison canteen helps smooth the rough places in their lives.

Howard wasn't satisfied. "That isn't the point," he said, tensely. "My mother sends me money, too, and they're stealing it from her. It's a crime; you have to take it to the district attorney and get them prosecuted."

"Okay, I'll see what I can do."

"That's not good enough," Howard said. "You have to succeed. Their crimes must be brought to light."

Mike admitted defeat. "I'll try," he said.

Howard then directed his attention to me. "Are you Mr. Barry's investigator?" he asked.

Mike said, "No, this is the lawyer I was telling you about, the one I've brought on as second counsel."

"Oh. Have you met Steve Scanlon?"

"No, not yet," I said.

"You should get to know him. He's got greatness in him. He's the kind of man who can control his fate." Thinking of what I knew of Scanlon's career, I wondered what Howard had in mind.

Howard went on. "I'm here for my beliefs. I didn't kill

anyone. They all know that. But I know God's plan for sending men like Scanlon to form colonies on the planets of other stars. I've been telling the truth to the world, and they knew they had to get rid of me." He leaned toward us, and his voice rose and took on an evangelical tone. "They knew I was exposing their plans, their corruption, all the evil inside their souls. They accused others, but all the time they were doing the same or worse behind their own doors. When I exposed them, they turned their power on me, to silence me. They're trying to silence me here, by keeping me from making phone calls. But I will not be silenced. If I am executed I will be a martyr, and my death will bring everything into the light and will destroy them. Their temples will fall around them, and the cities built on their corruption will be crushed."

Ulp.

"I hope you won't have to die to accomplish this," Mike said.

Howard deflated a little. "I would like to think that could be so. I don't want to die," he said, his face sad and worn. "Christ didn't want to die. He asked God to take the cup from his lips."

"I don't want you to have to go through that," Mike said.

Howard looked doubtful. "If you can expose them another way. I don't know."

"Showing that you were wrongly convicted would be a start."

"I guess." Howard brightened a little, as another thought came into his mind. "Do you read your Bible?" he asked me.

"Not as much as I probably should," I said evasively.

"You should. Start with the Book of Revelation. It will tell you everything."

"Okay," I said. "I'll do that."

"You'll see what I'm talking about."

I nodded.

"The Beast walks among us, even now."

From the papers in his file, Mike pulled out several authorizations for releasing records. "Howard, we need you to sign these, so that we can investigate your case."

Howard pulled them across the table and stared at the top sheet for a moment, frowning. "These are the same ones you asked me to sign before," he said.

"Yes," Mike agreed.

Howard pushed them back across the table. "I can't sign these," he said.

"But we need access to records to investigate your case."

Howard was firm. "Not these. You don't need information about me to expose the people who put me here."

"Okay." Mike put the papers back on the stack.

A couple of guards were moving down the row of cubicles, giving prisoners and lawyers the five-minute warning of the end of visiting time. As they approached our cell, Howard appeared to remember something and began riffling through the documents he had brought with him. He pulled out a transcript with handwritten notes between the lines and in the margins. He handed it to Mike. "Read this," he said. "It will tell you what's going on."

Mike took it and added it to his materials. "Thanks," he said.

The guard, a young Hispanic woman, came to our door. "Five minutes," she said, and we nodded. Howard glanced up at her and then began putting his papers into a large manila envelope. We sat, mostly in awkward silence, until she returned to take Howard back to the cell block.

"If you need anything," Mike said to Howard, "let me know." Howard nodded, then stood with his back to the cage door as the guard removed the metal cover from a smallish slot in the gate and reached through it to lock a set of handcuffs onto his wrists. That finished, he moved away from the door, and she locked the metal cover and then unlocked the door.

Howard's envelope was still on the table. He nodded toward it. "Would you slip that under my arm?" he asked Mike. He lifted his left arm as far as the cuffs would let him, and Mike slid the envelope between his upper arm and his body.

We followed them out and turned left toward the visitors' entrance, as the shuffling procession of Howard and the prison guard turned right, and the painted metal door to the interior of the prison opened and closed again behind them.

"Okay, that was intense," I said. "So Scanlon's an interplanetary colonizer, huh?"

"Yes, and the Beast of Revelations walks among us. And two courts found him competent to represent himself," Mike said, shaking his head.

8

Back home again, I let myself, my dog Charlie, and the two cats, Effie and Nameless, into the kitchen, and put groceries away, then checked my phone for messages; I've kept a landline in my house because cellphone service is nonexistent where I live. There were no voicemails. Then I called my neighbor, Ed Harrison.

Ed and I have a sort of buddy system that has grown tacitly over a half-dozen years in Corbin's Landing. Ed is a carpenter, cabinetmaker, and handyman, and I hire him now and again to build or repair things around my place. We both live alone, and after dark we can see the lights of one another's houses through the trees. We take care of each other's dogs; we buy groceries for each other when we go into town; and over time, we've taken to calling one another every day or so, on one excuse or another, but really as a sort of welfare check.

Ed answered at the same time as his machine picked up the call. "Sorry," he said, "I was on a ladder."

"No problem. I just called because I have groceries for you."

"Fine—bring 'em over. Want some coffee? I do, so I guess I'll start boiling water."

I changed quickly into rain boots, and bag over my shoulder, flashlight in hand, and with Charlie running back and forth in front of me on his short Corgi legs, started across my back yard and down the path through the woods between our houses. The path had been there when I moved in, but so overgrown it was barely visible. Ed and I had found it, and walking back and forth on errands had opened it up a bit, although it was still a narrow track snaking around tree trunks and rocks and, on a day like today, dripping with moisture from the oaks and redwoods overhead. It gave me a feeling that we were connecting with the history of our remote little settlement. I had found different things—an old glass marble, a fragment of patterned china, a Liberty head penny—on the path, and wondered who had dropped them there.

Once, in a maudlin moment, I had speculated that at some time in the past before either Ed or I lived in Corbin's, the inhabitants of the two houses had also been friends. "Could be," he had answered, "but it was probably made by rum runners or smugglers." The north coast had a checkered history: it was isolated, and a fishing boat could easily sail down from Canada, pull into one of the little dog-hole harbors and unload a cargo of cases of liquor or any other portable contraband, to be hidden in the barns and sheds of householders and moved in farmers' wagons down the old stage roads to Santa Rosa and points south.

Ed's door was ajar, the opening radiating warmth and light and a faint smell of wood smoke and wet dog. His dog Pogo, after a perfunctory bark, trotted out to touch noses with Charlie and get a pat on his big yellow head. Leading the small pack of dogs, I walked through Ed's crowded living room and into his kitchen, which smelled like coffee and cooking. Ed was at the counter, pouring hot water into his coffee press. Pogo assessed the proceedings and wandered off to a dog bed near the back door, where he sighed and flopped heavily down. Charlie examined Pogo's kibble dish and then lay down under the kitchen table.

"Got rained out of work today," Ed said, "so I made some chili. Recipe made a lot; would you like some to take home?"

"Sure," I said. "Save me cooking dinner—it's been a long day."

I sat down at the table, and he came over and began emptying the bag I'd brought. "Ah, Scotty's coffee—good stuff." He put away the rest—avocados, strawberries, butter, yoghurt, milk. "What do I owe you?"

"Twenty will do it."

He retreated to the back of the house and returned with a twenty-dollar bill and gave it to me. "Coffee should be ready," he said, and turned to the counter. He slowly pushed down the plunger in the press, while I got two cups from a cabinet above the sink and a gallon of milk from the fridge. Carrying our cups, we sat down opposite one another at the table. Ed knew me well enough to have left a lot of room in my cup for milk, and I filled it, watching the coffee turn the color of ice cream, then gratefully took a drink.

"So, did you take the case?" Ed said.

"Yeah."

"The crazy guy, right?"

I hung my head in mock shame. "Yeah, I guess."

Ed gave a laugh. "I could see you were going to." He paused for a second, and his face became more serious. "This is the one where the guy was supposedly killed by the Aryan Brotherhood?"

"The very one," I said.

"Jeez," Ed said. "You be careful. When I was living in Oregon I knew a guy who had some dealings with them. It didn't end well."

"Not what I need to hear," I said.

"It was a lot different from what you're doing. Guy was a meth cook down in the desert in San Berdoo, and the local bigwig thought he made them a bad batch. So they kept him prisoner in a house for a week, made him make them another one. He said the whole time they kept talking about whether to let him go after he finished or just kill him. In the end, I guess, cooler heads prevailed, and they took him home. He said he packed up and left that night for Oregon. When I knew him, he was a born-again Christian, said he never wanted to have anything to do with drugs ever again."

He was lucky, I thought. I'd known of cases—Howard's included, it appeared—where people were killed for less than that.

"Really," I said. "You didn't have to tell me that."

"I'm sorry," he said. "I didn't mean to upset you. It's just that I guess we're old friends at this point, and I don't want to see you put yourself in danger."

I reached across the table and took hold of his forearm. "Thanks," I said. "I don't think I'll be, but I feel better."

"Hey, we take care of each other," Ed said. "Watch out for your cup."

I sat back quickly and steadied it.

After I finished my coffee, Ed ladled about a quart of chili into a jar for me. By the time I got home, I'd decided that what it really needed to go with it was some corn bread. I called Ed and told him I was going to make a batch, and when it was done, I took half of it over to him, then walked back to eat my solitary, comfortable dinner in my own kitchen. I'd had enough of socializing; I was ready to be alone for a while.

9

"Shit. Shit, shit, shit, shit, shit."

I was pacing back and forth in my living room, holding both hands over my ears.

"Shit," I said again, more out of habit, at this point, than anything else.

I walked into the kitchen, still holding my head, gripping fistfuls of hair, then finally let go to retrieve a box of oyster crackers from the pantry, pull out a handful, and pop them into my mouth one and two at a time until I felt a little calmer. A call from Howard will do that to you.

It had been fifteen minutes cycling through a shorter version of the same rant as the prison visit, with a few more twists: we weren't helping him; he didn't kill anyone; he was in jail when it happened; this was all a conspiracy by the prosecutor, the judge, and the mayor of Wheaton to have him executed; Mike and I weren't taking his case seriously; he suspected we were in on the conspiracy; he would report us to the State Bar and sue us for malpractice; I had to come see him and bring an investigator and an FBI agent, or else. And on, and on, until the fifteen minutes the prison allowed for his call were up, and the line went dead in mid-sentence.

Howard made me wonder how many people were on death row because they were just pains in the ass.

I ate another couple of oyster crackers. At least I wouldn't have to talk to Howard for another two weeks. That was the deal Mike and I had made with him, that we'd each take one call from him a week. We lived up to our end of the bargain. Howard, on the other hand, called every couple of days. But since he had to call collect, I could refuse his calls. I'd even gotten to the point where I could do it without much guilt.

And then there were the letters. He sent Mike and me each about one a week—handwritten, the lines of oddly regular, rounded letters crowded together, on both sides of each page. He also wrote around the margins, top, bottom, and sides of every page, filling them with notes, quotes from statutes and cases, biblical passages—afterthoughts, perhaps, or meant to illustrate points in the letters; it was hard to tell.

I'd been working on Howard's case for less than a month, and already it had come to this.

"Crazy," I muttered to myself as I put away the cracker box and walked outside my kitchen door to breathe some fresh air and try to shake Howard out of my ears and brain. "I have clearly gone completely nuts."

10

The Brand. That's what the Aryan Brotherhood calls itself. White supremacists seem to love a certain offhand self-aggrandizement.

Not long after meeting with Mike I spent a morning reading Internet articles on the AB, my reactions alternating between irritated and queasy. The stories I read had a certain similitude, because they all seemed to be based on revelations by the same gang dropouts. Convicts and gang members like bullshitting their interviewers, and I took some of their accounts with a grain of salt, but they contained enough of what a scientist might call convergent data to give a lot of them a ring of truth. The photos showed a few of the most infamous of the AB shot-callers, old but scary-looking guys in prison grays, the blue-black tattoos on their necks and arms especially creepy against the pallor of wan, sagging skin.

At the state defender I'd handled a number of capital appeals involving defendants in street gangs. Gangs in general seem like violent boys' clubs for undersocialized adolescents. They have rites and insignia and signs, and rules and understandings that amount to the same thing: solidarity, loyalty, respect, and knowing your place in the hierarchy, never leaving, and never snitching. Street gangs are violent and dangerous, but mostly only in their own neighborhoods because they tend to occupy small territories and fight their turf wars with equally small rival gangs nearby. But prison gangs are another story.

Prison gangs are better organized, probably because they're run by men who are nominally grown-up. The structure still seems geared to men operating at the social level of teenagers, but the people controlling them are older and more savvy, and worse, into money and power. The major gangs—whites, Hispanics, and African Americans all have their clubs—are much bigger than the average street gang, with a wider reach and the ability to run ongoing criminal operations for profit. And through their families, former inmates, and supporters outside and on the prison staff, they recruit and operate both in and out of the prisons.

Judging from some of the crime stories related in the Internet pieces I was reading, the Aryan Brotherhood appeared to be pretty fond of gratuitous bloodshed. On the absolute loyalty vector, the Aryan Brotherhood claims to have a doctrine of "blood in, blood out," meaning that you have to do a killing for the Brand to graduate from being an "associate," a loyal foot soldier for the gang, to a full member, and that once you join, if you later try to leave the gang, you will be killed—presumably by some other wannabe hoping to "make his bones," another fine macho phrase for killing someone to qualify for a place in the club. That struck me as possibly unrealistic, if only because it would lead to an awful lot of carnage, but I found myself thinking it was probably better for the average person's health and wellbeing to stay out of the way of the AB and aspiring associates.

Where my reading started to connect to Howard's case was when the articles talked about people who get marked for death by the gang. Mostly they're snitches, suspected child molesters, or gang associates who have committed some infraction, like stealing drugs or money from the gang or failing to carry out an assignment from a member. In the colorful vocabulary of gangs, such traitors are "greenlighted," or in the Aryan Brotherhood's own term, "in the hat." What this means is that any gang member or associate, or someone with aspirations to rise in the gang, is allowed, even required, to kill them if they have an opportunity. Scanlon had told his buddy Sunderland that Lindahl had sold drugs for the AB in prison and had embezzled money from them, that he was in the hat, and that Scanlon had been given orders to better himself by doing him in.

For Mike, the challenge would be proving that Scanlon was telling the truth. Sandra Blaine, the prosecutor in both Howard's and Scanlon's trials, had argued, in her successful bid to keep Sunderland off the witness stand, that Scanlon's claim was an empty boast, an attempt to boost his stature among his acquaintances by claiming that his murder of Lindahl was something more exciting than a revenge killing done for whatever Howard could pay him in money and drugs. Freddy Gomez had claimed Scanlon told him he'd received five thousand dollars and eight ounces of meth from Howard—a claim even Blaine argued was probably an exaggeration after Howard's father had testified that he had given Howard money for his rent that month because Howard had been forced to spend part of his disability check to have a tooth pulled.

Eventually the content of the Internet articles started to repeat itself, and I figured I'd had enough of the wrinkles and skin pores of old gangsters.

After lunch and an hour digging planting holes for the last of the trees I'd grafted the year before, I spent the rest of the afternoon watching the video of a client confessing to drowning her two small children in the bathtub of their apartment. The videotape of the confession and the interrogation that led to it had been played at her trial, after a motion to suppress it had been denied; and the question whether the confession was legally obtained was an issue in the appeal. My client was a very young, developmentally disabled woman, a child herself, really, who had had two babies before she turned sixteen. She had drowned them and tried to kill herself with an overdose of pills after the babies' father acquired another girlfriend. Her case didn't involve the death penalty because she was a minor, seventeen years old, when she committed the crimes. She had been sentenced to life in prison. I could see there would be a lot to argue about in the way the police had cajoled and pressured her into confessing, but watching it all happen was hard, and the girl's confession itself, full of long hesitations, bouts of uncontrollable weeping, and apologies, with the homicide detectives feigning sympathy to keep her talking and suggesting incriminating details when her memory wavered, was painful to sit through.

I was relieved when I looked at the clock and realized it was time to meet my friend Harriet for the exercise class she had talked me into. I changed into a T-shirt and my stretched-out yoga pants, threw a raincoat on over them, called her to tell her I was on my way, and headed out the door. For once, I was actually looking forward to it.

Harriet was one of the first friends I made after retreating to Corbin's Landing. We had met one another at a garden club lecture at the Santa Rosa public library, after I asked a question about growing tomatoes over on the coast. She came up to me after the talk, a fairly tall, angular woman with short gray hair and a matter-of-fact manner, and we compared notes on where we lived and found we were nearly neighbors; her house was on the ridge, about a mile from mine. Since then, she had become not only my garden mentor but a substantial part of my social life, bringing me to garden club events and signing me up, along with her partner, Bill, for volunteer work for the community center and her church. She didn't mind that I wasn't religious, and I liked the feeling of helping people in a solid, tangible way, by things like serving food and giving away canned goods and school supplies.

Harriet and I had another bit of common ground: her first husband and their eight-year-old son had been killed many years ago, when the pickup they were in had been hit by a tractor-trailer. Her attitude, a quiet way of looking the worst that can happen to you in the face, lifting up your chin and moving ahead with the work of life, made me examine, finally, the way I'd let pain and self-pity control me in the years after Terry's suicide.

We traded driving to exercise class, and usually Harriet's friend Molly met us at Harriet's house, but today Molly was away babysitting a grandchild. I was glad, because I wanted Harriet to myself this time.

Harriet had been a court reporter, which gave us each a better understanding than most people of the other's work experiences. My work involved reading what reporters like her wrote down as they heard it in court.

The transcript of a criminal trial is seldom elevating reading, and I've seen my share of ugly facts and painful testimony. But before meeting Harriet I hadn't thought about the fact that the staff in the courtroom had to hear it all every day. The transcripts of the cases I handled were a tiny fraction of the hearings she had covered in her career. And I was reading words on a page while she had to watch and listen to the actual actors in the courtroom. "I heard a lot," she said to me once, "some really bad stuff—murders, rapes, robberies, child abuse. And you're not supposed to react to any of it in court. Believe me, sometimes that can be really hard to do. I had nightmares after some of those trials."

She was glad to retire, but she didn't have any problem with occasionally talking shop. When you're writing a legal brief, it's a real help to be able to run your ideas past some non-lawyer friends. Harriet was willing to hear me out, and she'd seen enough courtroom action to have a good sense of what works with jurors and judges.

"How are your tomato starts going?" Harriet asked, as we drove the short distance to the church hall.

"Not half bad," I said proudly. "They're getting nice and big."

"They're probably ready to put into four-inch pots," she said.

I sighed. "Yeah, more work."

She wasn't sympathetic. "You have to treat them right, or you'll lose them."

"I know," I said, feeling guilty about my plants, which were crowding each other out of their little six-packs. So I changed the subject. "I have a question for you: did you ever report on any cases involving the Aryan Brotherhood?"

Harriet considered. "I know we had some trials involving men in gangs like that. They tended to have funny names—Nazi Low Riders, and would you believe Peckerwoods? Skinhead gangs, kids with shaved heads and tattoos."

We were pulling into the church parking lot. "Let me think about it some more," she said.

The class was led by a young woman who seemed to love nothing more than to get us all dancing enthusiastically to pop tunes from the seventies and eighties. There were usually about twenty people there: women getting a little aerobic exercise on their way home from work, stay-at-home wives and mothers, and retirees trying to stay healthy. Once in a while a man came to the class, but they didn't tend to last long.

There was always a little chatter before the class, as people who knew one another caught up on each other's recent lives. One woman who raised chickens had brought eggs, and Harriet and I each bought a dozen.

There was no chance to talk during the dance routines, so it was only when Harriet and I were in her truck heading home that she said, "There was one case, a long time ago, back when I was working in Sacramento. Three guys charged with murdering someone from one of the big Mexican gangs, some kind of turf war. The DA said the defendants were with the Aryan Brotherhood. I'd never seen such a collection of scary-looking people. Real lowlifes. And half the witnesses were scared to death. Some of them just refused to testify, even when the judge said he'd put them in jail for contempt. They put extra security in the courtroom. Everyone was on edge. I've been trying to forget it; it's one of the cases that kept me awake at night."

In Harriet's driveway, as I was climbing down from the passenger seat, she asked, "You don't have a case with those guys, do you? The Aryan Brotherhood, I mean."

"Sort of," I said.

"Sort of?"

"It's a really old case."

"Huh. Well, be careful."

11

After I'd finished reading the material Mike had given me about Howard's case, I wrote a draft of a discovery motion and emailed it to Mike.

The motion was a pretty standard piece of legal writing, a request to be given copies of relevant material in the possession or control of all agencies involved in investigating and prosecuting the case against your client. The request is always to some extent blind, because while you know the general types of information a criminal investigation usually comes up with, you don't know what specific material the district attorney might have or know about that he or she isn't giving you. There's an art to writing a motion that claims your opponent has relevant material you're entitled to, when you don't know if they do or not. Fortunately, that technical problem has been solved by other, better lawyers than me, and I was able to get several good sample motions from an online criminal defense forum and crib shamelessly from them for my own.

One type of material prosecutors are required to turn over with or without a defense request is exculpatory evidence, that is, evidence found in the course of investigating the case that might suggest the defendant isn't guilty after all. A more enlightened Supreme Court held decades ago that prosecutors, as government officials, have a duty that goes beyond winning the cases they bring; they have to try to make sure that the result of the prosecution is just and fair to all sides. Part of this duty says that police and prosecutors aren't allowed to bury evidence that doesn't help their case; they have to make it available to defendants and their lawyers.

This ideal has one big weakness: that it's the police and the prosecutor—the players who are trying to get the defendant convicted—who decide initially whether a piece of information should be disclosed. Police officers and prosecutors don't usually know much about how to defend a criminal case; and it's easy for even a conscientious detective or district attorney to take an unduly narrow view of what evidence might benefit the defense. And some prosecutors and police officers see exculpatory evidence as an obstacle, adding confusion to a case whose outcome, in their minds, should be clear; some of them make the decision to pretend it doesn't exist, especially if the risk that the defense will find out about it is small. Even when a defendant is lucky enough to learn about the evidence after he is convicted, there are few consequences. A judge may grant him a new trial, but prosecutors and police officers are almost never punished for hiding evidence that might have kept a defendant out of prison in the first place.

Discovery motions are a standard part of most criminal cases, but Howard had fired his trial attorney before he could file one, and it had undoubtedly never occurred to Howard to prepare one of his own. Howard's first habeas attorney could have made a motion for discovery, but, for unknown reasons, hadn't. He had written a letter to Sandra Blaine, the district attorney who tried Howard's case, asking to see her files, and she had written him a curt response saying, in essence, "See you in court."

Mike sent an appreciative email after getting my draft, and then another with a copy of the motion after he'd made some edits and filed it; and for another couple of weeks, all was silent on the Henley front. Even Howard stopped calling; the silence from him seemed almost eerie.

I worked on a couple of the other cases I'd taken appointments on, went on hikes with Charlie, weeded my raised beds, planted beets and more lettuce, repotted my tomatoes, made yoghurt and bread, and generally enjoyed living like the backwoods foodie I had become. One day, after a late rainstorm, I went out with Ed and a couple of his friends to hunt mushrooms: the last boletes of the season, chanterelles, and morels.

I was about to call Mike, reluctantly, to find out whether something had happened to Howard, when he called me.

"Both the attorney general and the district attorney filed responses to our discovery motion," he said, "and the AG filed a motion for discovery from us. No surprises in them, but it looks as though Sandra Blaine's office is taking a personal interest in the case. I'll email them to you."

"That's not good." Blaine had been the prosecutor at both Howard's and Scanlon's trials. Now she was the elected district attorney of Taft County. "By the way," I added, "is something up with Howard? I haven't had any calls from him in a while."

"Yeah. He got rolled up and sent to the Adjustment Center."

"Shit. What for?"

"I'm not sure—apparently a combination of having too much paperwork in his cell and mouthing off to the guards who told him to get rid of it. He sent me a letter ranting about it. He thinks he'll be back on Grade A in thirty days."

"Could be worse, then."

"Yeah. It happens periodically. It's Howard; he can't shut up, ends up on someone's bad side, and they send him down there to let him know who's boss. But I have a favor to ask you."

"Sure."

"I'm supposed to go with Dan Connelly—the investigator I'm working with—to see a witness up in Crescent City on Monday, but I have a preliminary hearing that day I can't get out of. Can you go there and meet Dan?"

I didn't have anything scheduled on Monday except my exercise class. "I can do it," I said.

"It's a long drive, so you'll probably have to go up the day before. Dan's going to fly to Eureka and drive from there. He lives in Oakland, so it's easier for him to get to the airport."

I checked my calendar, just to be sure. Nothing going Sunday, either. *Nice to be so in demand,* I thought.

"Not a problem. Tell me about the witness." I hoped it wasn't some AB guy. I was starting to internalize Ed and Harriet's concerns.

"Her name is Ida Rader. She's a retired prison lieutenant. Used to be one of the Department of Corrections gang specialists. She knew Scanlon; he says he debriefed to her after dropping out of the AB."

"So what do we want from Mrs. Rader?"

"In part, to establish that Scanlon did write a debriefing document and that it was given to the Department of Corrections. And, anything else they might have from him. Whatever she remembers about Scanlon's history in the prison system. Her impressions of him. Whether she feels he was really connected to the Aryan Brotherhood and might have committed a killing for them."

"Okay."

"I've briefed Dan on what I want to ask her. But I wanted to come along because I'll probably subpoena her for the hearing, and I wanted to get a feel for how to approach her on direct examination. I'm hoping you can help me there."

"You mean, is she unfriendly to the defense? Will she be honest? Evasive? Like that?"

"Exactly. Dan goes up to Crescent City from time to time; he's been working on a case with some witnesses up there in Pelican Bay. I'll ask him to get in touch with you. Place is kind of a depressed area; he can probably tell you the name of a decent motel."

12

Crescent City is at the far north end of California, almost at the Oregon border. From where I live, it was a long day's drive, up the coast and inland, then north through the redwood forests. The forest scenery is punctuated by cabin resorts and old-fashioned tourist attractions: drive-through trees, a cabin built of a single redwood log. I'd made a couple of trips to the Eureka area years ago on another case, and the names of the old lumber towns and ports along the way—Fortuna, Trinidad, Scotia, Samoa—recalled drives down steep and potholed streets and witness interviews in rundown bungalows and convalescent homes. A lot of the highway was two-lane road, or sometimes a single lane where construction crews were repairing the damage from the winter's inevitable rock slides. But the weather was clear, and the redwoods in Humboldt County made the second-growth trees around my little acre seem pretty ordinary.

Near the end of the drive, the highway skirted the Pacific, with forested hills and green valleys to the east and the rocky coast to the west. I had expected Crescent City to look like someplace in the Pacific Northwest, but it turned out to be more of a seacoast town, a collection of weathered buildings surrounding the bay, under a wide open sky. My motel was part of a row of similar ones that bordered the water's edge, near a sizeable marina. After checking in and dropping my overnight bag in my room, I went out and treated myself to halibut tacos at a restaurant a little down the highway, then read in my room until I fell asleep.

I'd meant to sleep in, enjoying the luxury of not being awakened by Charlie and the cats, but I woke up at six anyway, so I took a walk around the marina. Gulls keened overhead, and the morning was sunny but chilly, with a sharp breeze that made my eyes water. The marina was half full of a mix of well-worn fishing and pleasure boats with names like *Skipjack*, *Moray*, *Katherine*, and *Chelsea*. At that hour, there were few other people around. A young man with a heavy dark beard was hosing down the steel cleaning tables and concrete floor of a fish cleaning station, amid the strong metallic smell of fish scales and blood. At the edge of a parking lot a woman in a fleece jacket and scarf was walking a big, placid yellow dog; I thought of Charlie and wished he were here with me.

After returning to the motel I ate a leisurely waffle in the breakfast room, then went through my notes for the interview. I showered and changed into the outfit I'd brought for the interview: dark gray slacks, a light sea-green pullover, and a black cardigan. I was trying to strike the right tone: professional, but casual and unintimidating—or so I hoped. I almost never wore work clothes anymore, and even the people at Corbin's Landing who did were hardly slaves of fashion. I fretted in front of the mirror, wondering if I'd lost track of how women were supposed to dress. But I'd gotten my hair cut the week before, and I felt appropriate, at least from the neck up, in my neat salt-and-pepper bob.

Even after all that, I had a couple of hours to kill before meeting Dan and Ida Rader, so I checked out of the room and went for a drive through the town. It wasn't a pretty place. There was a park of sorts along the shore of the bay, and along the edge of it a business district, such as it was, a utilitarian mix of one- and two-story stucco buildings housing car parts stores, a Grocery Outlet, repair shops, building supply stores, and so forth, all in some shade of beige or off-white and in need of repainting. Behind it were two-story apartment buildings, little offices housing bookkeepers, tax preparers, and insurance agents, and blocks of weatherworn houses, paint chipping on door and window frames. It all had an air of windswept near-poverty that reminded me of some towns in Alaska.

In a tiny bakery where I stopped for a midmorning coffee, a collage of old newspaper clippings gave another reason for the resemblance: several blocks of Crescent City had been leveled by a tsunami after the huge earthquake that devastated Alaska in 1964. The woman behind the counter, seeing me reading, struck up a conversation about it. Gesturing out the window toward the damaged area, she said, "Most of the business district was just wiped out. They rebuilt some things, but the town hasn't ever really recovered."

That probably went some way toward explaining why the town had welcomed the construction of the Pelican Bay State Prison, a supermax prison isolated a few miles outside town like a modern Alcatraz, tracts of forest playing the role of the San Francisco Bay as a barrier between it and effective escape.

Dan called a little before noon to say he was at the restaurant where we were meeting Mrs. Rader. His voice was a companionable, unflappable-sounding baritone, undoubtedly an asset for an investigator trying to gain the confidence of skittish witnesses. I drove over to meet him.

The Light Station restaurant was in a wooden building painted a maritime gray, near the marina. Picture windows looked out on the highway and the bay beyond it. The restaurant had two dining rooms. A lone man in slacks, collared shirt, and a windbreaker, who I guessed was Dan, was nursing a coffee in the rear one, near a big stone fireplace. He stood up when he saw me, and we introduced ourselves.

"I don't know much about Mrs. Rader," I said, after I'd ordered myself a Diet Coke. "How did Mike find her?"

"Scanlon told us about her. He knew her first as a guard in Soledad, and when he was sent to Pelican Bay he ran into her again there; she'd transferred and was a lieutenant in the

SHU, the security housing unit, where Scanlon was being housed because of his violent history and AB connections. When he decided to drop out of the AB, she was the person he went to for help getting out. He says she's a good cop. She's also an expert on gangs in California prisons, testifies in court a fair amount."

"She must be a tough cookie if she was a guard in Pelican Bay."

"Yeah, I'll say," Dan agreed. "She's picked some tough prisons to work in, between here and Soledad. I can see how she became a gang expert. Those places must be an education all by themselves."

I was taking a drink from my Coke and watching the door out of a corner of my eye when a woman walked in. She had to be Ida Rader. She was the right age, and from her posture and the way she scoped the room, I could tell she was law enforcement. She confirmed my guess about her identity by turning and walking to our table.

We introduced ourselves and shook hands. Ida was three or four inches taller than me, which would make her about five feet four or five. Not big for a prison guard, but she had an athletic build. Her hair, which must have been blond when she was younger, was cut short and almost white. She was wearing cowboy boots, jeans, and a white cable-knit sweater.

"Hope I'm not late," she said. "My husband and I were out looking at a used truck."

"Not at all," Dan said.

She took a seat at the table and glanced around the room. "This isn't a bad place," she said. "Crescent City isn't a restaurant town—people here don't have the money. But the food here is pretty good. I like the petrale sole, when they have it."

The young server brought us menus, and we ordered. Ida and Dan got pints of a local draft ale. I got another Coke. "Designated driver," I joked, by way of excuse. I've come to terms with the fact that at not much over five feet tall, I don't have the capacity to drink and work. We chatted while we waited for our food to arrive.

"How long have you been at Pelican Bay?" Dan asked.

"I'm retired now. But before that I was there for almost fifteen years. Jack—my husband—and I transferred here in 1999."

"Was he a guard, too?"

"A supervisor. He's retired now, too."

"So you decided to settle here, then?"

She nodded. "Yes. We really like it up here. We bought a ranch, raise beef cattle. But what about you? You came all the way up here to talk to me about Steve Scanlon?"

It was my turn to talk. "We're representing a guy, Howard Henley, who's on death row because he was convicted of hiring Steve Scanlon to kill someone for him."

"Right," she said. "Your partner, Mr. Barry, mentioned that when he called me."

I went on. "Scanlon told a couple of his buddies that he'd

done the killing for the Aryan Brotherhood. But the DA decided he was lying to make himself out to be a big shot."

"Really?" Ida looked surprised. "Well, he wasn't. Lying about something like that would be a pretty dangerous thing to do. Those guys don't like it when outsiders claim to be connected with them. Who'd he kill, by the way?"

"An ex-con named Jared Lindahl."

"The name doesn't ring any bells. Do you know why he was in the hat—I'm sorry, why he was marked to be killed?"

"Scanlon said he was told Lindahl had been running drugs in prison without paying the tax."

Ida rolled her eyes. "Right. Another dangerous thing to do."

"Yeah," I said. "He was also robbing people in the trailer park where he was living. Some folks there said he'd taken drugs and money from our client and pistol-whipped him; that was our guy's supposed motive for hiring Scanlon."

Ida almost smiled. "Sounds like a public service killing to me. What's your guy doing on the Row?"

"It's a long story," I said. "Among other things, he's psychotic, and he represented himself at his trial."

"Ah."

Our food came at that point, and for a few minutes we concentrated on eating. Then Ida returned her attention to us and asked, "What do you need from me?"

This time Dan answered. "Scanlon said we should talk to you."

"Really?"

"He said he debriefed to you and told you about the Lindahl killing. Also that you knew a lot about the Aryan Brotherhood and what was going on around that time. And he said you were a good cop and treated him fair—he wanted me to pass that along to you."

For a second her careful expression appeared to lighten a little. "I tried to treat everyone fairly," she said. "Poor Steve. He didn't start out so bad. I always felt sorry he got involved with the gang stuff."

"Sounds like you met him a while ago," Dan said. "Can you tell us something about him, what he was like?"

"Yeah. Back in Soledad, in the nineties. I remember him because he was younger than most of the guys on my tier. He was maybe nineteen or twenty. He was desperate to belong, to be in with the big guys."

"And I guess the big guys among the white inmates were the Aryan Brotherhood?"

"Yeah. AB, Nazi Low Riders. Steve was willing to do any errand, whatever it took to be accepted. He wasn't someone likely to rise high in a gang; he wasn't that bright, and his temper was a bit of a liability. We kept an eye on him because you could tell he was the kind of kid likely to get into trouble."

"Did you talk with him much?"

"Not a lot. As a guard, you don't let any of the guys get too close. But enough to get a sense of what was going on with him and whether to be concerned for his safety.

"He did get stabbed in the yard, I do remember that. I wasn't around when it happened, but apparently he mouthed off at someone who took offense. After that, he really threw his lot in with the AB, because he felt he needed the protection."

"So he became kind of a foot soldier for them?" Dan asked.

"Yeah."

"He told us," Dan said, "that before he paroled, he was instructed to take out Lindahl, because he was paroling to Taft County, and Lindahl was there, too; and that after he was paroled he got a sort of reminder letter from the guy who made the order. Does that seem like something that could happen?"

"Oh, yeah. It's not uncommon for the AB to order hits on someone outside from in the prison. They're usually ordered and approved by people fairly high up in the hierarchy, but the gang has all kinds of ways of communicating back and forth between the prisons."

"The name of the man who sent the letter was Cal McGaw. Was he in Soledad with Scanlon?"

"Not that I know of. I don't recall the name. But Scanlon was transferred to Folsom, and there were a lot of AB there. He may have met McGaw there. There's a lot of communication among inmates, and it doesn't seem unreasonable that this McGaw would know that Steve was about to parole to an area near Lindahl. But unless McGaw was a full AB member, he'd probably have been just a conduit for an order from someone higher up than he was."

"Scanlon mentioned someone named Corker. Does that name ring any bells?" Dan asked.

"Oh, yes. That was Bensinger, Walt or William, I'm not sure of his first name. He was called Corker because he supposedly made his bones in a stabbing in Corcoran."

"According to Steve, he was the source of the order about Lindahl."

"That's interesting," Ida said. "He was high enough in rank to do that. Do you have the letter?"

"Unfortunately, no. Steve said it was in his car when he was arrested, and he never saw it again."

"Pity. It might tell you something. Or maybe not; those letters are often in code."

"So Scanlon may be telling the truth about the order and where it came from."

"It could be. If that's what he said, I'd be inclined to believe him."

"Any particular reason why?"

"A couple. First, Steve was pretty straight up—not perfect, but basically someone you could credit when he told you something. That was one of his better qualities. And second, it's dangerous to go around saying the AB ordered you to take someone out when they didn't. Saying something like that is likely to make you a target."

"So you think of him as pretty honest, someone you could trust."

Ida gave a short laugh. "I don't know that you can say that about any of those guys. No, I wouldn't trust them."

"I take your point," Dan said.

"I mean that a lot of inmates are pretty manipulative—little games going all the time. With Steve, it was more 'what you see is what you get.'"

"Did you know Steve in Pelican Bay?" Dan asked.

"Not well. I was a lieutenant in the Security Housing Unit, the SHU." She pronounced it "shoe." "At first Steve was in general population. I guess he must have been there because of the killing you're talking about. But then he got convicted for attempted escape and assaulting a guard and went to the SHU for that and for being a validated AB member. It's where they put the most dangerous guys and the real hardcore gang members. I talked to him when he first arrived there, but I don't recall having any contact with him until he asked to see me to debrief."

"Steve wasn't hardcore, though, was he?"

"Not in the sense of being anyone with any power. He never got anywhere in the AB beyond being a low-level associate. No, he was in the SHU more because of the escape attempt and assault. Stabbed a guard in the neck and almost killed him. And, as I said, he was a validated AB associate."

"Steve said something about that incident," Dan said.

"It was a big deal up here, needless to say. They tried him here, and he got a life sentence for that on top of whatever term he had before."

"He knows he's never getting out of prison," Dan said.

"Yeah," Ida agreed. "Waste of a life."

Dan nodded agreement and moved on. "How did he come to debrief? He tried to tell us about it, but in all honesty he's not good at stringing two thoughts together."

Ida smiled again. "Yeah, that would be Steve. Give me a minute here." She waved the server over, and we ordered coffees all round. When she left, Ida went on. "Steve was in the SHU, and as you can figure, he had no friends there. Guards didn't like him, and the gang higher-ups were very unhappy with him because he had brought a lot of heat on the gang. There was a big crackdown after the incident, and a lot of guys who'd just been doing their time were validated as gang members and sent to the SHU. From what I was hearing, they more or less wrote him off as too much of a loose cannon.

"But they did give him one last chance: some kid was celled with him who had gotten on the wrong side of the powers that be by failing in some assignment, and Steve was supposed to take care of him. Steve apparently came to believe that the kid didn't really deserve to be killed—like I said, he has his good qualities—and he tried interceding on his cellie's behalf with… I think it was Ransom and Perry, who were running the tier at the time. He thought he'd succeeded because nothing happened, and eventually his cellie transferred out. The guy who replaced him, Bill Jennings, was another AB associate Steve knew and trusted. But then after they'd been together for a couple of months, Jennings jumped Steve in his sleep and tried to cut his throat."

"Jeez, was he hurt badly?"

"Yeah. I remember for a while it was up in the air whether Steve was going to live. He had several stab wounds and lost a lot of blood, and he got a pretty nasty infection from whatever it was Jennings used to stab him with. Jennings flushed the weapon, so no one really knew."

"He has permanent nerve damage in one arm and hand, he says, from defending himself."

"Not surprising," Ida said. "Anyway, he asked to see me while he was in the infirmary, and I went over there. That's when he said he wanted to debrief and get transferred somewhere else. He was really done with the gang—shocked, actually, that they went after him. I wasn't in that debriefing program; I was just a tier lieutenant. But I told him I'd tell the right people and what he needed to do to start with, which was write a detailed autobiographical statement of everything he'd done with and for the gang, and everything he knew about them. He called for me again a couple days later and handed me this long, handwritten document. I read it and then passed it along to the investigators, and I guess they took it from there."

"Did Steve mention the Lindahl killing in the debriefing document?"

"I don't know; I didn't read it closely. But when he talked to me in the infirmary, one of the things he was upset about was that he'd done a hit for the AB in Wheaton, and this was the thanks he got. I guess that's the one you're asking about."

"Did he say anything about another motive for the hit?"

"No, not at all."

"And I guess he never mentioned Howard Henley."

"Not that I recall. I never heard the name before Mr. Barry called."

"Do you know if the prison still has the debriefing document?"

"I'm sure they do, in their file on Scanlon. But if you want it, you'll have to subpoena it. It's a confidential record, and I wouldn't be allowed to give you details about it, even if I remembered what was in it."

Dan looked down at some notes. "Do you know the names Scotty Maclendon or Mack Gentry?" I hadn't heard the names before, but I didn't interrupt.

"Yeah. They were both in Pelican Bay when I was there, and presumably when Steve was, too. Gentry's dead; he was killed by an AB associate in some kind of power struggle. I don't know whether Maclendon is still at Pelican Bay or not."

She glanced at her wristwatch. "I'm going to have to get home soon. Was there anything else you wanted to ask me?" She gestured to the server and told her we needed our checks.

"I guess one last question," I said. "Mike talked with you, I think, about testifying at the evidentiary hearing in our case as an expert on the Aryan Brotherhood in the state prison system. Is that something you can do for us?"

"Yes. I've testified in that role before. I can send you a CV, if you'd like."

"That would be great," I answered. "And we'll probably also ask you about your experience with Steve, if that's all right."

"Sure."

The check came, and she reached into her purse and put thirty dollars on the table. "Oh, that's okay," Dan said. "We'll take care of it."

"Let me do this," Ida said. "I testified in a trial not too long ago where one of the attorneys made a huge deal about the other buying lunch for a witness."

We stood and shook hands with her, and she walked briskly out the door.

"Not bad," Dan said, as we waited for the server to bring back his credit card. "She'll make a good witness."

"Yeah," I said. "Mike will be happy."

I started for home right after lunch, hoping to catch as much daylight for the trip as possible. The restaurant had an espresso machine, and before leaving town I picked up a triple latte and a double chocolate cupcake the size of my fist. It was going to be a long ride through the big woods to the next cup.

13

I prepared a response to the attorney general's discovery motion for Mike to file, and had settled back into my hermit routine, planting my tomatoes, watching my beet plants sprout, and looking forward with lively expectation to a trip to the women's death row to see the client in a case I'd just agreed to work on, when Mike called.

"Well, the Wheaton court has assigned a referee to conduct the hearing, and he wants us in court next month."

"They've appointed one already?"

"Yeah, a local judge. Looks like your name isn't on the proof of service; we'll have to sort that out with them. Anyway, his name is Raymond Brackett. I did a little research on him, and he seems to have been a prosecutor and then a defense attorney, but that's all I know, except that he works fast. He's set a hearing on our discovery motion."

"Okay," I said. "When will it be?"

Mike gave a date in the middle of May. "You free then?"

I glanced at the calendar on my computer; my visit to my

newest client was early in the month. "I'll have to cancel my exercise class," I said.

Mike didn't miss a beat. "Oh, come on; there's nothing like a trip to Wheaton! We can drive there together. I'll make arrangements to examine the exhibits in Howard's trial and Scanlon's, and maybe introduce you to some of Howard's family," he added, "if you don't mind spending an extra day."

"In Wheaton?" I said. "Be still, my beating heart."

He laughed. "It's a date. See you the morning before."

Mike and I drove to Wheaton together for the hearing, our first appearance before the habeas referee—the judge appointed to take evidence in Howard's habeas case. After the scruffy suburbs of the Bay Area, we cruised at 80-plus miles an hour through the underbelly of California corporate agriculture and right-wing water politics. Vineyards and orchards of fruit and nut trees covered the hills down into the valley, under a cloudless sky. Some trees near the freeway had been left to die from lack of irrigation next to signs that pronounced the area a dust bowl produced by the water policies of Democrats in Congress. Other signs, along the road and at gas stations, advertised in Spanish for field workers.

To fill the time, we made small talk about our cases and our families and tried the various FM stations available along the way, a choice of angry talk radio, smarmy religion, and country or Mexican music. "Next time," I said, "I'll bring an audio book."

During the drive, I brought up the visit with Ida Rader. "I liked her," I said. "She seemed straightforward. And she makes a good case that Scanlon was probably telling the truth about the AB being behind the killing. Dan and I both think she'd be a good witness."

"I hope so," Mike said. "We need whatever we can to corroborate Scanlon."

At the south end of the valley lay Wheaton, the seat of Taft County. I'd worked on a post-conviction case there once before, a kidnap-robbery-murder after a drug deal gone bad. My client, a black man on the run from a parole violation in Los Angeles, had gotten the death penalty; his partner in crime, who was local and white and related to the county sheriff, had somehow never been charged.

My investigator, who had grown up in Taft County, had accounted for the outcome by the history of the place. The area had been settled by white Southerners: Confederate sympathizers before and after the Civil War, and later, Okies escaping the Dust Bowl, who found a familiar set of attitudes among the farmers and oilmen of the region. The Ku Klux Klan had flourished here long after it had died out, or gone underground, in the rest of the state; there had been lynchings in the 1920s and Klan marches in Wheaton as late as the 1980s.

When I had been there before, the place simmered with

suburban intrigue. My investigator and local lawyers had filled me in on an eye-opening array of scurrilous details about local politics and general bad behavior around the courthouse: who was sleeping with whose wife or husband, secretary or clerk; who was hiding a cocaine or alcohol problem; who had taken bribes. At the courthouse, and around town, there seemed to be a lot of women in their thirties and early forties looking like they spent a lot of time at the gym, dressed a little too young, makeup a little too thick, hair a little too big.

The town itself was a pretty ordinary place, a downtown of blocky two- and three-story office buildings, doctors' and lawyers' offices, bail bondsmen, dollar stores, and bodegas, surrounded by suburbs of one-story houses ranged around shopping malls.

One of the silver linings to visiting Wheaton was a Hilton hotel near the civic center that let rooms at the state government rate. Over Corona lagers and plates of chiles rellenos in a fancy Mexican restaurant, we talked about the discovery hearing.

"Damn," Mike said, topping up his glass from the bottle. "If we could only find that letter Scanlon says he had. But it's hard to tell whether he's even telling the truth about that."

"Well, we've got our hearing tomorrow," I said. "Let's see what turns up."

What turned up the next morning was Sandra Blaine.

Ms. Blaine was, as prosecutors go, a legend in her own

time. She loved high-profile cases, and she prosecuted them with fanatic self-righteousness and apparently complete indifference to the rules against concealing and lying about evidence, defying gag orders, putting on perjured testimony, and accusing her opponents, in court and out, of lying to the jury and worse. But the good citizens of Taft County saw her defiance of court orders and her grandstanding in court as passion and zeal, and eventually elevated her from the ranks of deputy prosecutors to the district attorney of the county.

As we walked in, I saw her at the counsel table talking with a man whom I figured must be the deputy attorney general appearing for the hearing. I'd seen only a photo or two of Blaine in newspaper clippings; in person, she was quite attractive, with a clothes-horse figure, long dark hair and wide-set dark blue eyes, and the kind of presence that turned heads as she moved through the courtroom. She must have been well over forty, but she looked ageless.

She probably charms judges and colleagues into agreement, I thought—but that idea was quickly dispelled. She seemed to be lecturing the deputy attorney general, a tallish bland-faced man, who was listening with an expression of condescension combined with something like wariness. Trial-level prosecutors don't involve themselves that often in post-conviction proceedings a decade after the trial. And the deputy attorney general probably knew something about her: in a half-dozen cases over the years, appellate courts had found convictions she had obtained were tainted by one type or another of prosecutorial misconduct.

The deputy attorney general caught sight of us and came over to shake hands. Sandra Blaine turned and stood where she was, unsmiling.

"Frank Willard," he said. No drama, just the bureaucratic civility of a government lawyer doing the job the public assigned him. "My plan this morning is to submit your discovery motion on our written opposition." He glanced back over his shoulder, to where Sandra Blaine was looking at some papers on the counsel table. "But I think Ms. Blaine may want to make some argument."

The court clerk and reporter emerged through a door at the front of the courtroom and set up at their stations, and Willard returned to the prosecution side of the counsel table. The bailiff announced to the world at large that all should rise and come to order because Department 6 was now in session, and Judge Brackett, stocky and broad-shouldered in his black robe, entered through a door behind the judge's bench. He sat, and the bailiff announced to the three or four people who seem to haunt the spectator seats at even the most routine court hearings that they could, too. Mike and I, and Willard and Blaine, stayed on our feet.

"In the matter of Howard Henley, petitioner," the clerk said from her desk, "please state your appearances for the record."

"Michael Barry and Janet Moodie for petitioner Howard

Henley," Mike said. Willard and Blaine each answered that they were appearing for the people.

"Sorry if I'm late," the judge said. "We had a hearing in chambers in another case. We're here on Mr. Henley's motion for post-conviction discovery, then."

"Yes, Your Honor," we said in scattered chorus.

"Is Mr. Henley by any chance related to the folks at Henley-Bishop Motors?"

Mike answered. "Yes, that was his father. I believe Mr. Henley's brothers run it now."

"Ah," the judge said. "Well, in the interest of full disclosure, I bought my truck there. Good people; best service department in this part of the state."

"Thank you, Your Honor," Mike said. "I think the Henleys would be pleased to hear that."

The rest of the hearing held few surprises. The judge granted the attorney general's motion for discovery. As to ours, Willard, as he had said, told the judge he had no argument beyond his written response to the motion. Sandra Blaine, on the other hand, stood up, the light of offended justice shining in her eyes, and argued that Henley had been given all the discovery he was entitled to at the time of his trial, that his first post-conviction attorney should have made the motion and that we were too late in bringing it now, and that we had no right to any of the prosecution's material on Steve Scanlon because he had been tried separately.

The judge listened impassively to Blaine's argument and

then mine and ruled that we were entitled to all the discovery we had asked for except that given to Scanlon's attorneys in connection with his trial.

"We have a records release from Scanlon," Mike said. "And this is a case where the defendants were tried using a lot of the same evidence. There is likely to be evidence in the prosecutor's files relevant to both men."

"I know," the judge answered. "That was in your motion. But the statute doesn't include discovery from a codefendant."

I wrote a quick note and passed it to Mike.

"Even if it's exculpatory of Mr. Henley?" Mike asked. "Your Honor, the prosecutor has an obligation to produce exculpatory evidence. I would think that would include such evidence even if it's in a codefendant's file." He glanced at my note. "Furthermore," he added, "since an order to show cause has issued in the case, discovery is no longer limited by the statute."

The judge thought for a minute. "You're right about that," he said. "Mrs. Blaine, I will order the district attorney to provide the discovery requested by Mr. Henley regarding his own trial to his attorneys a reasonable time before the hearing. What if I order that your office review the discovery from Scanlon's case and, if you find anything relevant to the issue in the order to show cause as to Mr. Henley, that you hand it over to his counsel?"

"I object to that," Blaine said. "It's just a fishing expedition, and it would require me to expend valuable time retrieving and reviewing the files. I can't delegate it, because no one else in the office knows the cases well enough to decide what might qualify as relevant."

The judge didn't seem sympathetic. "I can give you two or three months to do the review," he said. "Do you think you can handle that on your schedule?"

"I'm scheduled to try the Verdugo triple-homicide case next month." Even without knowing the case, I sensed this was a play to put a political price on the judge's decision against her.

He didn't bend. "You should be able to work around it."

"I can only try, Your Honor," Blaine said. Even with hardly any audience, it was a bravura performance: the hardworking prosecutor hard-pressed by an unreasonable court.

From there, we went on to scheduling the hearing on Howard's habeas case. We agreed on a date in October, with Blaine to provide the discovery ordered by the court no less than thirty days before it began. At our request, the judge set a telephone status conference in August to assess how the discovery was going.

As soon as we were out of earshot of Willard and Blaine, Mike said, "We may have done pretty well getting Judge Brackett."

The morning was still young, and we headed down to the first floor and the end of a long hall, to the exhibit clerk's office.

The clerk set us up in a bleak little workroom with bare

walls, no windows, and a metal table, where we arranged our computers and a portable scanner. There was only one box of exhibits from Howard's case, because most of them had been re-used in Scanlon's trial. We photographed some enlarged photos of Howard's trailer, inside and out, with our phones, and scanned court documents from his prior criminal cases and psychiatric records from the hospital where he'd been in Florida, even though we probably had them already.

Mike brought the box back to the clerk and helped her carry in the three boxes that held the exhibits in Scanlon's case. There wasn't much more to them: crime scene and autopsy photos; the autopsy report; bullets in evidence envelopes, and the criminalist's report giving their caliber and the brands of guns that could have fired them; more criminal records from past cases of Scanlon, Lindahl, and some of the prosecution and defense witnesses. Mike had already received copies of most of it in Gordon Marshall's files.

"That's enough paperwork," Mike said, as we packed our laptops away. "Anyway, there's someone we should meet while we're here."

14

Dorothy Henley met us at a Denny's Diner about a mile from the courthouse. "Everyone calls me Dot," she said, as we introduced ourselves. She was white-haired, slender and slightly stooped, and she walked with a cane ("My doctor wants me to have a hip replacement, but I've been putting it off."). Her skin had the powdery paleness of old age, but her blue eyes were bright and attentive. Her cotton skirt and blouse were inexpensive, but unfaded and neat. Under her free arm, along with her purse, she was carrying a photo album.

We found a booth under a window, and Dot set the album on the table beside her placemat, as she sat down. "I thought you might want to talk about Howard," she said, "so I brought some pictures of him for you to see."

The server who brought our menus greeted Dot by name. "I come here a lot with a couple of my friends," Dot told us after she had left. "We like the senior menu. I was hoping Kevin and Bob could join us, but they were both tied up today. Kevin may be around a little later. And Corinne is in Oregon, of course."

"Maybe some other time," Mike said. "We're coming back for more hearings on the case in the summer and fall."

"What did the judge do today?" Dot asked.

"Told the district attorney to give us material from their files and set a hearing to start taking testimony. He wants to start it on October 16th."

"Well, I'll be there," she said. "I don't suppose they'll bring Howard back for it, will they?"

Mike shook his head. "I doubt it. There's no reason to; he won't be testifying. And I don't think he wants to come here; he's used to being at San Quentin, and it's pretty disruptive getting moved back to jail."

Dot nodded. "I guess I can understand that. Though it's hard to tell anything with Howard. His letters and his phone calls—between you and me, they don't always make a lot of sense."

Mike and I nodded in agreement. "I know," we said at the same time.

"I sent him a birthday card a few weeks ago, and he sent me a letter that just said, 'Dear Mom, I got a horse,' with something like a kid's drawing of a horse in it." She shook her head and chuckled. "I had no idea what he meant by it." Her expression grew sober. "It's sad, though. He really shouldn't be there; he's too ill."

We agreed.

The server came back, and we gave her our orders. With the menus out of the way, Dot opened the photo album and turned it so we could see the pictures. "I wanted you to see Howard the way he was." She described various photos: a snapshot of Howard at seven with the family dog; a photo of him in a Boy Scout uniform; another of him in a suit, at the wedding of a relative; a school portrait of him in his senior year of high school. In his unsmiling stare into the camera in one picture, or the shadows around his eyes in another I imagined I could see hints of the sickness that would engulf him. Experts say that signs of later mental illness can sometimes be detected in children, although they're often so subtle that even close family members seldom see or recognize them.

"He was a bright child," Dot said, "and very well behaved, a responsible boy. He was in Boy Scouts, and he had a paper route all through high school, till he passed it on to Kevin, and his grades in school were always good. Lyle and I were so proud of him. He had such promise, until his breakdown in college. After that, he was never the same."

Over lunch, we talked about families. Dot asked about ours, and on learning my husband had died some years ago (I didn't elaborate), she was sympathetic. "I still miss Lyle a lot, even though it's been ten years," she said. "But at least he lived a long life. It's harder when they're younger. Kevin's wife, Sue, passed at forty-three—she had a really aggressive form of breast cancer—and he was just devastated. I didn't know what he was going to do for a while. I really feel it was his kids who got him through it—they remind you why you need to go on."

I asked her about her own life.

"In most ways, I've been pretty blessed," she said. "Lyle and I were happy together, and we made some lucky decisions along the way—especially buying into the dealership. We've done well, and when Lyle decided to retire, Robert took over in his place. Robert and Kevin have stayed close to us; they take good care of me these days."

"How did your family handle Howard's problems?" Mike asked.

Dot sighed. "It was a struggle. Lyle was so patient with him. We paid for psychiatrists to treat him, and they'd give him medications, and things would seem to be all right for a while. But then Howard would stop taking them and refuse to see the doctor, and he'd end up in his room for weeks on end, not eating, and talking to himself, until we'd threaten to make him leave unless he agreed to go to some other doctor. Lyle found him a couple of jobs, and Howard would try for a little while, but then something would happen, and he'd stop coming to work or say something and get fired.

"One day he just lost control and got in a fist fight with Lyle. He was raving—crazy religious stuff, saying we were all damned, things like that. We called the police. They sent him to a mental hospital. But the hospital couldn't keep him, because he wasn't completely helpless; that's what they told us. They gave him medications for a couple of weeks, but that was all. Lyle didn't want to file charges because he didn't want Howard to end up in jail. So he was released. But he was angry with us for doing that to him. He packed up his belongings and bought a motorcycle with his savings, and left."

"Was that when he went to Florida?"

"Well, we didn't know where he was for a long time, except when he called asking me to send him money. He wasn't speaking to Lyle. Once or twice he called needing bail money because he'd been arrested. Then he disappeared completely for about two years, and we couldn't find out what happened to him.

"Then one day he just showed up at the house. I hardly recognized him; he looked like he'd been homeless for a long time—dirty, thin as a rail, and some of his teeth missing. He wouldn't say anything about where he'd been. Lyle gave him the apartment over our garage and walked him through the paperwork to get SSI, so he'd have a little income. We tried to get him to see a doctor, but he wouldn't. Then one day he had an argument with Lyle over cleaning the apartment and threatened to burn down the garage; and Lyle told him he'd have to get a place somewhere else.

"We found him another apartment and helped with his rent and brought him groceries every now and then. It still wasn't easy; he'd keep getting evicted for being disruptive and threatening the neighbors, and we'd have to find him someplace else. Once he got arrested for disturbing the peace, and an old warrant came up out of Los Angeles—I guess he must have lived there for a while in his travels—so he was sent down there. It was a drug possession charge; he ended up spending a few months in jail for that and for failing to appear in court."

"What happened after he was released?" Mike asked.

"We don't know for sure. We thought he was living somewhere in LA, but we didn't hear anything from him until they called us from the hospital in Ventura."

"What happened?"

"He'd been in some kind of accident—hit by a city bus. Nothing too bad, they told us, a broken ankle and some scratches. But he'd gotten some kind of infection that put him in the hospital, which is why they called us; I'm surprised he gave them our names. They were worried about whether he was lucid enough to give consent to be treated. We went down there. He looked awful, and he was fighting them about giving him antibiotics; he'd gotten really paranoid and kept saying the city was trying to kill him so he couldn't sue them. We convinced him to let them treat him, and when he was recovered enough, we brought him home."

"Ah," I said. "He's talked a lot about that."

Dot sighed. "I know. Our family lawyer looked into it and filed an injury claim of some sort with the city, and there was a settlement. Nothing very big; Howard wasn't that badly injured, and the driver claimed Howard was jaywalking.

Howard agreed to it, but then he had buyer's remorse, and he always blamed us for pressuring him into it."

"What happened to the money?"

"He used most of it to buy a truck and the rest to pay a deposit on that place in the trailer park. I know it was all gone at some point because he was always short of money. We heard from a friend of Kevin's who's with the police that the trailer park was full of drug users and dealers, but we couldn't talk him into moving out of there."

"Do you think he got involved in drug dealing there?"

"I don't know. Someone could have talked him into it, I guess. But I know Ms. Blaine said he was this big-time dealer, and that couldn't have been true."

"Why?"

"He was always needing money from us. You can't live on SSI unless you're really good at making that little bit stretch, and Howard wasn't capable of that. Not that he didn't try: he was very frugal. But he'd have to call Lyle just about every month for a little to tide him over. Lyle bought him a cellphone—nothing fancy, no email or Internet—so he could call when he needed to. Not long before the time he was supposed to be hiring this Steve guy to kill that other man, Howard was calling Lyle asking for money for his rent because he'd broken a tooth and had to pay a dentist to have it pulled."

"Did he ever talk about being robbed by Jared Lindahl?"

"Not specifically. But a little after that time he called

Lyle, he called again. I remember because he didn't usually contact us more than about once a month. He said someone had robbed his cabin and stolen his TV and cellphone. Lyle got another phone from the company store, and took it to him. When he got back he told me Howard looked like he'd gotten the worst of a fight—he had a black eye and bruises. Howard wouldn't tell him what happened; he just rambled."

"Was he angry?"

"Lyle didn't say." Dot shook her head. "But Howard was always angry about something."

Something moved in my peripheral vision, and I looked up and saw a suntanned middle-aged man in work clothes standing next to the table. Dot saw him at the same time, and her eyes lit up. "Kevin!" she said.

He leaned down to kiss her cheek and give her a squeeze on the shoulder. "Hi, Mom," he said.

Dot introduced us. "These are Howard's lawyers, Mike and—" She paused.

"Janet," I said, with my best forthright smile.

"We were talking about Howard," Dot said to Kevin. "Can you stay a bit?"

"Yeah, for a little. We're waiting on a plumber who's running behind schedule."

Dot scooted over in the booth, and Kevin sat down next to her.

"Do you really think you can help Howard?" he asked

us. "I mean he's crazy and all, but we really don't think he did this."

"We're doing our best," Mike said. "It's hopeful that we got an order to show cause; it suggests that the California Supreme Court, at least, has some question about whether he's guilty."

"That's good news, right?" Kevin asked.

"It is," Mike said.

"You'll have to forgive me," Kevin said. "I'm no lawyer, and Howard's case has had so many twists and turns it lost me a long time ago."

Mike did his best to explain the process of appeals and habeas corpus proceedings in death-penalty cases, pointing out that of all the habeas petitions filed by death-sentenced prisoners in the state Supreme Court, in only a small fraction does the court see enough of a possibility of serious error to order the trial court to show cause why the defendant shouldn't get a new trial. At the end of it, Kevin seemed just as baffled, but too polite to say so.

"I guess all we can do is hope for the best," he said. "To be honest, though—sorry, Mom—I'm not sure he should be allowed to go free. He really ought to be locked up someplace, for his own good. And ours," he added. "We've all had to block him from calling us. Howard and his problems have really torn our family apart."

Dot gave him a sideways look, but she didn't disagree.

Kevin continued. "Bob really can't stand him. Some of

it's understandable. Back when they were young, Howard gave Bob's name a couple of time when he got arrested—I guess maybe to keep the police from finding out about warrants against him, or maybe just because he was crazy, I don't know. But it caused Bob a lot of trouble to clear his name. Once he even got picked up on a warrant against Howard and spent a few hours in jail. It was an even bigger deal to him because he's all about being some kind of big shot here in town—Chamber of Commerce, Rotary Club, all that. Howard's troubles have been a huge embarrassment to him. Bottom line, he's not anxious to help Howard. He doesn't want him to be executed, but I don't think he wants him coming back here, either."

Dot nodded. "It's been hard for him. Corinne felt it, too. I believe that had a lot to do with why she moved away."

A cellphone ringtone sounded from somewhere nearby, and even though it wasn't mine, I instinctively turned toward my purse. Kevin pulled his phone from his pocket, listened for a few seconds, then said a word or two. "Gotta go," he said. "Plumber finally showed up." He turned to Dot. "See you Friday?" he asked.

"Oh, I wouldn't miss it."

"Great. We'll be by around seven." He bent down and kissed her again, and then walked quickly toward the door.

Dot watched after him for a few seconds, and then turned back to us. "I'll have to leave in a few minutes. I'm taking a quilting class at the Adult School."

We walked out together. At the door, we thanked her, and Mike said, "Thanks for seeing us; and it was good meeting Kevin."

Dot smiled. "He's a good person."

"I can see that."

"The hearing is, when, October 16th?"

"Yes," Mike said.

"Good. I'll write that down. I'd like to go, hear what they have to say." She turned to me. "Nice to meet you, Ms. Moodie."

"It was great meeting you, too; please, call me Janet."

"Janet, then. I hope everything goes well with Howard's hearing. Will you be seeing him any time soon?"

"I'm planning to visit him next month," I said.

"Please say hello to him, and send him our love," she said, "and would you ask him if he got the quarterly package I sent him?"

"Sure will," I said.

"They seem like a nice family," I said to Mike as we walked to his car. "Not like the ones you usually find in mitigation investigations."

"Yeah. Makes our lives a little easier."

I felt almost guilty for agreeing. Most of our clients' families were, to put it kindly, troubled; and though I generally felt sympathy for their hardships, it was mingled with judgment for the fact that the parents, at least, bore a lot of the blame for how their child had turned out. Howard's kin were more relatable, a middle-class family on which the misfortune of Howard's mental illness had been visited through no fault of theirs.

"Gives you kind of a 'there, but for the grace of God' feeling, doesn't it?" I said, lamely.

15

After leaving Mrs. Henley, we drove out to the crime scene.

"Dan tells me they've spruced the place up a bit," Mike said. But even with some new paint on the common buildings and oiled roads between the trailers, the place still looked blighted. The trailers were old, their aluminum paint oxidized and the wooden latticework around their bases rotting and broken in places. A few were shabbily well kept, as though their owners had made some effort at maintaining or improving them, planting flowers and shrubs in the narrow strips of dirt at their fronts and sides. One had a minuscule patio next to it, with a plastic table and a pair of chairs on a bit of artificial turf. But many were surrounded by trash half buried in rank green weeds, and behind their windows I saw torn curtains and broken blinds. There were few people outside—a middle-aged man sitting on a folding lawn chair, beer in hand, and a woman taking a bag of trash to one of the dumpsters at the front of the park.

We had a copy of a map of the park from a police report,

with Howard's trailer marked on it. We drove there first and knocked on the door. No one answered. The woman we had seen earlier was walking by, and called to us, "The man who lives there is at work." We thanked her, and when she was out of sight I took a few pictures of the trailer. I'd seen photos of it in the trial exhibit, and it was still run-down all these years later, but not as ragged as some: the blinds in the windows were in good repair, the planting strip was weeded, and there was a small vinyl storage shed at one side.

After that we drove to Lindahl's cabin. The place where he'd once lived was outside the bounds of the trailer park, but connected to it by a dirt track. His was at one end of a line of three or four such cabins scattered in the woods behind the park, along the bank of a creek. When the police had asked people in the trailer park whether they'd heard the gunshots that killed Lindahl, a couple said that people sometimes used a clearing in the area behind the cabins as an informal target range, going out there to shoot at cans and bottles. Besides, it wasn't a place you'd rush out to check if you heard a shot; as one park denizen put it, "You don't go near the folks out there; they're crazy."

Lindahl's cabin looked as if no one had lived there in a while. The parking strip in front of it was green with small weeds, with no sign of tire tracks. The windows were filthy, and the wooden stoop in front of the door was rotted through. The door was locked. We walked around the cabin seeking signs of life and saw none. Lindahl's body had been found in the clearing behind the cabins; the police surmised he might have been target shooting when he was shot, though they hadn't found a gun at the scene.

As we were walking back to the car, we saw a man walking toward us from the direction of the other cabins. "Can I help you?" he asked.

It wasn't a friendly question; it was clear that he wanted to know what we were doing snooping around. He was wearing old jeans and a faded black T-shirt with the name and logo of what I guessed was a heavy-metal band. He was perhaps forty and in pretty good shape, someone who probably did physical labor for a living. Given that he was living in a place like this, I guessed he was an ex-convict or a drinker; he didn't have the vague, half-starved look of a drug user.

Mike answered him. "We're lawyers," he said, "working on an old murder case that happened here."

The man stopped, outside of handshaking distance, but close enough to talk. "I heard about something like that happening," he said. "When was it?"

"1999," Mike said.

"Huh. Yeah, I wasn't around here then. Only been here about a year." He glanced over at Lindahl's cabin. "It's been vacant since I've been here. Someone was killed there, huh?"

"Yeah," Mike said. "You wouldn't happen to know who owns it, would you?"

"No. I pay my rent to Kelly Properties over on Main Street. Maybe someone there knows."

Mike thanked him.

"Have a good one," the man said, and we wished him the same. He walked back in the direction he came from, glancing back once at us, as we got into Mike's car and drove off.

Although it didn't really seem to matter, we decided to stop at Kelly Properties just because we had the name and we were in town. An agent there knew about the area behind the trailer park. They managed it for the owner. His lot had three cabins on it; the lot on the end that held Lindahl's wasn't his. "You'd probably have to go to the county recorder and find the deed," she said.

We decided to forego the pleasures of the recorder's office; it was getting late, and we had a long drive back. "Well, home we go," Mike said cheerily, as we settled ourselves in his car. "I'll have to ask Dan to canvass the trailer park and see if there's anyone there who was around when Howard lived there."

By the time I reached home it was well after midnight. After coffee and the drive through the dark along the cliffs of Highway One, I was too wired to sleep. Ed had left me a voicemail, checking on whether I'd gotten back safely, but it was too late to answer. I racketed around the kitchen for a while, wiping cabinets and counters and mopping the floor. When that failed to work off the caffeine and adrenalin, I brought down my precious bottle of Grand Marnier from its cabinet over the sink. A small glass and a Nero Wolfe novel picked randomly from the shelf of paperbacks in my living room did the trick, and after a half-hour I was finally out for what remained of the night.

16

It felt as though I was barely home from Wheaton when Sandra Blaine's motion showed up in the mail. She had decided that Judge Brackett had a conflict of interest because he had defended Steve Scanlon in a couple of cases in juvenile court. I thought she was being a whiner and said so, in measured legal language, in the response I sent to Mike for filing. But Judge Brackett took the path of least resistance and issued an order two weeks later recusing himself from the case. The order also vacated the dates for the habeas hearing and status conference.

While we waited for a new judge, Mike and Dan went on a tour of prisons, visiting a few Aryan Brotherhood dropouts who Scanlon had told them might have some background on the hit on Lindahl. I worked on the rest of my cases and made a couple of long drives of my own to the Central Valley, to visit my client in the women's prison and interview witnesses in her hometown. Then, with a sigh of relief at not having to endure the oven-like heat of inland California for a while, I drove to San Quentin for a day of visits to clients.

It was summer, and I'd worn a white oxford cloth shirt under my black jacket. When I took off my jacket and put it on the belt of the X-ray machine, the guard there appraised my ensemble and said, "That shirt is a little too light. You can see the outline of your bra through it." I stopped taking off my watch. *Don't fuck with me,* I thought. *I didn't get myself out of bed at dawn and drive three hours to get here to be told my clothes are too sexy for a prison visit.* What I said, though, was, "I'm sorry. I didn't know."

The desk guard who had processed my paperwork came to my rescue. "She's okay," he called from behind me. "Let her through." I gave both guards a look that I hoped expressed only gratitude. The guard at the X-ray machine turned her attention to the TV screen that showed the inward secrets of my jacket, shoes, plastic case of money and pens, and file folder. I cleared the metal detector without further incident, put on my jacket, watch, and shoes, slid out the door into the prison grounds, and walked the couple hundred yards of sidewalk to the main prison gate, paying little attention to the view of the dark blue bay and the misty hills beyond it. *Oh, fuck you, fuck you—just fuck you all,* ran the resentful mantra in my mind. A visit to Howard was enough without some minor bureaucrat worrying about whether some inmate might glimpse the shadow of my utilitarian sports bra underneath my mannish blazer.

Howard wasn't the only client I was visiting that day.

First I stopped to talk to Arturo Villegas, whose appeal I had taken the previous year. He was worried for his family. His parents were undocumented and in fear of being found and deported. Immigration agents seemed to be everywhere in Los Angeles arresting people. His family hadn't visited him for his birthday because they were afraid to apply for a visit and travel from Los Angeles. His younger sister—the pride of his family—was enrolled in Cal State and living at home, and his younger brother had just started high school; they were US-born, at least, but he didn't know what they would do if his parents were taken away. His parents couldn't afford to hire an immigration lawyer, and they didn't know if one could even help them. Lately, they had been afraid to talk about the issue over the prison phones, so all Arturo could do was call them every week or so to see if they were all right. The price Arturo was paying for his crime included one that people on the outside didn't generally see: the pain of being unable to help when those you loved were in trouble.

I told him I'd make some calls to see if there were free legal services available for his parents, and said to tell his sister she could call me if his parents were picked up.

Howard was my last visit that day. Because he was in the Adjustment Center for the latest in an ongoing series of small infractions of prison rules, he was not allowed a face-to-face visit, nor could I buy him anything to eat or drink. Instead, we each sat in an airless, closet-sized room with a glass partition between us, and talked over bad telephones.

Howard was more lucid and less demanding than usual. His letter-writing campaign had for once paid off, in a small way. He'd received a sympathetic letter about his plight from an NGO in the Netherlands; he held it up to the glass for me to read and promised to send me a copy. He had been getting visits from a prison chaplain, though Howard didn't think much of the man's knowledge of the Bible. Howard spent a long time recounting in microscopic detail their disagreements about the meaning of the Book of Revelation.

"I told him about my case," he said.

"Howard, you know you're not supposed to talk about your case to people outside your legal team," I said. The warning was a formality at this point; Howard had spent the last decade and a half talking about it to anyone he could corner.

"I told him I'm innocent. I explained the conspiracy. He was pretty shocked. Not surprising. Everyone is when I tell them about it and that I was in jail when Jared Lindahl was killed. They all wonder why I'm still here."

"Well, I hope we can get you out soon."

"How is Steve Scanlon? Have you met him yet?"

"No, but Mike has. I gather he's okay."

"Good. He's done his best to help me."

I'd been nonplussed by Howard's calmness. Finally, I asked him point blank, "Howard, are you taking a new medication?"

"In fact, yes," he said. "They're making me take Risperdal."

"How did that happen?"

"They thought I was suicidal, but I wasn't. Anyway, they sent me to the psych ward and got a court order, so I have to take it for a year, they say."

The things that happen between visits, I thought. No one from the prison had told us any of this. "Well, you seem calmer," I said.

"I'm just tired all the time," he said. As if to prove his point, he yawned. "If you don't have anything else to tell me, I'll go back to my house and take a nap." He gestured behind him to the guard stationed behind the no-contact booth, and within a minute, he was being handcuffed. He turned away without a goodbye, and I was free to go.

I hadn't even reached my house when the next ax fell.

17

"I suppose I shouldn't have been surprised that they've assigned Judge Redd to Howard's hearing," Mike said, when I called him, after listening to his voicemail. "Actually, I'm a little surprised they didn't pick him first, since he was the trial judge."

"Is it really that bad?" I asked. As far as I could tell from reading the transcript of Howard's trial, the judge, except for keeping all evidence of the Aryan Brotherhood's involvement in the murder away from the jury, had more or less sat back and let Howard bury himself.

"Well, his nickname locally is Judge Dredd."

"Ah," I acknowledged.

"Howard's Luck," Mike sighed. "Again."

At some point we had given the name to the endless series of misfortunes and reversals that seemed to follow Howard through his life.

"I wish I had a nickel," I began singing, "I wish I had a dime; I wish I had a boyfriend, to kiss me all the time."

"What's that?" Mike asked.

"An old hopscotch song. Just seemed right for the moment somehow." I went on. "My mother took my nickel, my father took my dime; my sister took my boyfriend, and gave me Frankenstein."

"Huh," Mike said. "Sounds about right."

"And the funding cut?" I asked.

"Pretty bad," he said. "I talked with Mary, the claims person, and she said the court is taking the view that most of the investigation must have been done already, when Gordon Marshall had the case, so we didn't need all the money I was asking for. She said I could ask them to reconsider, but she didn't sound real hopeful. The only good news is that the court approved money for Ida Rader to testify as an expert."

"So what do we do now?"

"I'll have to assign less work to Dan," Mike said, "and you and I do more of the investigation. I can do unpaid work, but I don't have the money to pay a lot of expenses. I'll make sure you're paid for your time."

"Don't worry about that," I said, esprit de corps rising grandly above the mundane thought that I had a living to make. "In for a penny, as they say. What do we still need to do—aside from the hearing, of course?"

"Well, Dan and I have gone to see most of the guys we know about. There are a couple more we need to visit, one in prison and one out. Then there's the discovery litigation. By the way, Judge Redd's clerk called this morning about setting a date for a status conference. He wants to set dates for the hearing and find out how the discovery has been going. He thinks we can do it by telephone, save a trip down there. He wants to do it at eight in the morning, a week from Friday. Does that work for you?"

It did, and I said so.

"Fine. I'll let her know."

"Have we heard anything about discovery yet from Blaine?" I asked.

"Not a peep. We'll see what she has to say at the hearing."

18

The morning of the hearing on our discovery motion was cool and foggy, and the whiteness of the light inside my little house reminded me of snow. While I puttered around the kitchen, feeding dog and cats, grinding coffee beans, and pouring cold cereal, I mused about paying Maggie a Christmas visit to see real winter and the Northern Lights.

After breakfast, as I waited for the phone call and shrugged a flannel shirt over my jeans and cotton tee, I felt grateful that I didn't have to be in a suit and even more grateful that I didn't have to be in Wheaton, where the daytime temperature at this time of year would probably top out at well over a hundred degrees.

The phone rang. It was Mike conferencing me in, and soon I could hear the judge, Frank Willard, and Sandra Blaine. For the benefit of the court reporter transcribing the call, the judge recited the nature of the hearing, and we stated our appearances.

Judge Redd didn't waste time. "So, before Judge Brackett

recused himself, you had a hearing set for October, right?"

We all murmured agreement.

"And discovery compliance the middle of September?"

More murmurs of assent.

"Well, unless something has changed, I'd like to keep those dates."

More murmurings, this time with an undertone of uncertainty, as we all presumably checked our calendars. Willard and I came back saying both dates were still good for us. Mike said he now had a preliminary hearing on September 18, the date set for discovery compliance, but the October hearing date was still clear. The loudest whining came from Sandra Blaine, who said she had conflicts on both dates.

"How is the discovery compliance going?" the judge asked. "That should be almost ready by now, shouldn't it?"

Blaine hemmed and hawed. She had been so busy with other cases; it had been very difficult to conduct the review.

"How far along are you?" the judge asked. She had to admit that she hadn't yet gotten the files from storage.

The judge was not amused. "You've had all spring and summer, and it's nearly Labor Day. You have almost a month before the 18th. Surely you can do your review and make the materials available to Mr. Barry by then. I don't want to have to continue the evidentiary hearing because you haven't provided timely discovery."

Blaine hedged. She was sorry she hadn't been able to

get to the files, and she couldn't do it now because she was leaving on Labor Day weekend for a three-week vacation in Europe. The judge was unimpressed. "I'm sorry, Mrs. Blaine," he said, "but I'm not letting this hearing be delayed any more than necessary. I tried Mr. Henley's case. It seemed fairly simple. I can't imagine that the district attorney's files would be particularly extensive or that there was anything of significance that wasn't given to Mr. Henley or his advisory counsel. You should be able to assign someone in your office to get them from storage and go through them for work product or whatever. I'm ordering you to do that and to have the discovery available to Mr. Barry and his co-counsel by September 18th. No more excuses; is that clear?"

"Yes, Your Honor," Blaine said. I wondered if she wasn't thinking she might have had a better bargain with Judge Brackett.

"Good. Mr. Barry, did you say you had another hearing on September 18th?"

"Yes, Your Honor," Mike said, "but Ms. Moodie can take care of reviewing the discovery."

"Good. Mrs. Blaine, find someone from your office to take care of it, and let Mr. Barry and Mr. Willard know who that person will be. Can you do that by the end of the day today?"

"May I have until Monday, Your Honor?"

"Okay, Monday."

Blaine wasn't finished. Her next problem was that in

the time after Judge Brackett had recused himself, another department had set one of her cases for trial on October 11, and she was sure it would go for at least a week, and perhaps two.

"How about continuing the hearing to November 1st?" the judge asked.

Mike liked that, and I, as usual, had nothing else I was doing. There was a ragged chorus of, "Thank you, Your Honor," some probably more sincerely meant than others, and we all hung up.

Mike called me right away. "Well, that didn't go too badly."

"Better than I expected. It may just be me, but I get the impression Judge Redd isn't exactly fond of Blaine."

"Well, he probably knows her pretty well; my guess is he can tell she's stonewalling. Glad he reacted the way he did."

"Maybe he won't be so dreadful after all."

"You will be able to go to Wheaton on the 18th, won't you?"

"Yes, no problem."

"Great. I want to be there to see the files as soon as we can. I don't want Willard to get there first; he might talk them out of giving us stuff. I just hope they don't have the bright idea of calling him before the date. Not much we can do about it, though."

"We have to send Blaine and Willard our discovery, too. Are you taking care of that?"

"Yeah. We don't have anything to give them at this point but a few interview reports from some of those old-timers Dan and I saw. Now that we know the hearing date again, I'll have to send subpoenas to the Department of Corrections for debriefing documents on Scanlon and a couple of other people. I'll get Annie to do those. It's good to be moving again."

19

In early September I flew up to Alaska to see my sister Maggie in Fairbanks.

Maggie took a few days off from her job in the IT department of the university, and we spent my visit picking blueberries and low-bush cranberries, feeding and running her wildly energetic pack of sled dogs, soaking in the hot springs at Chena, and catching up on each other's lives. I admired the raspberries and giant cabbages in her garden, and she envied my ability to grow tomatoes.

"You've become a real end-of-the-roader down there," Maggie said one day as we drank gin and tonics on her deck on one of those gold afternoons where the summer sun seemed to hang forever in the sky above the spruce trees. "You may as well move back here."

I'd hated the four years I'd spent in Anchorage, following my parents' quixotic decision to move there from California. But Fairbanks was different. On visits to Maggie and her husband Pete over the years, I'd grown to love the vast and forbidding Alaska interior; and now that I'd gotten over my youthful resentment at being forced to live thousands of miles from any center of culture, moving back north didn't seem quite so unrealistic—at least in the summer. It would be nice to be near my family, I thought, especially with Gavin so far away in Australia. "Alaska is beautiful," I acknowledged, "but I'm too settled where I am. I don't think I could get used to snow again." Or eight-month-long winters, I admitted to myself.

I was on the second leg of my trip, visiting my other sister Candace and her enviably perfect family outside Anchorage, when Howard's case lurched back into my consciousness. An email arrived from Mike: "Bad news. The state Supreme Court cut my investigation funds request in half. We'll need to talk when you get back." Maggie would have cursed mightily in sympathy with me over the bad news, but Candace and Emil didn't have much pity for convicted murderers or the money problems of court-appointed lawyers. So I shut up about it, listened to Candace expand on the accomplishments of her children, and enjoyed the hikes we took in the state parks around Anchorage, the panoramic view of the mountains from her living room, and the salmon Emil barbecued for us the evening before I had to leave.

I barely had time, it seemed, to collect Charlie and do my laundry from the trip, when it was time to head back to Wheaton.

20

Before leaving I called the district attorney's office and talked to the deputy district attorney who had been assigned to pull the prosecution files in Blaine's absence; he confirmed that they would be ready and waiting for me. I also called Dot Henley, to let her know I'd be in town and invite her to lunch, if I finished my review in time.

The Central Valley in mid-September was still breathlessly hot outside the windows of my air-conditioned car, and beyond the irrigated fields and orchards, the hills were dusty tan after the rainless summer. The air was hazy with the smoke of distant wildfires, and now and then I passed a fire truck on its way to or from the mountains.

Wheaton was quiet on a warm Sunday night, and I ate dinner at the Mexican restaurant where Mike and I had gone before, surrounded by families gathered around festive plates of chips and guacamole and fajitas. Back in my room, I fell asleep watching a forgettable romantic comedy on the hotel's movie channel.

At the district attorney's office the next morning, I was greeted by a young man and woman who seemed hardly out of college. The man was the deputy prosecutor who had been left in charge of giving me the Henley and Scanlon discovery, the woman a paralegal who was assigned to sit with me while I reviewed it.

The prosecutor, whose first name was Adam, handed me a business card and a manila envelope. "Copies of CDs and cassette tapes," he said, making a disapproving face. "I would have put them on a flash drive for you, but we don't have the equipment, so the best I could do was copy them onto a DVD."

They showed me to a vacant office, where a small stack of boxes stood on a desk and another stack on the floor beside it. "The ones on the desk are Henley's, the ones on the floor are Scanlon's," Adam said. "We're still in the process of scanning the discoverable material, but because of the court's order, we're making the originals available to you to review today. We should be able to send you the scanned copies in a few days." The paralegal, whose name was Candace, volunteered to make photocopies of anything I wanted. They seemed a little worried that the compliance wasn't on schedule; apparently Judge Redd was not to be trifled with.

Candace found a chair in a corner of the office and sat, reading a textbook of some sort, while I set up my computer and portable scanner and pulled a stack of file folders from the first box.

Most of it was the usual stuff you find in case files: police reports, coroner's investigator reports, crime-scene photos, the autopsy report and photos, rap sheets of the defendant, the victim, and some of the people interviewed about the crime. A lot of the pages had numbers stamped or handwritten in their corners to identify them as discovery materials; those would have been given to the defense before the trial. I had a list of the numbered pages we had already in the files of Howard's previous attorneys. As for the rest, I scanned some and had Candace make copies of others. It was a tedious process. When Candace and I had to leave the office for her lunch break, I wasn't quite through the files of Howard's case. I called Dot and postponed our meeting till the next morning, and then ate a lonely and unceremonious lunch at a sandwich place near the courthouse before hurrying back for the afternoon.

The letter almost escaped my notice. It was the middle of the afternoon, and I was in a slump that even the giant iced coffee I'd brought back from my trip into the noonday heat hadn't lifted. I was skimming through documents from the files of Scanlon's case, scanning or having copied anything I didn't remember seeing before.

The jail deputies had intercepted several "kites," letters sent between jail inmates, from Scanlon to other men in the jail, and had given copies to the prosecutor. I was leafing through them when I turned a page and saw a fax cover sheet and behind it a photocopy of an envelope addressed to Steve Scanlon and a two-page letter. The cover sheet was from a parole office in Wheaton and addressed to a detective in the Wheaton police department. On it was a handwritten note reading, "Letter confiscated during the search of Steven Scanlon's vehicle on February 6, 1999."

On the envelope the sender was given as Calvin McGaw, the return address was Folsom Prison. The letter itself was handwritten; between that and the poor quality of the fax copy I decided I didn't have time to try to read it. None of the documents—the cover sheet, the letter, or the copy of the envelope—had discovery numbers on them.

I scanned them and then gave them, with the kites, to Candace to copy. Best not to draw attention to it, I thought.

Most of the rest of the files were daily transcripts of Scanlon's trial. I leafed through them and was able to finish reviewing everything from Scanlon's case before Candace's quitting time. With a smile I thanked her and picked up my computer and backpack full of photocopies.

Over the noon hour, when I knew I wasn't going to finish reading the files in time to drive home that day, I'd called the hotel and extended my stay for another night. Now I called Mike's office, but he had left, so I called his cellphone and left a voicemail, saying, "Just found something; give me a call."

Mike called back within ten minutes, and I told him about the letter. He was quiet for so long I asked if he was still on the line. "Yeah," he answered. "This could be huge;

I'm just trying to think what we should do. Can you email it to me?"

I said I could, and as soon as I was off the phone, I opened my computer and sent it to him. Impatient, and lacking much else to do, I decided to make a transcript of it, in an attempt to decipher it. It was dated late December of 1998, and the parts I could read seemed innocuous. "How are you?" it began. "Hope all is well with you.

It's been a while, and I thought I drop you a few lines, let you know how I'm doing here. I'm still in the hole. The way [ill.] people are talking I may [ill.] get out in less [ill.] to be a stool pigeon. That's fucked up isn't it. Maybe one of these days things will change and they will put me back on a mainline. Hell, I haven't really been in trouble for a long time! I intend to keep it that way too! I go to my parole board hearing in April. I'm not looking for them to give me a parole date this time. Hopefully in a few years they will. Well I hope you've been in good health. Are you still working? How are your homies there? Hope you [and your?] family shared a nice Christmas together and hope you have a great year in '99. Are you taking up martial arts like you wanted? I think you could [ill.] go somewhere.

Mail room is holding up my outgoing mail for some reason. My wife says it took a couple weeks to get my last letter. Let me know if you get this late. Well, my friend

that is about it. You take care and get back at me when
you can.
  Your friend,
  C. McGaw

It read like a pretty typical prison letter, though strangely lacking in anything but generalities. McGaw didn't have much to say to his friend Steve.

If there was anything encoded in it, I couldn't see it.

21

Dot Henley's house was down a country road outside of Wheaton. It was an ample two-story house, half-timbered in a sort of mock-Tudor style, in a neighborhood of upscale houses on several-acre parcels surrounded by white-painted horse fencing. A Prius and a small SUV were parked at the top of the driveway, and farther down a pickup truck stacked with landscaping tools was pulled over at one side. Two men were mowing the lawn and pulling weeds among the shrubs and trees in the front of the house. The morning was already warm, and a range of hills was visible in the distance across the hazy expanse of the valley.

Dot Henley answered the door at my ring. I apologized for standing her up for lunch, and she said, "I understand. I hope you got everything done you needed to."

"I did," I acknowledged.

She led me into a cool and spacious living room, decorated in pale colors, with large windows looking out to the front of the house, comfortable sofas and chairs gathered around a glass-topped coffee table, and framed family photos and pretty china knick-knacks on side tables. The fireplace was behind an old-fashioned painted screen for the summer, and a fan turned gently below the high ceiling.

At the other side of the coffee table, a middle-aged man in a suit was just standing up from an armchair. "This is my son Bob," Dot said. Bob reached out and shook hands with me. "Pleased to meet you," he said. He seemed serious, but not unfriendly.

Bob was a little taller than Howard and heavier-set, but the family resemblance was visible in his face, with its high forehead and gray eyes set deep in their sockets. His face had a healthy tan, though, instead of Howard's prison pallor, his cheeks and lips were more filled out, and his iron-gray hair was short and well cut. Dot pointed out the similarity. "Bob and Howard were a lot alike when they were younger," she said. "They both take after Lyle." Bob looked as if he wished she hadn't said that, but didn't say anything.

Dot asked if I wanted coffee, and I said I did and offered to help her with it. "Bob, would you like your cup warmed up?" she asked. He thanked her and handed it to her.

I followed her into a kitchen worthy of the house, a big, comfortable room with lots of counters and oak cabinets and a center island. It merged into a spacious family room with a stone fireplace and French doors onto a shaded patio.

She set down Bob's cup and took two others from a

cabinet. "Maybe I'll have some coffee myself," she said. "I hope you don't mind Bob being here. I didn't mean for him to ambush you, but he insisted on stopping by when I told him you were coming to see me."

"No, no, that's fine. I'm glad to get to meet him," I said. "I love your house."

"I've always liked it here," Dot said. "Lyle had it built for us. I love this kitchen. It was perfect when we had a big family and did a lot of entertaining."

"I can see that; it's really nice."

She nodded. "But to tell the truth, the house feels too big for me now. My kids don't want to give it up, though. I've been talking with Kevin about maybe selling it to him and moving into a nice condo nearer town."

Dot poured coffee from a coffeemaker next to the stove and asked if I wanted milk or sugar. When I said I liked milk, she said, "So does Bob. It's in the refrigerator door; would you mind getting it?" I did, and added some to his cup and mine. We carried the cups back out to the living room and set them on the coffee table.

Bob was back in his armchair, reading something on his phone; he put it in his pocket as we came back. I sat down on the sofa, reached for my cup, and took a sip of coffee.

He spoke first, to me. "I just wanted to meet you," he said, almost apologetically, "get to know Howard's new attorneys. His case is important to us—I guess that goes without saying. It hasn't been easy putting up with Howard all these years, but the bottom line is, he's family, and he doesn't deserve to be where he is."

"I definitely agree," I said.

"Mom and Kevin tried to explain to me what's going on with his case. He's got a hearing scheduled about whether he's actually innocent of the murder, is that it?"

"More or less. The court is asking what evidence there is that he didn't commit the crime."

"Well, I'm glad they're asking that question. Howard isn't all there, but he's not a killer. And the idea that he'd hire someone and pay him was just b.s., pardon my language. Ray Donahue, the lawyer we retained for Howard, told me the guy who really killed him told a couple of people that Howard didn't have anything to do with it. He figured he'd have no trouble getting him off at trial. But then Howard fired him," Bob rolled his eyes, "and the rest is history."

"Yep," I agreed.

"I got no love for Howard, in some ways," Bob continued. "He messed my life up pretty bad when we were young. Stole my identity, which got me put in jail and fired from a good job. It took years, and a lot of help from Ray, to finally clear my record. I was ready to let him rot in jail, for all I cared. I even voted for what's-her-name, Blaine, when she ran for district attorney. But Dad and Mom here pushed me to forgive him, and I guess I have. I wish you good luck, hope he gets off death row."

I thanked him.

"One thing, though. If he's freed, is there any way you can get him into a hospital, or at least keep him from coming back here?"

"To be honest, I don't know," I said. "I know there are some fairly strict legal requirements that have to be met before a person can be kept in a mental hospital against their will, but I'm no expert on that area of law."

Bob nodded. "Yeah, I know something about that. We've been through it with Howard. I've asked Ray, and he says the same thing. It's a shame, really. Howard is his own worst enemy; there's no way he should have been out on his own. I sure don't want him back here, especially since Dad isn't around to deal with him."

"I wish I could be more helpful."

"It's the system." He shrugged and shook his head, and said with a chuckle, "Maybe we can just pay him to live someplace like Mexico or Costa Rica."

"It might work," I answered.

He stood up. "I'm glad we got to talk. I've got to get back to work now. Just wanted to come by and meet you and say my piece."

I stood, too; this seemed like a good time for me to move on. Bob shook my hand again. "Thank you for working on his case, and good luck. I'll get the door, Mom; see you later." He bent down and kissed Dot's cheek and headed out the front door.

I helped Dot carry the coffee cups back to the kitchen.

"I should go, too," I said. "I need to drive back up north today."

"I hope Bob didn't make you uncomfortable," she said, as we walked toward the front door. "He really wanted to come meet you, but I didn't think he'd say all the stuff he did."

"It's okay," I said. "It's a difficult situation for your family, and it's good that he was able to let us know how he felt."

"He did that," she said, with a small smile. "Well, we all wish you and Mr. Barry success."

I thanked her.

The morning was growing hot, and the hills were nearly invisible behind a layer of smoky air as I walked out to my car. The SUV was gone, but the Prius and the gardeners were still there. Dot's family took good care of her, I thought. It would be easy to envy her if you didn't know about Howard.

22

At home, I read through the reports and other papers I'd copied, and listened to the recordings on the DVD.

Among the numbered discovery documents from the district attorney's files of Scanlon's case were a few reports we hadn't seen before of interviews with people in and around the trailer park. One of the people questioned was Freddy Gomez, the pivotal witness against Howard. He told the police that he'd heard from other people in the park that Lindahl had beaten up Howard and robbed him. Howard wasn't really a drug dealer, Gomez said, just a sort of babysitter for another guy's drug business. The guy, whom he refused to name, ran the business out of the trailer park and had taken to leaving some product with Howard when he was out of town because Howard didn't use, unless you counted smoking weed now and then, and, whatever else people might think of him, Howard was absolutely honest about money. If Lindahl took drugs and money from Howard's place, Freddy said, they belonged to the other guy, who would not be happy about it. Nothing in the reports suggested that the police tried to find out the identity of the mysterious dealer; presumably the discovery of Scanlon's confession to the murder and Freddy's later accusation against Howard had foreclosed that line of inquiry.

Another resident interviewed said that Freddy had gone to Lindahl's cabin after the killing and taken a gun belonging to Lindahl. She said the gun was hidden in the cabin, but Freddy knew where it was. Freddy told her he'd tried to sell it to a gun dealer he knew named Indio, but Indio wouldn't take it. Freddy denied all of it, saying the girl was a heroin addict and had made it all up.

Among the cassette tapes reproduced on the DVD were the recordings of Freddy Gomez's statement to a detective about seeing Henley give a gun to Scanlon. We had the transcript of that interview, and there were no surprises except for one point where Gomez hesitated when asked to describe the gun, a brief hemming and hawing followed by, "Oh, right, it was a revolver, looked like a .38." The pause and the "Oh, right," were not in the transcript. It was easy to imagine that someone gave him a cue, but with just the audiotape there was no proving whether any such thing had happened.

Except for the transcript of the taped interview, none of this had apparently been given to Howard or his lawyers. Many prosecutors would have handed it over, but Blaine's reputation was that she was one of those who generally decided against giving up information when she felt she could get away without doing it—who "tacked close to the wind," as the Supreme Court put it when writing about prosecutors' obligation to disclose exculpatory evidence. Looking at the material, it would be easy to rationalize that none of it obviously pointed to Howard's innocence. The letter, of course, was a different story.

The name "Indio" rang a bell. Mike had said Steve Scanlon had told him and Dan he'd bought the murder weapon, a Smith & Wesson .38, from a guy he knew only as Indio and, because he needed money, had sold it back to him afterward.

So now what?

"Well," Mike said, when I called him. "We've got to see Scanlon again and show him the letter. Dan has been trying to locate this guy Indio, but it's just about impossible with nothing but a nickname."

"What about McGaw? Shouldn't we try to authenticate the letter through him?"

"Dead," Mike said.

"Damn, these guys don't live long, do they? What did he do to get on the hit list?"

"Nothing, actually. His death certificate says he died of a stroke."

Rimshot.

"Can you come with me? Dan's going to be working on locating and interviewing witnesses from around Wheaton. And with the court cutting my investigative expenses, I can't afford to pay him for three or four days of travel out of town, but you may be able to bill the court for attorney time. If not, I may be taking advantage of your offer to do some work for free."

"Sure—when do you propose to go?"

"As soon as I can arrange a visit and find some cheap plane tickets to Salt Lake. I'll let you know."

23

"This place is really in the middle of nowhere," I said. "It's like a prison in the sky."

"People probably think twice about escaping," Scanlon said drily.

"I would think so." I didn't feel very conversational. After what seemed like an endless day—a redeye flight to Salt Lake City followed by an eternity of winding, lonely mountain highway, rock walls, and scrubby pine forest—my head ached and my stomach wouldn't stop churning. Mike said it was probably the altitude; I wasn't sure I cared.

Wasatch was a modern prison, all concrete and metal. We had been escorted into a pod, a five-sided space, which contained several attorney visiting rooms, each a glass-fronted segment surrounding a central court with tables and backless stools. Everything in the pod seemed to be made of steel and bolted to the floor. In our visiting room, the table surface was brushed stainless, and the chairs were painted metal with fake leather cushions on their seats. The lighting was fluorescent and shadowless; it made my headache worse. One other visiting room was occupied, but the central court was empty except for an occasional guard or inmate moving through on an errand.

Steve Scanlon had been brought out without handcuffs, escorted by a single guard. He had greeted Mike and me with an almost courtly courtesy—how do you dos, handshakes, a polite question about how we had found the drive up here. Someone had taught him good manners, it seemed. He was fairly tall—I'd guess a little shy of six feet—and lanky. Even at forty-plus, he was good-looking in a likeable, boyish way, clean-shaven, with straight light-brown hair parted on one side.

"How does being here compare to California?" Mike asked.

Scanlon seemed close to cracking a smile. "A lot better," he said. "It's high security—they've got one guy with a death sentence here—but I'm not locked down. I get to go to the yard with the other guys on my unit—it's a pretty normal life, for prison. Fucking cold outside in the winter, though." He spoke easily, in a slight central California drawl.

"What about retaliation from the AB?"

Scanlon shrugged. "Could happen," he said. "But the Brand isn't as big up here, and I'm probably no big deal to them at this point. Business seems to have kind of slowed down in the last ten years or so; couple of big federal RICO cases took out a lot of the higher-ups and shot-callers. I'm not afraid, really. When you go, you go." He shrugged and gazed briefly out the window into the court. "And it's not as if I have much to look forward to."

"Well, we need you to stay alive," Mike said.

"I'll do my best. How is old Howard?"

Mike turned to me. "Not bad," I said. "I saw him a couple of months ago."

"Still crazy?" Scanlon asked.

"Yeah, but he's calmed down a bit."

"That's good. In the jail he was so wound up everyone thought he was going to have a heart attack."

"Did you see him a lot?" Mike asked.

"Not a lot; I kept my distance," Scanlon said. "But I heard him—and heard about him."

He gave a sideways glance through the windows and got down to business. "So you may have the letter McGaw sent me."

"We think so," Mike said. He leafed through the manila folder of papers he had brought, pulled out a copy of the letter, and placed it in front of Scanlon.

Scanlon glanced at it. "Have you talked to McGaw? I haven't heard anything about him; don't hear much through the grapevine these days."

"He passed away," Mike said.

Scanlon didn't seem particularly surprised at the news. "Huh—what happened?"

"A stroke, according to his death certificate. He was out of prison when he died."

Scanlon chuckled. "Imagine that. Guy like McGaw, after all he did, dying in his bed—now that's irony. So, I guess you're asking me if this is the letter."

"Yep," Mike said. "And maybe you can help us understand where the hidden message is in it."

"Okay." Scanlon read slowly through the letter, occasionally shaking his head. When he had finished, he said to Mike, "That's it, all right. Kind of hard to read. McGaw's handwriting wasn't the best. But I can't say I'm good at decoding what he was saying. I didn't really try at the time. I just considered the source and took it as a reminder of what I was supposed to be doing. The stuff about stool pigeons I figure was some kind of reminder to stay loyal. The homies probably meant Lindahl. And I remember I took the Christmas thing as a way of saying they knew what I'd been up to, and the 'are you still working' and delayed letters as his way of saying, 'Why are you screwing around out there?' 'Cause I'd been out on parole for a while at that point. The martial arts part probably just meant what it said; I'd been practicing in prison, and he thought I was getting pretty good. How'd you find it, anyway?"

"It was in the district attorney's files of your case," Mike said.

"Son of a bitch," Scanlon said. "They never told us they had it."

"Did you tell the Corrections Department about it when you debriefed from the gang?"

"Definitely. I told them I had the proof if they could find it."

"We've been trying to get your debriefing paper—the one you wrote—from the Corrections Department," Mike said, "and the attorney general has been stonewalling us. I'm afraid they're trying to keep it from us until the last minute and then use it to impeach you when you testify, try to show you're a liar."

"Sounds about right," Scanlon said.

"We're going to have to ask you to tell us everything you remember writing in it, everything about your criminal history, so we aren't blindsided."

"You have my C-file, don't you?" Scanlon asked.

Mike nodded. "Yes, and a bunch of court records. But that's just the stuff you were convicted of, and the disciplinaries you picked up. We need to know what else you told Mrs. Rader."

"Hoo, boy," Scanlon said.

Mike's paralegal had made a timeline of Scanlon's brushes with the law, and Mike started going through that with him.

"How old were you when you were first sent to prison?"

"Eighteen. I'd been in the Youth Authority before that, but they let me go."

"How long were you in for that time?"

Scanlon thought for a moment, counting the years on his

hands. "Six years. Right up until I paroled and then popped Lindahl. It wasn't supposed to be that long, but I lost good time because I kept getting in trouble."

"What kind of trouble?"

"Bunch of stuff, mostly getting involved in other people's fights and mouthing off at the guards."

"Where were you during that time?"

"The first place they sent me was the fire camp at Owens Valley. I guess I flunked out of that, so they sent me to DVI, then to Soledad, and from there to Folsom."

"Where did you first run into guys from the Aryan Brotherhood?"

"Probably Soledad, really. There were some at DVI, but I wasn't there that long. There were definitely AB at Soledad. Lotta guys with the shamrock tattoos. They were pretty much in charge of all the white guys there."

"How did that work?" Mike asked. "Did you have to join them in some way?"

"Actually, no," Scanlon said. "They didn't want just anyone. Basically, you could mind your own business and be left alone, as long as you didn't screw up or mess with them. If someone from one of the other races messed with you, they'd have your back because they took care of the whites."

"So did you voluntarily seek them out, then, to get involved?"

"Yeah. Like I said, I was pretty immature, and wanting something bigger than me to get involved in, you see. You might say I was seeking a cause. And these guys, they were like, you know, real men. They had a code and rules for how to behave, and it all made sense to me then. And then, if you were a young white guy and they thought you might have promise, they'd kind of take you under their wing and teach you how to survive. Mack Gentry did that for me—taught me how to make knives, handcuff keys, whatever. I looked up to him; he was like the perfect white man."

"Do you know where Gentry is now?"

"Yeah, he's dead."

"Damn."

"Yeah. He was killed in the Pelican Bay SHU. Some kind of fight among the higher-ups. I was debriefing when it happened. It made me feel I'd done the right thing to get out."

"Did you meet McGaw at Soledad?"

"No, Folsom. But he helped me, too. Taught me to get a little more control over myself."

"Can you remember what you told them in your debriefing statement about who you knew and what you were involved in there?"

Scanlon closed his eyes and lowered his head for a moment, thinking, before turning back to Mike. "I was trying to see the pages in my head, to remember what all I wrote. Let's see, there were an awful lot of stabbings there. It was a violent place. Kites went around all the time saying that this or that guy was in the hat or ought to be taught a lesson or just gotten rid of. I didn't get to see most of them because I wasn't a member or really high up, so I wasn't in on the business of making the lists. I'd just hear that we didn't like so-and-so, and that was a signal that he should be taken out."

"Were you ordered to stab anyone?"

"Yeah. I mean, it wasn't like a direct order, but you knew you were expected to carry them out. There are no 'maybes' about it. They don't tell you, 'Do this.' It's just if I say I was AB, and you were an associate, and I told you, 'If you ever see John, we don't like him,' you'd pretty much know what you have to do."

"Did you follow those orders?"

"Oh, yeah, you don't have any choice."

"So you stabbed people in the prison?"

"Oh, yes. I did a few. I wrote up the ones I remembered. Guy named John, who was supposedly a child molester, and some guy whose name I can't remember, who disrespected Corker. I threw him over the tier rail. He survived, but he never said who did it to him. Claimed he didn't remember. Smart, actually. There were a couple of others, stabbings in the yard; I don't even remember their names anymore.

"Don't get me wrong; I wasn't always just following orders. Sometimes I volunteered when I heard about someone on the list."

"Why did you do that?"

"At first more or less just for the excitement, because it

was new, to see what it was like. What kind of shocked me was that I didn't feel nothing inside after the first or second time. I remember thinking, man, shouldn't I feel sorry or feel bad? I guess I decided the way to deal with it is I just see it as a game of Monopoly. He didn't pass go, he didn't get his two hundred bucks. He knew the rules just like I did, so that's his fault. I don't know if that's a good way to look at it, but it helped me.

"And also at the time I had ambitions. I wanted to rise up in the ranks, maybe get to be a member. So I put the word out I was up for whatever."

"And at some point you were told in some way to kill Lindahl?"

"Yeah. All without just coming out and saying it, of course. I heard he was on his way out because he'd stolen drugs or something like that—maybe been given some product to sell and put it up his own nose. I don't know. But he wasn't paying the tax. He paroled before they managed to act, and then I guess McGaw knew I was from the same town as Lindahl and I'd be paroling, too, in a few months. So arrangements were made, you might say."

"So McGaw wasn't the one who ordered the hit, just the one who arranged it with you."

"Right. The order came from higher up the chain somewhere, maybe Corker Bensinger, who was a major player in Folsom, maybe someone higher than him."

"And then you paroled, and what happened?"

"Well, it was kind of late in the year, close to Thanksgiving, and what with that and Christmas and all, I was spending some time getting to know my family again. I even worked for a few weeks. Thought I might try to stay out of trouble. Kept putting off this thing with Lindahl till tomorrow, next week, whatever. It was kind of a jolt, actually, getting that letter from Cal. I guess, realistically I was on my way back to prison by then; I'd started doing burglaries and small-time robberies—for entertainment as much as the money. I was getting bored living a respectable life. Anyhow, I'd been told before I paroled where Lindahl was staying. I knew the trailer park because I'd grown up around there, and a cousin of mine that I was always pretty close to was living there—I'd crashed at her place a couple of times when I was a kid, and while I was out I stopped by once in a while to see how she was doing. Kind of a welfare check, if you know what I mean; she had her problems."

"Is she still around?"

"No. She died maybe five years ago. My sister wrote to tell me. She had cancer, I think, but it took her pretty quick."

"What did the letter from Cal mean to you?" Mike asked.

"Well, I saw it as kind of a reprimand. It came out of nowhere. I hadn't heard zilch from those guys since paroling, and then here's this letter. Made me think I'd better get going, because if I didn't finish the job before getting sent back to the joint, there would be problems for me there.

"Anyhow, I set things up with Freddy Gomez, first to

help me buy a gun for the hit—I'd been doing robberies with one I found in a drawer in my parents' house, and I wasn't about to use it in a murder—and then to introduce me to Lindahl. Freddy was kind of an AB wannabe, but he was too into drugs to ever go anywhere. I didn't tell him anything about my plans, told him I was looking for a partner for some robberies. So he gave me a cellphone number for this guy Indio, and I got in touch with him and bought a good gun, a Smith & Wesson .38, 'cause I didn't want anything to go wrong. Then Freddy brought me up to Lindahl's cabin one afternoon. And I got to know Lindahl, did a robbery with him the next day. The day after that I went to his place with Freddy and some beers, and we hung out for a while, drank beer, smoked weed, talked guns. Then I suggested we go to the clearing and do some target shooting. I sent Freddy out for more beer, so it was just Lindahl and me. We went out back and shot a few rounds, and then I waited until he wasn't looking and just popped him in the back of the head, like that," Scanlon mimed shooting a handgun two-handed. "He just dropped, without a sound. I figured he was dead, but I shot him another couple times anyway, just to make sure. Then— God knows why, I guess I was kinda ripped—I took his watch and a police scanner he'd had with him."

"Then Lindahl had his gun on him when you killed him?"

"Yeah. I heard they didn't find no gun out there. Little son of a bitch Gomez probably came back and took it. I didn't take it, 'cause I didn't know where he got it or what it might have been used for."

"Freddy's the one who turned you on to Indio, right?"

"Yeah."

"We've been trying to find Indio. Can you tell us any more about him?"

He closed his eyes for a second, then opened them. "I'm trying to remember. All Freddy gave me was the name Indio and the phone number. I remember being surprised when I met him, because I figured with a name like Indio he'd be, like Mexican or Indian, you know? But he was this kind of heavy-set Anglo guy, light hair, not too old, maybe early thirties. Freddy said he worked in the oil fields with his brother."

"Do you know anything more about him?"

"Nothing, really. My guess is that he must have been kind of affiliated with the AB, but not an associate—just, like a sympathizer. Freddy was sort of an AB hanger-on, and he said the guy was safe to deal with."

"How much did you pay for the gun?"

"Three hundred. I had some money just then, wanted a good gun."

"Where did you get the money?"

"I had some from a couple of store robberies."

"So Howard didn't give it to you?"

"Hell, no. No drugs, either. Howard didn't even know this was happening. Nah, I was broke when I heard the cops were after me and I was gonna have to take off. I'm not a planner; spent my last money partying. I was afraid to even try a robbery until I was out of the area. That's why I called Indio and sold the gun back to him instead of getting rid of it somewhere. Got a little cash and a cheap .22. Stupid move, but I was desperate."

"Do you know what he might have done with the gun?"

"Not for sure. We talked a little when I gave it back to him. He was some sort of amateur gunsmith; said he could switch out the barrel and the firing pin of a gun so it couldn't be identified."

"I guess that means it's probably gone for good," Mike said.

Scanlon shrugged. "Probably."

"Anything else you recall about Indio?"

"I heard Freddy Gomez gave him up when he ratted on me, and he was busted not long after that. He was in the jail while I was there, though I didn't see him. I heard they'd set up some kind of sting to get him."

"I take it you told Corrections all this in your debriefing."

"Not about Indio. I don't think I said anything about where I got the gun, and they never asked. They were interested in AB, and Indio wasn't, that I know of."

By prearrangement with Mike, I had been writing down a declaration for Scanlon, in the event that he didn't manage to stay alive until the hearing. It wasn't long, just a statement that he had been an associate of the Aryan Brotherhood;

that he had been told before he paroled to kill Lindahl when Lindahl got out of prison; that the letter we showed him from McGaw was the one he had received reminding him of the order. It also said he had gotten the murder weapon from Indio and sold it back to him afterward. And it said Howard Henley had nothing to do with killing Lindahl, didn't know Scanlon was going to kill him, and never gave Scanlon anything to kill him with. It contained a sentence saying it was signed under penalty of perjury—which, it occurred to me, would be a moot point if we actually had to use it.

Eventually we ran out of things to ask, and Scanlon was becoming a little restless. I gave him the declaration, and he read it intently, initialing each page, signed it at the end, and pushed it back to me. Mike pressed the button that signaled the guard, and while we waited we said our goodbyes and told Scanlon as much as we knew about when he might be transported to California to testify.

"I don't know if they told you," Scanlon said, "but some deputy attorney general and an investigator came to see me, I guess a month or so ago. Asked some questions about who in the AB told me to kill Lindahl, if it wasn't Howard. I got the feeling they were trying to trip me up or something. I told them I wasn't giving up any names to them. The AG wasn't too bad, but the investigator was another story altogether."

"How?" Mike asked.

"Well, as they were getting ready to leave, and the AG

was at the door waiting for the guard, the investigator started threatening me."

"How?" Mike asked.

"He leaned over toward me and whispered that if I didn't work with them they'd bring me back to California and arrange for me to be put in general population."

"Damn!" Mike and I both said.

"Yeah," Scanlon agreed. "I told him I was telling the truth, and I wasn't afraid of dying. Told him he could put his threats where the sun don't shine."

"That was a hell of a thing for him to say," Mike said.

"Yeah," Scanlon said. "But they pull that kind of shit all the time."

"I believe it," Mike said. "I heard of cases where they threatened a witness with a perjury charge for saying he'd been pressured to lie at trial."

Scanlon nodded knowingly. "Then they count on no one believing you when you say what they did."

The guard showed up and we went our separate ways, Scanlon back to the cells, and us past the usual succession of guard posts and sally ports to the brightness of the outside world.

Mike and I didn't say much as we walked back to the car. A dry wind blew grit at us from the bare ground that surrounded the parking lot. I felt cold, from more than just my headache and the thin air. Listening to Scanlon had felt like hearing a voice from beyond the grave. I don't think I'd ever met someone with so few illusions left about his life.

As we drove out, I looked back at the prison, sprawled across a desiccated primordial plain, snow-dusted mountaintops visible in the distance.

Yeah, I'd think twice about escaping into that.

24

I came home wishing for more time to get my affairs in order before the hearing. I had to help Mike prepare for it, mostly by writing more discovery requests for prison records and a motion to open up the hearing to take evidence on a claim that Sandra Blaine had suppressed exculpatory evidence at Howard's trial. I also had to prepare and submit some bills to the courts for work I'd been doing on other cases: I needed the money to get my driveway graded and some patching done on my roof before the winter rains, and to get myself through the winter. Howard's case was not shaping up to be particularly lucrative. And my son Gavin and his fiancée, Rita, were getting married in Melbourne, and I was taking a week off in December to fly to Australia for their wedding.

Howard, who'd been let out of the Adjustment Center, called several times. Because I thought he might be anxious about the upcoming hearing, I didn't want to limit him to the usual once every two weeks, so twice a week or so, I spent the fifteen minutes the prison system allows for inmates' phone calls listening to him rant about the conspiracies that had landed him in prison, until he was mercifully cut off, usually mid-sentence.

Harriet talked me out of skipping our exercise classes, and I had to admit she was right. Dancing and sweating to old ABBA songs and cooling down to Carole King ballads made me feel less jangled after Howard's calls and nostalgic about my youth, before law school and grown-up life and Terry, and now Howard.

One afternoon, she and I made the trip to the big mall in Santa Rosa, where she bought a machine saw for Bill's birthday and helped me choose a couple of professional-looking suits I couldn't afford for the hearing.

I took another day off with Ed to start a batch of cider, with apples from our trees and some expert help and the loan of an apple press from Vlad, who ran the brewpub down on the highway. We stashed the big bucket of fermenting juice in my garage, where it filled the space with the heady smell of apples, yeast, and alcohol.

I was just starting to feel settled in my old life when Mike called again.

"Want to make another prison visit?" he asked.

"Aw, really? How come nobody we need to see lives someplace nice, say, like San Francisco?"

Mike laughed. "Just our luck."

"Where is this prison? Not Utah again, I hope."

"No, much closer; Folsom."

"Folsom," I said. "Of course. Who's there?"

"Keith Sunderland. Dan hasn't been able to find him till now, but he just checked the prison inmate locator site again, and there he was. He must have been sentenced recently; we probably couldn't get a good address for him earlier because he was in jail."

"When do you want to go?"

"I'd like to see him before we have to go back to Wheaton. Are you free next week if I can get a visit?"

I sighed inwardly. "Yeah."

2 5

Folsom Prison, made legend by Johnny Cash, is hidden behind what is now an upscale suburb of Sacramento, the state capital. The complex, down a country road out of town, is huge. From the building where visitors are processed in, Mike and I and a handful of lawyers and friends of prisoners rode in a gray-painted shuttle bus that threaded its way through a maze of gray, barrack-like concrete buildings, dropping visitors off at first one visiting area, then another. We were at the fourth stop.

Inside a vestibule, a guard in a booth examined our visitor badges; then an inner door of metal and glass slid open and let us into the building. Another guard showed us into the visiting room, an auditorium-like space with tables and chairs set up throughout it. A row of doors along one side marked the attorney visiting rooms. *I am spending too much time in places like these,* I thought, as I took it all in. The guard unlocked the door to one of them. "You'll be in here," he said. "You're seeing Sunderland, right?"

Mike nodded.

"He's on his way down, should be here soon."

Sunderland was brought to us by a different guard. If his date of birth in the police reports was correct, he'd be in his mid-fifties, but he looked older. He was tall, but gaunt, his prison blue shirt and jeans hanging loose on his lanky frame. His thinning salt-and-pepper hair was neatly combed straight back from his lined, sallow face, and his dark eyes glinted with a mix of curiosity and suspicion.

Mike introduced us, and Sunderland shook his proffered hand and then mine. I offered to get food from the vending machines along the far wall. Mike asked for a coffee with sugar, and Sunderland said he'd have the same and a cinnamon roll if they had one.

When I returned, Mike and Sunderland were talking at the table in the attorney room. I distributed coffees and food and sat in a chair next to Mike.

"Keith just told me he and Scanlon are related," Mike said.

"Yeah," Sunderland said. "We're first cousins. His mother and mine are sisters. We grew up together, more or less, though we weren't really close because I was quite a bit older than he was. I guess that's why he thought of my place when he was on the run. I was living between Wheaton and the Nevada border, and we were family."

"You were living in El Dorado then," Mike confirmed.

"Yes."

"Did he call you before coming, or just show up?"

"He called, said he needed to get out of town until something cooled down."

"Did he say what?" Mike asked.

"Not then. He was pretty cagey in the phone call. It wasn't until after he got up here that he told me what was up."

"What did he tell you?"

"He said he'd killed someone. He didn't think he was suspected, but he figured he'd lie low for a while until he was sure he was in the clear."

"Did he tell you anything else about it?"

"Yeah." Sunderland thought for a few seconds. "Not all at once. Bits and pieces kind of came out as we spent time together. Steve is a talker, never could keep his mouth shut for long."

"Do you remember what he said about it?"

"Some. I told my parole officer pretty much everything at the time. Then they asked me some of it at Steve's trial."

"What did he say?"

"Oh, God, let me think; it's been a long time. I remember he said he'd done a hit for the Aryan Brotherhood because that was new to me. I had no idea he'd gotten in with those guys. But he'd been in prison most of the time since he turned eighteen, so I guess I shouldn't have been surprised. He never had good judgment, Steve."

"Did he say who he'd killed?"

"No, I don't think he said a name. But he did say someone

else was in custody. I remember asking him if he was worried that guy might inform on him, and he said no, he didn't know nothin' about it. Just some crazy guy off the street. He figured the guy would only be in jail for a few days, till the police figured out it wasn't him."

"Did Steve ever mention getting a letter from an AB guy about the hit?"

"Yeah, he did. He seemed kind of proud about it, like it was some sort of recognition."

"Did you ever see it?"

"No, I wasn't interested. The whole thing kind of scared me. I'd been in prison, and I never wanted to get anywhere near those gangs. Besides, I'm part Cherokee, on my father's side. I don't want nothin' to do with that white nation stuff. He said he had it in his car; it could stay there, as far as I was concerned."

"How long did Steve stay with you?"

"Two days, and then he took off. Asked to borrow some money. I gave him fifty dollars, and he gave me a watch worth about half that."

"And then you went to your parole officer and told him what Steve had said?"

"Yeah, I did, and I paid for it, too."

"How is that?"

"My parole officer violated me for receiving stolen property and associating with criminals, and I spent another year in the joint."

"Did you tell him about the letter?"

"I'm sure I did."

"Were you ever interviewed by Detective Springer, from the Wheaton police?"

"Yeah. I guess my parole officer contacted the police there, and the guy came to see me in jail."

"Do you remember what you told him?"

"Pretty much what I'd told my parole officer. It was all out by then anyway, no point in playing games."

"Did you mention the letter?"

"Yeah. This detective seemed to want to prove Steve was lying about the AB connection. He kept asking me whether Steve talked about doing the crime with this guy Henley; and he seemed kind of ticked when I said he didn't. I told him to look for the letter if he didn't believe me."

"Then you got called to testify."

"Right. Twice. I really didn't want to, because of Steve. I was kind of glad I didn't have to the first time. But the district attorney subpoenaed me to Steve's trial."

"No one asked you about the letter, did they?" We'd read Sunderland's testimony, and we already knew the answer.

"No. I figured it didn't matter to them."

Mike questioned Sunderland about his criminal record, which would surely be used to attack his credibility if he testified, and said he'd be getting a court order for Sunderland to testify at the hearing, though we didn't know yet when he'd be scheduled.

"Okay," Sunderland said. "You said Steve's gonna be there, too?"

"I did," Mike said.

"Glad to hear he's trying to help your guy out. Steve isn't a bad guy, at heart; sometimes he'll do the right thing. Any chance we could be brought down at the same time? Haven't seen him in years."

Mike said the scheduling was up to the judge, so he doubted it, but he'd see what he could do.

When the guard came to get him, Sunderland shook our hands again.

"Thank you for seeing us," Mike said.

"Any time," Sunderland said. "I'm not going much of anywhere for a while."

26

"Son of a bitch," Mike said. "What a day!"

We were back in Wheaton, walking down the sidewalk from the courthouse to the parking lot. The air was weirdly warm, still and muggy, and the sky looked ready to rain on us at any moment. Earthquake weather, they call it here in California.

"Yeah," I said. "I need a beer."

"I need more than that," Mike said.

Howard's evidentiary hearing had escalated into a war. Sandra Blaine had advanced into the courtroom under full sail, alight with indignation that her integrity had been questioned by the legal team of a convicted murderer. That we'd expected. But Frank Willard had surprised us by bringing extra forces, in the form of a sandy-haired fireplug named Joe Laszlo. Joe was built like a wrestler and shone with the flame of righteousness and ambition; moreover, he fancied himself a legal scholar. So he spent the morning of the first day asking the judge to quash every subpoena we'd issued for prison records on the ground that we should have asked for the records in discovery. We won that round after telling the judge that we had, in fact, requested them from the attorney general, but they hadn't been produced. Laszlo followed that up by arguing that the records were hearsay, and we spent half an hour arguing about technical hearsay exceptions. And so it went.

Blaine insisted on joining in the argument about expanding the scope of the hearing to include Howard's claim that the prosecution had concealed exculpatory evidence. The gist of her contribution was that she didn't conceal the letter because she had no idea it was in her file or how it came to be there. And it didn't matter anyway because there was nothing in it that would have appeared exculpatory to a reasonable prosecutor. And it would have been irrelevant and hearsay at Howard's trial because Scanlon didn't testify to authenticate it.

The judge denied the motion to expand the hearing, but pointed out that the letter was already relevant to one of the questions before him, namely whether evidence existed at the time of Howard's trial that might have led to a different result. "It doesn't seem strong," he said, "but I don't know at this point what other evidence Mr. Henley's attorneys are proposing to present."

Better than nothing, I thought.

Ida Rader had flown down from Eureka to testify in the afternoon. I picked her up at the local airport, and we discussed her testimony over lunch at a Chinese buffet Mike had discovered not far from the courthouse. The food was acceptable, but more importantly, the restaurant was big enough that we could easily find an out-of-the-way table where we could talk in relative peace and quiet. Laszlo spent the afternoon objecting, it seemed, to every second question Mike asked Rader.

She recounted her background as a prison guard, first at Soledad, and then at Pelican Bay, and finally as a lieutenant in the Security Housing Unit there, which housed a number of gang members. After she detailed her training and experience in the Department of Corrections in learning and teaching the operations of prison gangs, Laszlo didn't wait for Mike to ask that she be qualified as an expert before objecting. The judge allowed Mike to ask her how many times she had been involved in litigation and testified as an expert witness and then overruled Laszlo's objection.

After losing that round, Laszlo objected again on relevancy grounds when Rader began to explain how the Aryan Brotherhood worked and its structure. The judge asked Mike why the history of the gang mattered to this case. Mike said it was needed to explain Scanlon's position in the AB and the manner in which he received the order to kill Lindahl. "It supports his confession as to his true motive for the killing." Grudgingly, with a comment that Mike appeared to be inserting unnecessary complexity into what should be a fairly simple hearing, the judge allowed her testimony.

Rader continued. Basically, she said, the gang's origins could probably be traced back to around the 1960s or 1970s, to groups of white inmates that initially formed for their own protection. "What eventually happens is, you have a small gang that's dedicated to some ideology, social change," she said, "but they always evolve pretty quickly into a criminal organization. The AB did that in the 1970s. And then around 1980, the groups in the different prisons here in California organized into a structure, with a three-man commission at the top, a general council, and then the general membership. Below that are associates, men who aren't full members, but maybe want to rise through the ranks and become members, or just stay loyal foot soldiers. And kind of at the fringes are people who are sort of hangers-on for the protection the gang gives them, or wannabes." Laszlo moved to strike her description as hearsay and speculation; his objection was overruled.

"In recent years," Rader went on, "the Aryan Brotherhood has been hurt by a series of federal racketeering prosecutions. Some of the gang leaders have ended up in federal supermax prisons, and others have taken deals to become witnesses for the government. It's not what it used to be, but it's still a threat."

One of the ways the gang made money—"and they actually have quite a bit"—was by controlling drug sales in the prisons. "They've figured out ways of bringing drugs in, through visitors and even prison staff. They sell them themselves, but some come in through freelancers. Anyone selling drugs in the prison has to pay a tax to the AB on their sales: last I heard, it could be anywhere from 15 to 50 percent, depending on the prison."

Another objection from Laszlo. And so it went.

The gang enforced its authority with violent retribution. "If you don't do what they tell you, they will kill you. They will threaten to kill members of your family on the street, and sometimes do that, too."

"Can one person in the AB give an order to have someone killed?"

"Yes, generally, if he is high enough in status. But I think some orders require more than one person."

"An associate can't give such an order?"

"In general, no."

"If somebody was in a position of having to pay the Aryan Brotherhood money and couldn't do it or didn't do it, what would be the consequence?"

"He would be given a pretty short time limit and told if he doesn't pay it, he's going to get hit. He would be stabbed, strangled, beat, whatever. If they could kill him, they would."

"What if the inmate paroled before that happened?"

Laszlo objected, but the judge allowed her to answer.

"Well, if they could get their hands on him, they'd kill him on the street. That would serve two purposes: it would punish the guy for cheating them and show the inmates in prison that the AB can get them wherever they are."

"How would the gang do that?"

"They have associates and members that parole. They may send somebody else out to do it, like a brother, a cousin, a friend on the streets. One of them might do it for money, or just to help the Brotherhood."

Another objection, on the ground of speculation. Mike reminded the judge that Rader was testifying as an expert.

"So someone might do it just because they were asked."

"Oh, definitely. Or told to."

Mike asked her to explain gang validation and debriefing.

Rader gathered her thoughts for a second. Validation was a sensitive subject, a sore point between the Corrections Department and advocates for prisoners' rights; and Rader chose her words carefully. "Validation is the name the Corrections Department uses for the process of identifying active gang members. If a prison makes an official finding that an inmate is an active member or associate of a gang, it can take measures, such as housing them in administrative segregation, for the security of the institution. It's pretty regulated. The prison considers certain types of information—letters from gang members, group photos of the inmate with known gang members and associates, gang tattoos, their own admissions. A certain number—lately, it has been three—of pieces of firm evidence are required before an inmate can be validated as actively associated with a gang. An inmate who's been validated goes before the classification committee in his prison, and if they find he's hardcore or dangerous, he can be put in segregation or even what they call the security housing unit, or SHU, indefinitely."

"What is the SHU like?"

"The SHU is extra high security. Some men are double-celled, two to a cell, but the most dangerous inmates are kept in solitary confinement, although that's decreasing. The men there are in their cells for twenty-three hours a day, and their contacts with other people in the prison and things like family visits are highly restricted."

"Can inmates in the SHU communicate with one another?"

"Yes. They can talk between cells, and they have ways of communicating in code through the plumbing pipes, passing kites in law books—I don't know all of them. They pass messages from prison to prison through mail to their families, notes smuggled in by visitors; or sometimes inmates being transferred will memorize a message to be transmitted to someone where they're going. Prisoners can be pretty ingenious."

"So an AB member in administrative segregation could communicate an order, say to kill someone, even though he's in relative isolation."

"Yes."

"Do you know of someone named Walter Bensinger?"

"Yes—his moniker was Corker. He was pretty high up in the AB. He may at one time have been a member of the general council, I'm not sure."

"Scotty Maclendon?"

"He was another shot-caller."

"Mack Gentry?"

"Yes."

"Were they at Pelican Bay?"

"Yes, beginning around 2005, 2006. Some of them were in the SHU."

"Gentry was killed, right?"

"Yes."

Laszlo objected that Ida hadn't shown she was personally aware of Gentry's death, and the judge sustained it.

"You were at Pelican Bay at the time of Gentry's death, weren't you?" Mike asked.

"Yes."

"Were you personally aware of his death?"

"Yes, I was on duty when they found his body and arrested his cellmate. I saw the medics bring his body out of the cell."

I glanced at Laszlo. He was glowering, but for once, silent.

"Did you know Cal McGaw?"

"No. You mentioned his name to me, but I hadn't heard of him before that."

"You never worked in Folsom, did you?"

"No. I was at Soledad, then Pelican Bay."

"You were acquainted with Steve Scanlon at one point, weren't you?"

"Actually, we came into contact at two different institutions, first Soledad and later Pelican Bay." Ida then explained essentially what she had told Dan and me about her contacts with Scanlon. "Scanlon was young and impressionable and looking for someplace to belong. A kid like that will tend to gravitate toward the gangs. He wasn't all that bright, and he had a short fuse, so he got into trouble a fair amount. After he angered another inmate, who stabbed him, he threw in his lot with the AB, because he needed the protection of belonging to a gang."

Laszlo objected that she was speculating, and the judge told Mike to move on. "You knew he had gotten involved with the AB, though?"

"Yes. He told me, and I could see he was associating with that group on the yard."

"How would you describe Scanlon's intelligence and sophistication?" Mike asked.

"He was pretty inept socially. Not too bright, either; I'd put his intelligence somewhere around the low end of normal. But sometimes he has some insights. Once in a while he's not so clueless. He was kind of a bumbling kid."

"Did he eventually get transferred out of Soledad?"

"Yes."

"And did you come into contact with him again after that?"

"Yes, when he came into the SHU in Pelican Bay."

"Did you see much of him there?"

"Not really, until after he was stabbed."

Mike asked her to elaborate, and Laszlo objected. The

judge overruled him and let her go on.

"Scanlon tried to escape and assaulted a guard. The incident caused a crackdown on the AB in the prison, and he and a bunch of other AB guys ended up in the SHU. Later, Scanlon was stabbed by another AB associate and nearly died. When he was recovering in the prison hospital he asked to talk to me. I went to see him. He was kind of appalled that the gang had done this to him. He always felt he'd been a good soldier. He said he was ready to debrief from the AB."

"And what is debriefing?"

"It's a way of dropping out of a prison gang and getting protection from the prison system."

"How does it work?"

"It's a process. The inmate needs to write an autobiography of his involvement with the gang, you know, everything he's done with them, who he knows, who he doesn't know, any current plots to hurt staff, what kinds of things they do to transport weapons and drugs. The inmate has to be very, very candid about his activity with the gang, because the statement then goes to the investigation unit, and the people there are very competent and thorough. They have ways of verifying what you're talking about to see if you're lying or not."

"Did that happen with Steve Scanlon?" Mike asked.

Laszlo objected. "If she knows," the judge said.

"Yeah, he completed an autobiography and gave it to

me. It was pretty thick and rambling. I just kind of browsed through it and sealed it up, taped it, initialed it, and put it in a lockbox to be sent to gang investigations."

"Do you know what happened after that?"

"No, not specifically."

"What generally happens?"

"Inmates requesting debrief go on a waiting list, and the lieutenant and the sergeant and the gang investigation… it's kind of like first come, first served. I believe Scanlon was allowed to debrief—"

Laszlo objected, and the judge struck Rader's last sentence.

Mike moved on. "But at some point Scanlon was no longer an inmate at Pelican Bay."

"That's right."

"Before your testimony today, Ms. Moodie showed you a letter."

"Yes, she did."

Mike asked that the letter be marked for identification and then handed it to Rader.

"Is this a copy of the letter she showed you?"

Rader looked briefly at each page of the letter. "Yes, that appears to be the one."

"Addressed to Steve Scanlon from Cal McGaw, Folsom Prison?"

"That's what it said."

"Does that letter appear to you to contain any sort of coded message?"

"I would say, having seen letters between gang members, that there is probably some message encoded in it, but I couldn't tell you just what it might be."

Laszlo objected and asked that her answer be stricken, and the judge sustained the objection.

"When Scanlon talked to you after he was stabbed, did he mention a contract killing he did in Wheaton?"

"Yes. He said he'd done a killing for the Aryan Brotherhood in Wheaton, shot a man and went to prison for it. It was one of the reasons he was so shocked by what they did to him."

"Did he say he killed the guy for anyone else besides the Aryan Brotherhood?"

"Not to me, he didn't."

"Do you have an opinion in general based on your interactions with Mr. Scanlon over the years as to his credibility?"

Rader nodded slightly. "When any inmate comes to us as an informant, whether or not you've known them, you have to corroborate their information. But aside from that, I felt Steve was pretty honest with me in general. But, again, I never did an investigation following up on anything he ever said."

Willard started his cross-examination after the mid-afternoon break. He began by showing us, and then Ida Rader, a copy of Scanlon's debriefing statement. "That's one way to get it out of their grasping claws," Mike whispered to me.

After going through the statement with Ida Rader and establishing that it didn't mention Howard Henley, Laszlo asked, "Isn't it pretty common for criminals to try to enhance their stature by claiming association with the Aryan Brotherhood?"

"Not at all," she said firmly. "It's a dangerous thing to do; they'll punish you if they hear of it."

"Is it common," Willard asked, "for someone who has done a killing for the Aryan Brotherhood to tell a lot of other people about it and who was behind it?"

"Actually, that would be fairly common," she answered. "The AB doesn't mind word like that getting around because it enhances their power to have people know they're capable of killing people who go against them—even more so if it's someone on the street. It shows their reach."

Not getting the answers he wanted, Willard retreated to asking Rader about her direct examination testimony, his questions dripping with sarcasm and incredulity.

After a brief redirect by Mike, the judge said he had something else he needed to attend to, and adjourned the hearing for the day.

Dot said hello to us after court. She had come late, but had spent most of the afternoon watching the hearing. She was with another woman, whom she introduced to us as her best friend, Lillian.

A newspaper reporter, a baby-faced kid who seemed too young to be working at a grown-up job, had been assigned to the hearing. After court ended for the day, he stopped us and introduced himself—"Josh Schaeffer, for the Taft County *News Gazette*"—and questioned us about what had just happened and what we had planned for the next day. He didn't understand the legal maneuvering, but he'd clearly done some homework about Howard's case, and he seemed interested in what we were doing. The possibility that Howard might be innocent of the murder would make good, if controversial, copy.

At dinner, after driving Ida Rader to the airport for her flight home, I allowed myself the beer I'd longed for. Afterward, Mike and I worked for a while going over questions for the next day's witnesses and researching the arcana of hearsay law for arguments against Laszlo's wall of objections.

I slept badly, and woke up before dawn the next morning. The blandness of the hotel room—even though it was cleaner and better decorated than any place in my house—made me feel depressed and homesick. I missed my nest of a bed, with its aged down comforter, its nighttime population of cats, and pillows that smelled like me. After a half-minute wallow in self-pity, I shook myself out and showered in the brightly lit, pale tan and white bathroom. Made up and dressed for court, I met Mike in the café off the lobby. Today Mike was questioning Sandra Blaine, and we both fortified ourselves with eggs and bacon. *Morituri te salutamus.*

27

The morning started with testimony from Gordon Stans, the parole officer who had faxed the McGaw letter to the Wheaton police. Laszlo began by objecting to Mike's use of a subpoena instead of a discovery motion for the parole records, but subsided when Mike pointed out that the attorney general had not given us the letter in discovery, even though it was presumably in the files of their own client, the Department of Corrections.

Stans himself said the letter we'd found in the district attorney's files was the same as a copy still in the parole file. He had forgotten the case, he said, but after seeing the letter, the fax cover sheet, and a couple of his old reports, he remembered that he had been called in to do a parole search of Scanlon's car and was present when the letter was found. He recalled that he'd found it in the glove box. He had told the police officers doing the search that the letter was probably relevant to validating Scanlon as a gang member, and they had given it to him. He had sent the original to the Department of Corrections and faxed a copy to Dave Springer, the Wheaton police detective investigating the Lindahl homicide. He didn't recall the exact date when he'd sent the letter and copy, though he believed it was soon after the search of the car. (Laszlo objected that his belief was speculation; the judge agreed and struck that sentence.)

On cross-examination, Stans remembered that he had read the letter, and nothing in it had struck him as strange. He knew Scanlon was in with the AB, so he thought McGaw might be an associate; that's why he'd sent the letter to Corrections, in case they could use it when Scanlon was back in prison.

Detective Dave Springer was our next witness. He remembered nothing about the letter—not getting it, not sending it over to the DA's office. "The Lindahl homicide was over fifteen years ago, and I've worked on a lot of cases since then," he said, sounding a little aggrieved. He remembered talking to Freddy Gomez. "Freddy was a lowlife, but he'd given us good information at other times." The name Indio rang a faint bell. "But I'm a homicide detective. If Freddy gave me information about someone trading in stolen guns, I'd have passed it along to property crimes." The head of that unit used to be Marvin Ingalls; Ingalls was still around, working for the sheriff now.

Cross-examined by Willard, Springer expanded on his theories about the murder. He didn't really believe that Scanlon killed Lindahl for the AB. "Steve Scanlon was just a small-time con who got in over his head. He'd taken out this guy for Henley, and got caught. If he told the truth and named the guy who hired him, he'd be a snitch and probably end up dead in jail or prison, 'cause they don't like snitches there. So he figured out a good lie, made himself out to be a big shot by making up this story about it all being for the Aryan Brotherhood. Or maybe he really was AB and pulled a scam on Henley—he knew he was going to kill this guy Lindahl for the AB, but he let Henley think he was hiring him, so he'd get paid to do it. What does it matter? They're both guilty, whichever way you look at it. You know that he testified at his own trial and denied everything—denied the murder and ever having anything to do with those guys."

In Springer's opinion, the police had plenty of evidence that Henley had hired Scanlon. "The word around the trailer park was that Henley wanted Lindahl dead so he hired Scanlon and paid him in drugs. Freddy wasn't the only person saying that." Springer was sure the names and statements of other people who had said that were in his reports.

"I was just surprised Henley didn't do it himself," he went on. "Henley was a time bomb, a really dangerous guy." Mike objected and asked the judge to strike Springer's opinion and admonish him to stick to the facts, but the judge said, "I believe his opinion as a law enforcement officer is relevant."

Springer went on. "He really needed to be put away; the man was out of control and getting more violent over time.

It was only a matter of time before he killed someone. We're just lucky it was Lindahl instead of someone innocent, like a kid." Mike asked the judge again to strike Springer's opinion about Howard's dangerousness; his motion was denied.

Scanlon had, of course, lied to Sunderland about why he committed the murder. Regarding Christian Niedermeier, the other man to whom Scanlon confessed that the murder was an AB hit, Springer said, "He was in jail with Scanlon, but who knows if he ever actually talked to him. He probably heard some rumor, saw some newspaper story, and put it to good use. Inmates like him make up these confession stories all the time, trying to get plea deals in exchange for providing information."

On redirect, Mike asked Springer if he'd have said the same thing if Niedermeier had claimed Howard confessed the crime to him. Laszlo objected to the question as argumentative, and the objection was sustained.

"But you used Niedermeier as a witness at Scanlon's trial," Mike asked, "even though you found him unbelievable?"

"That was the prosecutor's decision," Springer said.

"Did you tell her you didn't think Niedermeier was a credible witness?"

"All this happened years ago," Springer said, defensively. "I don't remember if I did or not."

"But surely you'd have said something to prevent an injustice."

"I probably would have, if I thought there was one."

"Did you tell Mr. Scanlon's attorneys that you didn't believe Niedermeier was credible?"

"I don't think that's my job," he said testily.

"Whose job is it?"

"The prosecutor's, I'd think."

As we left the courthouse for lunch, Mike asked me, "Can you wait for lunch for a bit?"

"Sure," I said. "What's up?"

"I want to go to the sheriff's office and try to find Marv Ingalls."

The sheriff's office was in a different building in the civic center complex, and it took us ten minutes and a few wrong turns to find it. Mike asked the uniformed man at the counter whether Marvin Ingalls worked there. "Sure does," the man said. "He's a lieutenant over at the jail."

"Do you have a phone number for him there?"

"Yes, we do." He walked a couple of feet along the counter and ran a finger down a list taped to the vinyl surface. "Here it is. I'll call down there and see if he's in. Can I tell him what this is about?"

Mike handed him a business card. "I'd like to talk with him about a case he worked on." The man read Mike's card, nodded, and picked up a phone near the list. He dialed and waited, the phone to his ear. After a moment, he said, "Marv? This is Gonzalez at the desk. There's an attorney here wants to talk to you about an old case. He left me his number." He recited Mike's cellphone number from his card, then hung up the phone and turned to us. "He's probably at lunch; I left him a voicemail." We thanked Deputy Gonzalez and left.

"I saw a Panda Express across the street about a block from here; not as good as the buffet, but closer. Work for you?" Mike asked.

"Sure," I said. Visions of orange chicken danced in my head. I was feeling suddenly deflated and very hungry. "They have coffee?"

"Don't know, but I'm sure we can get some around there. Let's go eat and talk about what Sandra Blaine may try to do to us this afternoon." Mike strode off, and I followed, yawning, in his wake.

28

Sandra Blaine was all business as the clerk read her the oath. As she agreed to tell the truth, the whole truth, and nothing but the truth, she even managed to look a bit humbled by the solemnity of the ritual. I was impressed.

Mike questioned her about her decision to prosecute Howard.

"There were strong grounds," she explained. "People in the trailer park told the police that Henley was dealing drugs and that Lindahl had beaten Henley and stolen his money and drugs. There were people who said they saw him after the robbery with a black eye and swollen face. Henley had a motive to kill Lindahl, and people said he had been threatening to kill him and asking where he could buy a gun."

Blaine admitted that the district attorney had had to dismiss the first prosecution against Howard when records showed that Howard had been in the local lockup when Lindahl was killed. And a search of Howard's trailer had found no gun and no ammunition—and no drugs, for that matter, except a couple grams of marijuana.

"So the first time you ended up dismissing the complaint against him except for the misdemeanor marijuana charge?" Mike asked. Blaine agreed.

"So why did you charge him a second time?"

Laszlo's relevancy objection was sustained, but Blaine went ahead and answered the question on her own.

"Freddy Gomez came forward," she said, "and told Detective Springer that Mr. Henley had asked him where he could get a gun and someone to kill Lindahl. Mr. Gomez said he gave Henley contact information for another man who sold guns, and suggested to him that Steve Scanlon might be up for a paid killing because he was in the Aryan Brotherhood, so he was probably a killer. Gomez said he was at Howard's cabin a couple days later when Scanlon showed up. He saw them talk and Henley hand Scanlon a revolver."

Blaine didn't feel that Gomez was any less believable because he was a heroin addict under arrest and desperate for a deal that would get him back on the street.

"Did Freddy Gomez receive any compensation from the prosecutor's office for his testimony at Mr. Henley's preliminary hearing?" Mike asked.

"Not that I recall," Blaine said, with a defiant lift of her chin.

"Do you recall why Freddy was in jail?"

"Not offhand."

"Do you recall that it was for possession of heroin and felony assault with a deadly weapon?"

"No."

"For trying to run his girlfriend over with a car?"

"No," Blaine said, testily.

"And that he was looking at an attempted murder charge and a long time in prison?"

"No." She turned her head toward the judge, as though asking him why he wasn't putting a stop to Mike's badgering.

"Were you aware that after he testified in Henley's and Scanlon's preliminary hearings, Mr. Gomez was permitted to plead guilty to simple battery and was sentenced to credit for time served?"

"I don't remember."

"Didn't you make that deal with him?"

"Not if I wasn't prosecuting him, and I wasn't. Any plea bargain would have been made with the prosecutor in Mr. Gomez's case."

"So the fact that he walked free after testifying against Scanlon and my client didn't have anything to do with his testimony?"

Laszlo objected to Mike's question as argumentative, and the judge sustained it.

"You were aware," Mike asked, "that two men had come forward to say Steve Scanlon had told them he committed the murder for the Aryan Brotherhood?"

"I saw no credible evidence," she said, emphasizing

"credible," "that Scanlon killed Lindahl for anyone but Henley."

"Did you believe Sunderland's and Niedermeier's statements?"

"I had no reason to believe that they weren't truthful about what Scanlon told them. But I didn't believe Scanlon, or that the Aryan Brotherhood was involved."

Mike asked her why she had objected to them testifying at Howard's trial. "Don't you think the jury should have heard what Scanlon told them?"

Laszlo objected that the question was argument, and his objection was sustained.

Mike showed Blaine a copy of the McGaw letter and its envelope. She gave it a careless glance and handed it back to him.

"Do you remember seeing that letter before?" Mike asked.

"Yes," Blaine said. "Mr. Willard emailed me a copy about a month ago."

"Were you aware," Mike asked, "that it was in your files of Mr. Henley's case?"

"Not before talking with Mr. Willard," Blaine said, glancing down at the letter with the slightest shake of her head. "It has been many years since Mr. Henley's trial. But I certainly don't remember ever seeing that letter before these proceedings." Her voice held the merest hint of reproach.

"So you don't remember whether you disclosed this letter to Mr. Henley or his advisory counsel?"

"No," she said. "I'm sure I would have if it had seemed relevant."

"What about Mr. Scanlon's attorney?"

"Same thing. I just don't remember." She glanced at the letter again. "It's possible I didn't think it was relevant. It's hard to read, but it just seems like a sort of hello letter. I don't see anything about the case in it."

"But weren't you aware that Steve Scanlon told Keith Sunderland he had a letter from Cal McGaw in his car?"

"No." She turned her head again toward the judge and then swept her gaze from Laszlo and Willard to Mike and me. "Realistically, I doubt that I'd have seen any reason to disclose this letter if I did have it. It didn't exculpate Mr. Henley; on the face of it, it had nothing to do with Lindahl. There's certainly nothing in it that appears to support what Scanlon said about the Aryan Brotherhood ordering him to kill Lindahl. And it certainly didn't exculpate Scanlon. His defense was that he had nothing to do with Lindahl's murder; the letter wouldn't have helped him at all."

"Okay," Mike said. "That may be true of Scanlon. But wouldn't the existence of the letter be exculpatory as to Mr. Henley because it corroborated what Sunderland said Scanlon told him?"

Blaine's blandly professional manner buckled, and for a brief moment her face took on the pinched expression of a defensive bureaucrat. "I don't see it. But even so, this all assumes that I was aware of the letter at the time. I assume you're telling the truth that it was in my files, but I really do not remember it being there." Her tone combined slight irritation with wounded integrity. "I would never prosecute someone if I had any doubt they were guilty," she said. "I believe to this day that Howard Henley and Steve Scanlon killed Jared Lindahl." Sandra Blaine, defender of truth, justice, and the American way. She gave a moment for her audience to absorb her performance, then exhaled as if signaling that, as far as she was concerned, the questioning was at an end.

On cross-examination, Frank Willard lobbed Blaine a few softball questions, indirectly reminding the judge that the Henley and Scanlon cases were very old and one could hardly be expected to remember every paper in a case file after all that time; that the letter, viewed objectively, was insignificant; that Blaine was an experienced and dedicated prosecutor with honed instincts about the credibility of witnesses; and that she was both legally and morally within her rights in keeping the jury from being confused by unfounded claims about Scanlon's motive for killing Lindahl.

"They really closed ranks," I said to Mike and Dot Henley, as we walked in a slow group down the hall from the courtroom.

"I'll bet she knew about that letter," Dot's friend Lillian said. "She's a piece of work, she is. She prosecuted my nephew for attempted murder after he was attacked by his girlfriend's ex-boyfriend. Everyone said it was self-defense, but some jailhouse snitch got a deal for testifying that Donnie confessed he'd been planning to kill the guy. Blaine asked him on the stand whether he was getting anything for his testimony, and he said, no, he was just a concerned citizen. But Donnie's lawyer found out he'd told a couple of guys at the jail that he was getting a no-jail-time deal on his case in exchange for putting Donnie away. He called those inmates as witnesses, and Donnie got off—no thanks to Miss Blaine."

"Wow," I said. "That's pretty outrageous."

She nodded, with a snap of her eyelids. "Yep. And look what she did to Howard. She has a reputation. But people don't mind that sort of thing around here. They don't mind if she cuts a few corners as long as she gets the right man. That's why she's the DA now. I say, just wait until she does that to someone you know who's innocent, and see how you feel."

"When is the next hearing?" Dot asked.

"November 29th," Mike answered.

As we waved them off, Mike's phone rang. After a brief conversation, he turned to me and said, "That was Marv Ingalls. He says he can meet us at six thirty tomorrow morning at the hotel coffee shop."

"Son of a bitch," I mumbled. "Doesn't anyone here ever sleep?"

2 9

I, for one, slept that night, the sleep of the exhausted and relieved. We were coming back for more in less than a month, but I was just glad the hearing was over for now.

At 6:30 the next morning, when I made it downstairs to the coffee shop, Marv Ingalls, in uniform, was sitting in a booth, a cup of coffee in front of him. He looked like every cliché of a middle-aged cop nearing retirement—broad-faced, round-shouldered and getting thick in the waist. He stood up as I approached, and held out a hand. "Marv Ingalls," he said, his voice a gravelly tenor. His wide, weathered face, behind his smile, kept that expression of controlled vigilance that policemen seem to acquire in their training.

"Janet Moodie," I said, as we shook hands. "Mike Barry's co-counsel."

"Nice to meet you."

We sat. "I just got here; haven't ordered yet," he said.

Mike showed up as the waitress reached the table, and we

all ordered coffee and food. Marv ordered scrambled eggs, fruit, and toast without butter. "My heart," he said. "My wife and my doctor have me on a tight leash. So, what can I do for you?"

Mike did the talking. "We're trying to find a guy who was supposedly busted for dealing in stolen guns back in 1999, when you were in property crimes. All we know about him is that he went by the name of Indio and supposedly worked in the oil fields."

Marv cocked his head a little to one side. "You're the lawyers here on that thing about Howard Henley, then?"

"Yeah," Mike said. "How did you know?"

"Word gets around. Indio was part of that case. That's how we learned about him. I remember it pretty well because we set up a sting to get him. We didn't often get to do anything that elaborate, so it was pretty memorable."

"Were you personally involved in it?"

"Yeah. I remember homicide and the DA were trying to get him to give them information about Henley's case, but he lawyered up, wouldn't tell them anything. I surmised he had some involvement with one of the prison gangs, and he was afraid to snitch."

Our food came; Marv ate quickly, glancing at his watch from time to time.

"What happened to Indio?" Mike asked.

Marv took a bite of toast and thought for a few seconds. "As I recall he ended up pleading guilty and going to state prison." He shrugged. "Kind of a shame, really. Maybe he could have shed some light on what really happened with Henley and that guy he supposedly had killed."

"Did you know much about the case?"

"Not really. But I knew Henley, and I met his father a few times. Back when I was working patrol, old Howard was kind of a fixture, you know, the neighborhood loony, always having run-ins with the police. I don't know what evidence the DA had on him, but the idea that he'd have killed anyone—or had his act together enough to hire a hit man—" He shook his head. "It all struck me as pretty damned improbable. He was all noise, and a bit of a pain in the neck, but basically harmless, near as I could tell."

"Well, we're trying to prove that now," Mike said. "We're trying to find Indio, in the hope he might have something to say now. But we don't know his real name, so we're kind of stuck."

Marv took a drink of his coffee. "Forbush," he said. "Wayne or Dwayne, something like that."

"Great," Mike said. "That will be a big help in locating him."

"Hope so." Marv checked his watch again, then pushed his plate away. "I've got to get to work soon. Is there anything else you need?" He looked around for the waitress.

"No, you've been a real help," Mike said. "I'll get breakfast; thank you for meeting us. Oh, by the way, a couple weeks from now we'll be calling some prison inmates as witnesses;

they'll probably be housed in the jail. Can you tell me who I should call there to find out if they all got here?"

"Sure, no problem." Marv reached in a pocket and pulled out a business card. "The deputy to call is Eloy Santos." He wrote a name and phone number on the back of the card and handed it to Mike. Mike and I each gave him one of our cards.

He stood up, the holstered gun at his waist visible, and pulled on a heavy uniform jacket. "Gotta go," he said. "Good luck with your hearing."

After he was out of earshot, Mike said, "Well, that was a surprise."

I nodded. "Really."

"Funny," he said, "but it kind of adds to the pressure. You know, people say it's harder to defend someone who's actually innocent, and they're right. You feel like the stars ought to line up and everyone figure it out—especially with a case like this, with a confession from the actual killer, for God's sake—but here we are. The judge and the AG don't give a shit, and the hearing isn't even going well. I'd feel bad enough for any client, guilty or not, but this is a whole lot worse."

"I know," I said, at a loss for encouraging words. "I feel it, too."

"Yeah," Mike said, and he shook himself out of his mood. "Oh, well, let's see what we can find out about Indio."

"I can go find his court file, if you want to start back

now." We'd driven down in our own cars this time, so that we could work separately on witness preparation and whatever else might be needed during breaks in the hearing.

"Thanks," Mike said. "I'll take you up on it. I have a lot of other work to do, to pay for this case."

After checking out of the hotel, I drove to the county clerk's office. A look through the felony index gave me a case, *People v. Dwayne Robert Forbush*, whose filing date fell within the period between Howard's arrest and trial. I took down the number and joined the line at the desk.

Luck was with us; the file was still in the building, in the closed file archives. I gave the deputy clerk my ID and waited, reading emails on my phone, until she returned with the file. It was fairly thin, and I took it over to a long reading table attached to the wall, with chairs spaced along it. A couple of other people were seated there, poring through files and making notes, or filling out documents. When I set up my laptop and scanner, one of them gave me a sidelong glance. "You look like you do this kind of thing a lot," she said. "Are you a paralegal?"

"No, attorney," I said.

"Ah," she said, and returned to her work.

The documents in the file were what I expected: the complaint, the information (amended once), court minutes, abstract of judgment, a few motions and oppositions. I saw that Forbush's lawyer had gotten one count of the information dismissed, and that Forbush had, as Marv Ingalls said, pled guilty and been sentenced to state prison. There wasn't much personal information about him in the file, but several documents had his date of birth and his address in Hanover, a town near the oil fields north of Wheaton. There were affidavits and search warrants for his apartment and car and a storage locker he had apparently been renting. I scanned what I could, but many of the documents were stapled, and I didn't feel comfortable unfastening them, so I waited in line at the one public copy machine in the room. Since I was copying everything in the file, I didn't inspect them too closely.

In a couple of hours, I was finished. I sent Mike a text telling him my hunt had been successful and giving him Forbush's full name and date of birth and address at the time of his arrest, so that Mike could pass it on to Dan. With luck, we'd be able to locate him; with more luck, he might corroborate what Scanlon had told us. And now I had one more errand to run before I started for home.

I met Dot Henley at her house and, over coffee and some blueberry muffins I'd bought at a bakery in town, told her our tale of woe. "I hate to be asking for money," I said, "but the court doesn't want to pay for the investigation we need to do, and Mike is paying the investigator and travel expenses out of his own pocket. He doesn't begrudge doing that, but I don't know whether we'll be able to pay for everything we need to do."

Dot was surprised and sympathetic. "You're working so

hard for Howard. I didn't realize the court wasn't just paying for everything. Let me talk to Bob and Kevin, and I'll let you know what we can do."

I thanked her, and we talked a little about kids and our Thanksgiving plans before we said goodbye and I started for home. I hadn't told Mike I was planning to do this, and I hoped he wouldn't be upset. As court-appointed attorneys we weren't allowed to accept legal fees from anyone else to represent Howard, but the court didn't have a problem if we covered the expenses it wouldn't pay out of our own pockets or someone else's. If it would help Howard get a fair hearing, I was willing to beg a little.

It began to rain on my way home, and I drove the last miles of winding highway at a crawl in teeming darkness that swallowed up the light from my headlights. I was exhausted, tense, and dank as I unlocked my kitchen door, shook rain from my hair, submitted to lectures about abandonment from two angry cats, and got a fire going in my stove. The message lights were lit on both my home and office phones. My home phone had two voicemails, both from Ed, telling me he'd been over to do something concerning the cider in the garage. I could see lights on in his house so I called him to let him know I was back and would pick up Charlie in the morning if that was okay. What I needed now was not a walk through the dripping woods, but some kind of hot drink with a stiff shot of brandy in it and my own bed. The office phone could wait until tomorrow.

30

I could tell it was late when I woke up. Somewhere behind the rain clouds the sun had risen, and the light was gray outside my bedroom windows. The house was chilly again—banking a fire so that it burned through a long night was not one of my talents—and the phone in my office was ringing. I decided to let it go to voicemail, put on bathrobe and slippers, and padded out to the kitchen to make coffee. While the coffee brewed, I got a fire going, noticing with a sigh that the wood rack was nearly empty. The day was presenting me with a mass of small tasks, none of them anything I really wanted to do.

After downing a cup of coffee, I called Ed, then changed into jeans, sweater, jacket, and boots and headed for his place, carrying a couple pounds of Peet's Coffee I'd bought for him as a thank-you for taking care of Charlie.

As soon as I knocked on Ed's door, I heard Charlie and Pogo bounding toward it, barking. Ed called out, "It's open!" I pushed my way in past a wall of enthusiastic dogs.

In addition to the usual smells of wood smoke and dog this morning, I detected a strong overtone of pine disinfectant. Forced by the rain to work indoors, Ed was cleaning his kitchen floor. He propped the sponge mop against the counter and looked toward where I was standing in the doorway. "How'd it go?" he asked.

"The usual," I said. "Killer prosecutor, lying cops."

"No AB guys?" Ed asked.

"Not yet. So far it's been the detective and the DA. Amazing how no one remembers anything when it might help your client. And one good witness, an expert on prison gangs who knew the shooter, Scanlon."

"Hope it goes better from here," he said.

"Me too." I handed him the coffee. "Thanks for keeping Charlie for me. I'll have to ask you again in a couple of weeks, if you're around."

"Let me check my busy calendar," he said, raising his eyes heavenward. "Nope. Nothing going on till I don't know when."

"Thanks," I said. "The judge seems to be doing this hearing in his spare time, a couple of days at a time, until we're all too exhausted to go on."

"Bummer," Ed said.

"Well, I should leave you to your exciting morning and go home to mine," I said.

He gave a brief laugh. "Have fun. Check the cider; it's smelling pretty good."

With Charlie trotting beside me on short, determined legs, I walked back home through the dripping woods.

No good news ever comes in a voicemail, I thought, as I piled the armload of logs I'd picked up from the woodpile onto the rack, added one to the stove, and set a couple of others on its top to dry. I exchanged my boots for felt clogs and hung up my jacket, then made myself another cup of coffee and a bowl of cereal and carried them into my office.

There were a couple of voicemails from the state prison phone exchange—no way of knowing who they came from, just an automated voice saying I had a collect call from an inmate at San Quentin—and then one, and another, from someone I knew. Abby Stanhope, the lawyer who had been appointed to represent Walter Klum in his habeas corpus case all those years ago, had called me twice while I had been away in Wheaton. I called her back, got an automated answering system, and left a voicemail in her mailbox. Then I booted up my computer and read through my emails and a newspaper or two as I ate. As usual, the news worth reading about was bad. I had opened up the research file in one of my appeals and was starting to read through my notes when Abby called back.

"Janet, hello. I must be a voice from the distant past at this point."

"No problem," I said. "Good to hear from you. How's Walt Klum these days?"

"Well, that's what I'm calling about." The briefest of

hesitations. "We have a problem."

I rolled my eyes heavenward and uttered a silent *damn*. This was not the time for Walt to have a problem. "What is it?" I asked.

"I don't know if you know, but the state Supreme Court just denied his state habeas petition."

"I didn't," I said.

"Well, it was really recent, just a couple of weeks ago. Anyhow, now we have to file a federal petition, and Walt doesn't want to sign the form."

"Oh, jeez," I said. "And I guess the clock is running?"

"Yep."

A generation ago, Congress passed a law designed to make it harder for federal courts to grant new trials to criminal defendants. One of the new hurdles they had thrown up was a statute of limitations for filing a habeas corpus petition in the federal court after losing in the state court system. A defendant had one year to file his federal petition, and if he missed the deadline he was out of luck.

Because Walt was under a death sentence, there was another wrinkle. Once the state Supreme Court denied his state habeas petition, the state could immediately set a date to execute him. But if he filed a simple request telling the federal court that he intended to file a federal habeas petition and asking that court to appoint him an attorney, the federal court would issue a stay of execution until it had had a chance to hear his case. For most defendants in his position, the choice between continuing to fight their cases and being executed within a few months doesn't require a lot of thought. But most people have a firmer hold on life than Walt.

"This just came at a really bad time for him," Abby said. "His sister—Edna, the older one—died a couple of months ago."

"I'm so sorry," I said. I remembered Edna. Mike and I had helped her navigate the prison visiting process, and she had traveled from Oregon a couple of times a year to see Walt. She had also called a few times to warn us when Walt's phone calls or letters seemed unusually depressed or delusional.

"Yeah," Abby said. "He feels like he doesn't have anybody now. I think the denial of his state petition just convinced him there was no reason to go on."

Oh, God, I thought. "You mean he wants to be executed?"

"To be honest, I don't think he's really thought it through. Right now I'm just trying to find anything that might turn him around. He liked and respected you and Mike, and I thought it might help if you could go see him. Sound him out, show him he still has people who care what happens to him."

"Absolutely," I said. "I'll see how soon they can fit me in. He's not refusing visits, then?"

"No. He's always come down, except once or twice when he was sick."

"That's good. Have you talked to Mike?"

"Yes," she said. "He's going to try to get a visit on the 28th. I gather you both have a hearing in Wheaton."

"Yeah."

"Lucky you. I had a case there once—awful place."

"Tell me about it. I'll set up a visit and let you know what happens."

"Great! Take care."

"You too."

This was a bad time for Walt to go off the rails, I thought, and followed that up by asking myself whether there was a good time. I had been through this with a couple of other clients over the years. It was uncommon, but not uncommon enough, for defendants on death row to decide, usually temporarily, that they didn't want to go on with their cases. They might be worn down by the thousand daily frustrations of prison life, depressed and tired of the protracted legal fight, or anxious and trying to seize control of their situation by turning the fearful uncertainty of future execution into reality. The state is no help: unless you can prove that a client is too mentally ill to competently make the decision to be executed, the law takes the position that there is no difference between being executed involuntarily or voluntarily. The best you can hope for is to try to talk your client off the ledge and buy time for him to move through and out of his despondent mood—not that it always works.

One of my bitterest memories is of a former client,

Ronald Harmon, who managed to find a lawyer willing, for perverse reasons I never understood, to represent him pro bono and defend his right to be executed. Despite the pleas of his appointed lawyers and other people who had known him, including me, that Ron was bipolar and his decision the product of a deep depression, the federal district judge agreed with Ron's request to dismiss his case. A few months later, he was executed, in the usual unseemly media spectacle of retrospectives of his life and crimes, interviews with the family of his victim, photo spreads of the execution chamber, and op-eds for and against his death. I tried to visit him during that period, but Ron, angry that I had opposed his decision, refused to see me. Obviously, there is no way of knowing whether he would have ended up executed anyway at the end of an unsuccessful sequence of petitions and appeals, but I never resigned myself to the bland willingness of the system to allow a mentally ill man to meet an ugly, public, and avoidable death.

I scanned the paper copies I had made of the documents in Forbush's file, combined them with the ones I had scanned in the clerk's office, and emailed them to Mike, then called him.

"I just talked with Abby Stanhope about Walt Klum," I said.

"Me too," he said. "I said I'd go see him, but I can't until after Thanksgiving. I have to travel to Michigan for a week of witness interviews on a case, and then we're driving to San

Diego to spend Thanksgiving with Sue's parents."

"I'm not going anywhere, so I thought I'd try to set up a visit as soon as they'll let me."

"Glad to hear it. I told Abby I'd go see him on the 28th, on my way to Wheaton. Thanks for the Forbush files, by the way; I'll send some of the information along to Dan, see if he can locate him."

"Hope it helps. Do you want me to see Howard while I'm at the prison?"

"That's okay, I'll visit him on the 28th, too."

"Who do you have on board for the 29th?" I asked.

"Scanlon and a couple of former AB guys who knew Lindahl was in the hat and were aware of the order for Scanlon to take care of him. Maybe George Gettle, Howard's advisory attorney; I'm trying to reach him."

"Okay. Let me know if there's anything I can do. Good luck in Michigan."

Modern technology comes late to the prison system, but the current visiting officer at San Quentin, unlike his predecessors, let lawyers email their visit requests to him instead of faxing them. I filled out and printed the form asking to set up visits with Walt and, while I was there, Andy Hardy, my client waiting for a ruling on his habeas petition, then scanned and emailed them to the prison. I wrote letters to Andy and Walt letting them know I'd requested a visit and when to expect me, and spent a couple of hours researching a coerced confession issue for the appeal of the young woman who had drowned her children.

When it seemed that Charlie and I both needed a break, I bundled him into the car and, after a stop at my mailbox on the highway, drove down to the state park around the old Russian settlement at Fort Ross, where we took a short walk along the bluffs, with the windblown rain sheeting into my face and ruffling Charlie's fur. After that we backtracked to the real-estate and vacation rental agency that was my mail drop and office address, where my business mail was waiting for me in a mailbox in the hallway. Then I walked next door to Vlad's.

The little pub was empty except for a couple of pairs of off-season tourists waiting out the rain at tables near the wood stove. Vlad wasn't there, but I bought a growler of his pumpkin ale to take home, from the young woman who had the thankless job of tending bar and waiting tables that day.

That afternoon I worked out some of my snarled feelings about Walt's crisis and Howard's hearing by starting a batch of bread and spending a few minutes in the garage watching the occasional rise and burst of carbon dioxide bubbles through the airlock of the carboy of cider. Living processes, moving at their own pace, the rising of the bread and the slow fermentation of the apple juice, settled my mind and put the wrongs of the world into context for a while.

31

Well, at least it isn't raining, I thought, as I did a final inventory of my prison visiting gear—black slacks, white sweater, no-underwire bra, gray jacket, simple gold earrings and necklace, black raincoat with pockets emptied, manila folder of papers with no paperclips, transparent plastic cosmetic bag with pens, dollar bills, and change, a giant insulated mug of hot milky coffee, and a breakfast sandwich: almond butter and strawberry jam. I checked my wallet for my driver's license and bar card. Charlie went into his fenced yard, and the cats decided to follow him out. Then it was my turn to go out in the pre-dawn darkness, to my car.

The drive always seemed like an epic journey in miniature, from wild coast through gentle ranch lands, towns, and then suburbs and freeways. The commuter traffic on the last stretch was lighter than usual, and I arrived at San Quentin a quarter-hour early for my visit. The guards assigned to the front visiting office checked my ID and ran their eyes over my clothes and papers, and after a shoeless walk through the metal detector, I was free to move on, down the long walkway paralleling the staff parking lot and the bay beyond it, the water gray and choppy this morning, through the entry gates, and left to the old brick building with the cages for legal visits. The first clanking gate of the sally port opened and then closed behind me, the second one opened, and I was in the visiting area. The guard behind the Plexiglas window took my ID and said, "Hardy's down here."

Andy Hardy, my first visit that day, was waiting for the state Supreme Court to act on a habeas petition we had filed for him earlier in the year. It seemed inevitable that he would get an order to show cause and a hearing, as Howard had, because we had presented strong evidence that Andy was intellectually disabled, and under decisions from the United States Supreme Court it would be unconstitutional to execute him. In the meantime, Andy waited impassively for whatever might happen. But in the past few months his sister had died, and his mother had disappeared in a mysterious car accident. My guess was that she was dead, but Andy lived in hope that she would get back in touch with him. For now, though, he had only me and my co-counsel on the outside to answer his infrequent phone calls and buy him the quarterly packages of ramen, peanut butter, cookies, instant coffee, T-shirts, socks, shoes, and the like that helped supplement the bad food and rudimentary clothing supplied by the prison.

I turned right and walked along the aisle between the

rows of cages. A couple of men in prison uniforms glanced over at me from inside the barred cubicles, then turned away, seeing I wasn't the visitor they were expecting. Then I saw Andy sitting in one to my right. The cubicle had a barred window overlooking a service road, with a glimpse of the bay behind hedges on the other side. Andy's head was turned toward it, and he didn't see me approach.

"Andy?" I called quietly.

He turned quickly to face me, and his long pale face lit up with a shy smile. "Hi, Ms. Moodie," he said.

I asked him what I could get for him from the food machines, and he asked for a cheeseburger, chips, and an orange soda. "No ice cream," he added. "It gets too messy."

It took ten minutes or so to feed dollar bills and quarters into various vending machines and microwave the burger. I bought myself a bag of pretzels and a mocha—the chocolate flavor hid the sour cardboard taste of cheap instant coffee. I then added a dozen brown paper towels to the tray, walked back to the cages, and waited politely, holding the tray, while Andy and the guard went through the ritual of opening the cubicle door. It was the same every time and oddly uncomfortable to watch. The guard unlocked a metal panel in the door of the cage, and Andy backed up to it, holding his hands out behind him. The guard handcuffed him, he moved away from the door, and she slid it open to let me in. Once I was inside, she closed and locked the door, and the process was reversed as she unlocked Andy's handcuffs and removed them through the port. By the time she had finished, I had distributed our food on the small, chipped table and leaned the tray against it on the floor.

Andy sat down at the table. "Wow, I wasn't expecting you," he said. "When they told me I had a legal visit this morning I wasn't sure who it was."

"I'm sorry," I said. "I wrote you a letter, but I guess it didn't get to you in time."

"Nah. That's okay, though." He noticed his food, and devoted a few seconds to unwrapping the cheeseburger and opening the soda and the bag of chips. He held the bag out to me. "Would you like some?"

"I'm good," I said. "I have my pretzels."

"Yeah, you almost always get those. Guess you like them, huh?"

I shrugged. "They aren't as fattening as most of the other stuff."

"I don't like them. The salt feels funny on my teeth."

He'd said that just about every time I visited and bought pretzels, and I gave my usual answer. "I know what you mean. Guess it doesn't bother me as much."

He took a bite of cheeseburger—"Good," he said, his mouth full—and then devoted himself to finishing it. When he was finished, he wiped his mouth and hands with a paper towel and took a long drink of the soda.

"Thank you for the canteen money," he said. I'd put thirty dollars on his books a month ago, so he could buy some extra food and toiletries. "Got a dozen ramen and some instant coffee and shampoo. I was out of shampoo. And I still have some of everything left."

"Good for you," I said.

"Did you have a reason for coming to see me today?" he asked. "Have you heard anything about Mamma?"

I shook my head. "No, nothing."

He sighed. "I keep hoping."

"Of course. We'd all like to see her come back."

"I miss her and Carla all the time."

"Are you doing okay?"

"Yeah, better than I was."

The rest of our visit was taken up in small talk. Andy didn't ask any questions about his case; he was always content to let his lawyers handle it. He talked about his new neighbor in the cell next to his—much better than the previous one, who heard voices and had yelled day and night. That guy had finally been taken to the hospital after he began banging his head on the walls of his cell. Andy's new neighbor was a lot quieter and mostly kept to himself, though he and Andy had traded a few food items from their quarterly packages.

Andy asked how I was doing, how my garden was, what Dave, our investigator on his case, was up to these days. We talked about television and what movies had played recently on the prison channel. And then the guard gave the five-minute warning, and our time was up. Andy was handcuffed and escorted down the aisle toward the painted iron door that led back to the cellblocks, and I followed him and stood near the sally port with three or four other attorneys I didn't recognize, waiting for Walt.

I wondered if I'd recognize Walt when I saw him. I tried to remember how long it had been since I'd last paid him a visit—seven years? Eight? I needn't have worried; when he emerged through the iron door, a guard at his side, I knew him right away. He'd always had the stance of a strong man broken, big and broad in the shoulders, but hunched and a little bewildered, as if he couldn't quite figure out how he had ended up in this place. He was a bit thinner and more stooped than before, and his short, wiry hair had gone from salt and pepper to gray. He saw me, and a look of mild surprise crossed his blocky features. He and the guard turned away as he was led to his assigned cage, and I followed at a discreet distance.

Walt didn't want anything from the vending machines. "Not even a Dr. Pepper?" I asked him, as it came back to me that that had been his favorite drink. He shook his head. "I'll get a coffee, then, if you don't mind."

I got another mocha and hurried back to the cages and stood awkwardly balancing it and my manila folder and clear plastic bag of pens and money while the guard went through the handcuffing ritual. It was a different cage, in the other row; instead of a window it had a blurred view, through scratched Plexiglas, of the vending machines and a mural, painted long ago by another inmate. Walt wasn't paying any attention to it; his head was bent and his shoulders rounded. He looked worn out.

"Long time no see," I said, as soon as he was free of the cuffs. "How have you been?"

He lifted his head a bit to meet my eyes. "Not so good." He sounded tired, and his eyes and face were dulled by sadness.

I set my coffee and paraphernalia on the little table that nearly filled the cage. "Can I give you a hug?" I asked.

"Sure." I put my arms around him and hugged him for a second or two; he seemed to relax a little. "Come sit down," I said. I sat, and he settled, slowly and heavily, into the wooden chair opposite me.

"I just heard from Ms. Stanhope about Edna."

"Yeah." His eyes closed for a moment, then opened, and there were tears in them. "Yeah; I miss her."

"I was really sorry to hear it. I remember her; she was a really lovely person, and she loved you."

He nodded. "She was like a mother. She raised me after our mom died." I remembered that, too; Walt's mother had died young, of cervical cancer, but really of poverty and ignorance. Edna had told me that by the time her symptoms were bad enough that she couldn't put off seeing a doctor, the cancer had spread, and it was too late to do anything for her but give her morphine against the pain. Walt cried so much when they visited her in the hospital that they stopped bringing him.

"Abby Stanhope said you were feeling pretty bad, and she thought it might lift your spirits a little if Mike and I came and said hello."

"Thank you," he said. "Thank her."

"Is there anything I can do for you? Put some money on your books, or get you a quarterly package?"

He shook his head. "There isn't anything I want."

"Are they treating you all right here?"

"Mostly. Doctors want to change my medications, but I'm not sure. I don't feel like I can trust them."

"Why not?"

"They experiment."

"How?"

"They give me meds without knowing how they'll work. Some of them do, some don't and make me flip out."

"But do you feel that what you're on now is working?"

"I don't know, but at least I know how I'm going to feel after taking them." He stopped and thought for a few seconds. "I don't trust the guards, either," he said.

"Why? Do you think they may be messing with your food again?"

"That, and they've got something up their sleeve. I can hear them late at night, talking about me in the office on the tier. I hear them saying my name and laughing. I've been too afraid to sleep at night, so I end up falling asleep during the day. I'm tired all the time."

I decided to take the plunge. "Abby Stanhope says you

don't want to go on with your case. Is that why?"

He shook his head. "Not just that. All of it."

"Edna?"

"Yeah. And everything else."

"Like what?"

He sighed, and his shoulders slumped. "I don't know, I'm just tired of it all. I—I killed Irene and Tim, people I loved. Even Laura—she pushed me too far, but she didn't deserve to die for it. A day doesn't go by when I don't think about them. I don't have any defense for what I did, and they're going to execute me anyway. And with Edna gone I don't have anybody anymore. I just don't want to go on like this."

"I'm so sorry," I said. "It's really hard sometimes."

He nodded. "I really felt it about Edna. I knew she was sick, and I couldn't even be there to take care of her. I've just messed everything up in my life."

"I don't think she thought so," I said. "She knew you loved her and that you would have been there."

"Yeah," he said reluctantly. "The trouble is, I couldn't."

"I know. But she wouldn't want you to give up now," I said. "She never did. She kept coming to see you and staying in touch. It really mattered to her for you to stay in her life."

"Yeah," he said again. "But now she's gone." He lifted his hands to his face and bent forward, rocking as he cried almost silently, with deep, rough breaths. I remembered those paroxysms, that rending grief, and how they felt. I felt helpless watching him. All I could do was reach a hand across the table and press it on his big shoulder.

In a minute or so, he stopped, his face wet with tears. He found one of the paper towels I'd brought with my coffee, and wiped his eyes and cheeks with it. "I'm sorry," he said. "It just hits me sometimes."

"No problem," I said. "I often felt that way after my husband died."

Walt looked at me. "Did he? I didn't know."

"It was after your appeal was over—a little less than seven years ago."

"I'm sorry," he said again.

"It's okay now. Takes time, but it does get easier after a while."

"I don't see how." His voice was uncertain, and his hands were shaking. "I think I probably ought to go back to my house," he said. "Sorry. I just don't feel too well."

"Okay," I said. "Can I come to see you again?"

"Sure."

"I'll try to schedule things so that I can get a letter to you ahead of time."

He nodded. "It was kind of a surprise to see you," he said, with a wan smile.

I got up, walked the two steps to the door of the cage, waited until a guard appeared in the aisle, and waved until I caught his eye. He came over. "We're ready for Mr. Klum to go back," I said.

Walt had composed himself by the time the guard came

back with the handcuffs. We both stood, heads down, while he put the cuffs on through the door port. As the door slid loudly open, Walt seemed to wake up.

"Good to see you again," he said politely.

"You, too. Take good care of yourself. See you soon."

He turned away with the guard behind him, and I followed and watched as the metal door was opened and they moved into the corridor behind it. A couple of minutes after the door closed, the guard inside the windowed booth called over a loudspeaker. "Klum—cleared." He handed me my ID, and the sally port opened, letting me out into the gray afternoon.

3 2

On the drive back home, I fretted about Walt. With a statute
of limitations running, there could hardly have been a worse
time for him to be unsure whether to go on with his case.
I wasn't good at psyching people out or persuading them.
Lectures by psychologists at criminal defense seminars had
taught me a few techniques for listening to troubled people,
but that was all I had—that and what I'd learned about the
pain of grief after Terry died. In the hour or so I'd spent
with Walt I didn't think I'd accomplished anything, except
to confirm the bad shape he was in. I was grateful that he
was at least willing to see me and didn't feel I'd lost interest
in him after my court appointment ended.

I made a couple of stops on the way home, at a hardware
store and a supermarket. I knew I wasn't going to get home
before the end of business hours, so I called Abby from the
hardware store parking lot to report on my visit.

"Poor guy!" she said. "You see what a hard time we're
having."

"Yeah."

"Would you be willing to go see him again in a few weeks? We're trying to keep him communicating with us, especially through the holidays. So we're visiting him in relays. I have a really good investigator working on his case, a young woman. Walt has taken to her, in a sort of big brotherly way; she's good at cheering him up."

"That's a real plus," I said. When the state defender's budget had been more flush we had sometimes worked on habeas corpus cases as well as appeals, and I remembered a few bright and dedicated kids who'd interned with us. Their energy and unspoiled conviction was uplifting to the rest of us dealing with emotional fatigue from repeatedly watching years of hard work burned before our eyes by hostile courts. To clients, they were less intimidating than lawyers, and the men and women on the Row sometimes confided things to them they had never told their attorneys.

We picked a day for me to visit after I was back from Wheaton, and I said I'd check in beforehand in case there was something she wanted me to focus on when I saw Walt again.

Then it was Thanksgiving. I had let Harriet strong-arm me again into helping her serve the free dinner put on by her church in Santa Rosa. "I got so bored with making Thanksgiving dinner all those years," she explained, to justify doing twice as much work an hour away from home. Bill was one of the cooks this year, and he, Harriet, and

I bundled into their truck at five in the morning to make the trip, and returned at seven in the evening, footsore and spotted with gravy and whipped cream, and grateful for having homes and friends to go back to after seeing so many people who didn't.

Harriet invited me in for a glass of wine before I headed for home, and in her living room the three of us chatted for a while, winding down from the day. Bill gave me some advice on how to fix a slow leak I'd found under my kitchen sink and gave me some plumber's tape and the loan of a pipe wrench. He offered to fix it for me, but I saw Harriet shake her head and mouth a silent no, so I said I wanted to try handling it myself. Harriet asked me how my hearing was going.

"Not well," I said. "It's tough. Mike feels like it's his to lose. I mean, the man who did the killing confessed and said our client had nothing to do with it. You'd think that would be the end of it, but somehow no one wants to believe him. The fact that Howard is probably innocent makes it worse."

Harriet and Bill both nodded. "I remember a few cases like that," Harriet said. "Most everyone was guilty of course, but once in a while there'd be someone, you'd listen to the evidence and think, this guy really didn't do what they said he did. And then he'd be convicted anyway. Couple of times I remember even the judge was kind of upset by the verdicts, but there wasn't much anyone could do."

"Yeah," Bill said. "This is that Aryan Brotherhood case, right?"

"Yes," I said.

"They're dangerous characters."

I shrugged. "Not as much as they used to be, I gather. Our prison gang expert says some big federal racketeering prosecutions took a lot of them off the streets, and a bunch of the old guard have died or dropped out. The guys we've been talking to are all dropouts or people who were never that involved in the first place."

"That's good," Bill said. "I have to admit I've been a bit worried for you."

"Thanks," I said. "This is a really old case, and I don't think anyone in the AB cares much about it anymore."

"Good," Bill said. "We'll be keeping an eye out for you anyway."

I thanked them. I really didn't feel any fear of problems with the AB over Howard's case; Scanlon and the guys Mike and Dan had talked to had been surprisingly willing to try to help set an innocent man free. But living alone in the woods with only a nine millimeter in my night table and a Corgi guarding my door, I felt grateful I had friends looking out for me.

Bill's comment came back to me a couple of days later, when I was walking Charlie on the bluffs near Fort Ross. Charlie had run into the woods after a rabbit, and I was looking for him and calling him, to no effect, when I saw a man walking toward me. He was tall, young, and athletic-looking, and despite the chill wind on the bluffs, he was wearing a T-shirt and fleece vest. As he came closer I could see his arms were covered in tattoos. My heart began beating faster, and it was all I could do to tell myself there was no point in trying to run. When he got within talking distance, he asked me, "Are you looking for your dog?"

"Yes," I said, faintly.

"I saw him back there. Can I help you catch him?"

I thanked him, and we walked down the trail the way he had come, calling for Charlie together. In a couple of minutes, I saw Charlie crashing his way toward me through the undergrowth. "Rotten dog," I said to him when he reached me, as I bent down and put on his leash. I turned to the man. "Thank you," I said. "Are you visiting here?"

"No, but I haven't been here long." He spoke with an accent, maybe German or Dutch. "My name is Carl. I just started working at the brewery."

"Oh, you work with Vlad."

"Yes."

"You all make great beer," I said lamely.

"Thank you; that's good to hear."

"Guess I'll see you there sometimes, then."

"Maybe. But I work in the brewery, so I am not in the pub that often." His light blue eyes took in the view around him. "This is a beautiful place."

"I like it a lot." Charlie was pulling at his leash, anxious to get moving, so I said goodbye and thanked him again.

"Well, that was stupid of me," I said to Charlie after he was out of earshot, but even so, I headed back to the car, feeling anxious to be out of there and back in my own house.

33

All too soon—it was always too soon—it was time to drive back down to Wheaton: to pack my suitcase, gather my papers, leave food and water for the cats and walk Charlie over to Ed's. Charlie didn't seem at all sad to be left with Ed and Pogo, making me wonder what a dreary companion I must be if even my dog was glad to get away from me.

We were well into the rainy season in California, and the first winter storms had turned the hills along the interstate the velvet green of a pool table. The orchards of almond, walnut and peach trees were leafless, their bare branches dark against the green hills and silvery winter sky.

The hotel was decorated for Christmas, festooned with plastic spruce garlands and small winking lights; in the middle of the lobby stood a lavishly decorated tree with wrapped presents around it. The clerk at the desk recognized us. "Back again, eh?"

"Couldn't stay away," I said.

He chuckled. "Glad you like us."

After dropping my bag and suit hanger in my room, I met Mike in the lobby, and we went out in search of dinner. We settled on a Japanese restaurant. "I need something light—too much food last weekend," Mike said.

Over bento boxes of teriyaki, I asked Mike how his visit with Walt Klum had gone. He sighed. "Not too badly, I guess. I didn't change his mind, but he seems to be too broken down to remember why he didn't like me. I kept it low-key—actually, that was pretty easy; by the time I left I felt almost as sad as he was. I'm going to put some money on his books, so he can have a little canteen for the holidays."

I said I was planning to do the same. After that we talked about our plans for the hearing.

"I've got Niedermeier under subpoena, and they're bringing Sunderland from Folsom. George Gettle—the advisory attorney—is going to try to make it tomorrow afternoon; he's a court commissioner now, and he has a juvenile court calendar in the morning. And Ray Donahue, the lawyer Howard fired, is coming in, too. They'll both testify that they didn't get the letter. And Scanlon's here, too, though they have him at the state prison down the road in Wasco for security reasons. I wasn't sure he'd make it because of the holiday and the weekend, but I called on Monday, and they've got him."

"Full plate," I said.

"Yeah. I just hope we can get through Scanlon before we have to break."

We compared Thanksgivings. "You're lucky," Mike said, after hearing about mine. "Sue's mother still likes to have the family over and cook an enormous meal, even though these days Sue and her sister do a lot of the work. Still, Ruth bakes three or four pies and puts out all kinds of snacks. And you know how family visits are—hours of sitting in someone's living room telling old stories and trying to keep someone's brother-in-law from getting into politics."

"I guess there's some advantage to being too far away from your family to see them on holidays," I said, and then remembered, miserably, that Gavin and Rita were even farther away than my family in Alaska.

After dinner, Mike was anxious to get back to the hotel to prepare for the next day's witnesses. I offered to help, and he suggested I might do the direct exams of Donahue and Gettle, since they wouldn't need much preparation. At the hotel, he gave me some notes he'd made from his conversations with them, and we parted to spend the evening with our separate homework assignments.

We reached the courtroom at a quarter to nine the next morning. The usual audience was sitting on the benches in the hall: the two attorneys general, Dot Henley and Lillian, whose last name I had been told was Carver, and Josh Schaeffer, the young *News Gazette* reporter. Mike and I had read what he'd written about the first set of hearings; and he seemed bright and unbiased, and even inclined to favor the view that Howard was innocent.

Josh jumped up and collared Mike to ask him what his plans were for the day. Mike told him who the witnesses were that he hoped to call and left it at that.

A gray-haired man who had been talking with Dot also came over to us and introduced himself. "Ray Donahue," he said, shaking our hands in turn, with a firm, businesslike grip. I walked with him a little way down the hall.

"I'm going to be doing your direct examination this morning," I said.

"Okay," he said. "How is Howard, anyway?"

"Quieter these days."

"I guess that's something. He sure wasn't when I knew him. I felt bad for him," he added, "especially the way things went at his trial. If he'd only cooperated I could have won that case for him. What will you need from me?"

I told him we were trying to establish that Sandra Blaine had not given him the letter to Scanlon from McGaw.

"Your co-counsel talked to me about it and emailed me a copy. It was new to me. Where did you find the letter anyway?"

"There was a copy in Blaine's case file."

"Son of a bitch," he said, and quickly added, "Pardon my French. That sounds like Blaine. I'm surprised she didn't destroy it. Well, I never saw any letter, as I told Mr. Barry. I heard about it from that guy he confessed to—Sunderland, wasn't it? But since no one said they'd found a letter I assumed Scanlon was just blowing smoke."

"So you had a chance to talk to Sunderland?"

"Yes. I went to see him with my investigator, Jim Warren. He was in Mule Creek prison, if I recall, on a parole violation. I don't recall just what he said, but I remember it jibed with what he'd told his parole officer and the detectives. I'm working from memory, at this point. I don't have my file anymore. I passed everything on to Gettle after Howard fired me."

Everyone else had filtered into the courtroom, and we followed. A minute later the judge came out, and the bailiff called the case.

We began with what now seemed like the usual skirmishes over discovery. Mike brought up the AG's continuing failure to give us the materials we were supposed to receive about witnesses until the day they were supposed to testify. Laszlo grumbled about Mike's requests, accused us of withholding reports of our witness interviews until the last minute, insisted we didn't have the right to anything we'd requested, and then grudgingly handed over a small stack of documents. Among them were reports of their interviews of Scanlon and Niedermeier.

When Mike complained that we were receiving the interview reports the day before the witnesses were supposed to testify instead of a month before as the law required, the judge said, "Well, you have the documents. You should be able to read them in a day," and told us to call our first witness.

Ray Donahue took the stand. "Good morning, Mr. Donahue," Judge Redd said.

"Good morning, Your Honor." It was the greeting of two men who had known one another, in the courtroom and out, for a long time, and on the judge's side, which was the one that mattered, I detected a note of some respect.

Donahue testified to what he had told me: that he'd been retained by Howard Henley's family to represent Henley. He had read the police reports of Scanlon's confession of the Lindahl murder to Sunderland.

His investigator had interviewed Sunderland, and Sunderland had confirmed what was in the police reports: that Scanlon said he had been assigned by the Aryan Brotherhood to kill Lindahl. Laszlo objected that Donahue's testimony about Sunderland's statement was hearsay—he corrected himself, *double* hearsay. When I said we would be putting both Scanlon and Sunderland on to tie it up, the judge overruled the objection; and with an internal sigh of relief I went on.

Donahue continued: Sunderland also said Scanlon had told him he had a letter from someone in the organization confirming the order and that someone else who had nothing to do with the crime was in jail for it. He said that while he was representing Henley he had received some discovery from the district attorney, but he was sure that discovery had not included any letter to Scanlon. "Did you ever receive information that a letter like the one mentioned by Sunderland had been found?" I asked. Donahue answered that he had not. I showed Donahue the copy of the letter from McGaw, and he said he did not remember ever seeing anything like it before Mike had called and emailed it to him.

"Had you seen this letter while you were representing Mr. Henley," I asked, "would you have considered it significant?"

"Definitely," he said. "It was corroboration that Steven Scanlon was telling the truth when he said he'd committed the murder at the behest of the Aryan Brotherhood, and not Mr. Henley." Donahue said he would have made a discovery motion seeking disclosure of the letter from the prosecution, but he didn't have the chance before Henley asserted his right to represent himself. After Henley fired him, Donahue gave all his files of Henley's case to George Gettle.

I couldn't see what there could be to cross Donahue about, but Laszlo managed a few questions pointing out how many years it had been since he had represented Henley and the fact that he no longer had his files available to refresh his memory about the case. He questioned whether the letter would have been all that memorable, given that it said nothing about Lindahl or the killing. This was a mistake. Donahue hit back, repeating even more firmly what he had said on direct examination, that the existence of the letter supported Scanlon's confession, which exonerated Henley; it would have been an important piece of evidence at Henley's trial.

"If you could get it into evidence," Laszlo sniped.

Donahue gave him a look that summed him up as a complete amateur. "I'm pretty sure I could have," he said.

During the morning recess I made small talk with Dot and Lillian, while Mike talked with Niedermeier. From my reading into Niedermeier's criminal history, I knew he was about forty-five, but he appeared twenty years older. He was fairly tall, but bony and narrow-shouldered; his hair was sparse and needed cutting; his eyes were watery, and his cheeks sunken and leathery. He didn't hide the fact he was unhappy to be here.

Our next witness was Sunderland. Brought from the holding cell in an orange jail jumpsuit, he slouched, unshaven and resentful, in the witness chair as Mike questioned him, over routine hearsay objections from Laszlo, about his visit from Scanlon and Scanlon's confession of the killing to him.

He said, as he had in our interview, that Steve had called him, telling him he had to get out of Wheaton for a while and had stayed with him for a couple of days before moving on. When Mike asked if Steve had confessed a crime to him, Laszlo made a hearsay objection. Mike said Scanlon would be testifying to what he told Sunderland, and Laszlo revised his objection, stating Sunderland's testimony would be cumulative. The judge overruled both objections, but said all testimony about what Scanlon had said to Sunderland would be stricken if Scanlon didn't testify.

Mike continued.

"Steve Scanlon told you something about the murder of a man named Jared Lindahl, right?"

"Well, I didn't know the name of the man at that time, but yeah."

"What did he say?"

"He said it kind of in bits and pieces, but the gist of it was, he was in with the Aryan Brotherhood and had orders from them to kill some guy in Wheaton, and he'd gone and taken him out."

"Did he tell you someone else was in jail for the murder who didn't have anything to do with it?"

"Yes, he did."

Laszlo objected that the question was leading. "Please avoid leading your witness, Mr. Barry," the judge said.

"Did he say anything to you about a letter?" Mike asked Sunderland.

"Yeah, he said he had a letter from some guy in the AB—said it was sort of a friendly reminder to get on with the hit."

"Were you involved in any way with the Aryan Brotherhood?"

"No way. When I was in the joint I stayed away from all that stuff—just did my time. I was sorry to hear Steve got caught up with them, and just as glad when he took off; I really didn't want anything to do with their business."

Mike asked if Scanlon had seemed to have money.

"Not that I saw," Sunderland said. "He told me he was almost broke and waiting until he could get out of California to do a robbery and get some cash. He asked me for fifty dollars to help him get out of the state, gave me a watch as part payment. I helped him out by using my credit card to fill up his car."

On cross-examination, Laszlo walked Sunderland through his long and unsavory criminal history of armed robberies, burglaries, drug possession, and statutory rape. He was now doing ten years for shoplifting some steaks from a market, because he was what they call a habitual criminal. He'd gone to his parole officer to turn Scanlon in, because he didn't want to be involved in a murder. Sunderland made it clear that he thought Scanlon was a bit of a braggart and a little loose, especially for someone with aspirations to rise in the Aryan Brotherhood. Scanlon didn't show him the letter. He didn't know whether Scanlon's story about it was true or not, nor did he know whether Scanlon was telling the truth when he said the other guy in jail wasn't involved in the murder. He'd never thought of Scanlon as particularly truthful or honorable. Scanlon had been jumpy and paranoid while he had been staying at Sunderland's house. He might have been on meth, or just scared.

"Did you tell that to your parole officer and Detective Springer?" Laszlo asked.

"Probably not."

"But you're saying you told them the truth about what Steve said to you?"

"Yes, I did, and I paid for it, too."

"How is that?"

"My parole officer violated me for receiving stolen property and associating with criminals, and I spent another year in the joint."

"Why receiving stolen property?"

"That watch Steve gave me turned out to be stolen. I should have known better, knowing Steve."

On redirect, Mike asked, "When you told your parole officer and Detective Springer what Steve told you, did you tell them everything you remembered him saying about the murder?"

"I did."

"Did you deliberately hold anything back?"

"No. I was trying to be as honest as I could. I didn't want trouble."

Mike had found out Scanlon was in the holding cell at the courthouse and was going to see him over the lunch break. "Not a bad morning," Mike said, as we separated. He gave me the discovery Laszlo and Willard had given us, for me to read over before the afternoon session. There was a DVD and transcript of the attorney general's interview of Niedermeier, who, Willard said, had told them he had no memory of ever meeting Scanlon. And there were debriefing reports from Corker Bensinger and Scotty Maclendon. Progress was being made on some fronts, at least.

I declined a lunch invitation from Dot Henley, pleading the need to work through the break. With a made-to-go ham and cheese sandwich and a horrible coffee from a minimart near the courthouse, I settled into a small conference room at the county law library to listen to the interview on my computer and check it against the transcript. There wasn't that much to it: mostly Niedermeier protesting, in a slurred voice, that he just wanted everyone to leave him alone and he no longer remembered anything about Scanlon or the Henley case. I made markup copies of the rest of the discovery at the copy machine and ate my sandwich while reading and making notes.

When I got back to the courtroom, Mike was in conversation with another man. "Commissioner Gettle, Janet Moodie," he said, introducing us. Gettle seemed gentler and less dynamic than Donahue. Lean and a little stooped, he peered down at me through metal-framed glasses. "I'm glad to see Henley is getting a hearing," he said. "It's a case you don't forget." We went briefly over what I'd be asking him, and he said, "I gave my files to the appeal attorney, but I'm sure, as I stand here, that I never got any such letter. You know, we tried to call Sunderland as a witness, but the judge wouldn't let him testify about what Scanlon told him about the AB. If we'd had that letter, you know we'd have tried to present it."

When Gettle took the stand, Judge Redd didn't seem quite as impressed as he had been with Donahue. Even as a commissioner, it seemed, Gettle wasn't one of the club.

Gettle spoke briefly of how he had come into the case,

appointed by Judge Redd to be Howard's advisory counsel. "The judge called me the day Mr. Henley made his motion to represent himself. He said Mr. Henley had no legal background and was refusing to waive time, insisting on going to trial immediately, and he was sorely in need of advisory counsel. He asked me to come to court the next day, so he could make the assignment."

I asked why the judge had called on him.

"I had been advisory counsel in another case before him not that long before, and I guess he thought I'd done a creditable job." I saw the judge give a slight nod, as if agreeing.

"Had you heard about Mr. Henley's case before that?"

"A little, but I'd been in trial in a case in Visalia for a while, so I was a little out of the loop on local events."

"Did you talk with Mr. Donahue about Mr. Henley's case?"

"I'm sure I did." Laszlo's objection that he was speculating was sustained.

"Did you obtain Mr. Donahue's files?"

"I did."

"And did you read them?"

"Oh, yes."

"And you were aware that Steve Scanlon claimed he had a letter from someone in the Aryan Brotherhood regarding the killing of Jared Lindahl?"

"Yes."

"Was any such letter in the files you got from Mr. Donahue?"

"No."

"A letter like that would have caught your attention, wouldn't it?"

"Absolutely. I was hoping it would turn up."

"Did you receive any discovery from the district attorney after you were assigned as Mr. Henley's advisory counsel?"

"I believe we did."

"Was that discovery given to you or Mr. Henley?"

"I had arranged with the district attorney's office to have it given to me. I then made copies and shared them with Mr. Henley."

"Why did you decide on that arrangement?"

"Several reasons. I was concerned about Mr. Henley's custody status and the danger that material related to his case might get into the wrong hands in the jail. Also, his mental condition was such that I was concerned about his ability to keep track of discovery he received." Laszlo objected to Gettle's statement about Howard's mental condition as irrelevant and asked that it be stricken; Judge Redd denied his request.

"The bottom line, though, was that the discovery was given to you, and not him, correct?"

"Asked and answered," Laszlo piped up. The judge, for once, ignored him.

"Yes," Gettle said.

"Did the discovery you received include a copy of any letter to Scanlon?"

"No."

"When Mr. Henley presented his case at trial, wasn't he trying to show that Scanlon had confessed he had killed Jared Lindahl for the Aryan Brotherhood?"

"Objection, leading," Laszlo said. The judge overruled him.

"Yes," said Gettle.

"The letter Scanlon claimed he had from an Aryan Brotherhood higher-up would have been useful evidence for his defense, right?"

"Of course."

"So if he had obtained a copy of such a letter, you would expect him to try to present it as evidence, then?"

"Definitely."

"As far as you knew, Mr. Henley didn't have a copy of such a letter."

"True. I had no indication that he had."

Laszlo's cross-examination began with asking Gettle pretty much what I had asked him, and getting the same answers. I made a few "asked and answered" objections, which were overruled, but I didn't much care.

Then Laszlo moved to a different topic. "You knew that Mr. Henley had been the subject of a hearing relating to his mental competence to stand trial?" he asked.

"Of course," Gettle answered. "He was found competent

to stand trial and to represent himself."

"Was he cooperative with you in preparing his defense?"

"He wasn't required to be," Gettle said. "He was representing himself; my role was only to give advice, which he was free to take or not."

Laszlo pressed on. "Did he cooperate with you?" I objected to the question, but the judge overruled me.

"Not always," Gettle replied, "but sometimes. He objected to my being appointed, but when the case came to the penalty phase, he asked the judge to appoint me as his lawyer. So there must have been times, at least, when he respected my advice."

"If he had a copy of the letter to Scanlon, would he necessarily have shared it with you?"

"I'd like to think so," Gettle said. "He clearly wanted to present evidence of Scanlon's confession and prove his actual motive. He tried very hard to do so at his trial. Had the letter been available, it's hard to imagine that he would not have tried to introduce it."

Laszlo made a snide comment: "So you could at least imagine that he might not let you know if he had such a letter." I objected to it as argumentative and asking the witness to speculate, but Laszlo sat down without waiting for the judge to rule. I didn't feel any need for redirect examination, and Gettle, released from the stand, left the courtroom with what I thought was an encouraging glance in our direction.

"Okay," Mike whispered, as I settled into my chair.

After Gettle's testimony, Laszlo argued that we still hadn't proved the letter hadn't been given in discovery and that we would have to call Brian Morris, the lawyer who had represented Howard in his direct appeal, to testify that it wasn't in the files he received from Gettle. Mike pointed out that among the exhibits to the habeas corpus petition filed by Gordon Marshall was a declaration under penalty of perjury from Morris stating that no letter fitting Scanlon's description was in any files he'd received from Howard's prior attorneys and investigators. Laszlo objected that the declaration was hearsay. Judge Redd, seemingly tired of the issue, agreed with Mike. "Mr. Morris is an officer of the court, and we have his declaration. This hearing seems to be becoming awfully long, and I don't know what we would gain by bringing Mr. Morris here just to repeat what he has already said in a sworn statement."

Our last witness for the day was Christian Niedermeier. He appeared nervous and on edge; as the clerk gave him the oath, his eyes kept moving from one person in the courtroom to another, as if seeking someone he recognized.

"Good afternoon, Mr. Niedermeier," Mike said. "I understand you're not very happy to be here."

He glanced quickly at Mike, as if startled to hear him speak. "No, I'm not," he said, with a querulousness I associated with long-time alcoholics.

"Your Honor," Mike said to the judge, "Mr. Niedermeier

asked me earlier if we could close the courtroom for his testimony. He has concerns for his safety. I gather he suffered some repercussions for his testimony at Mr. Scanlon's trial."

Laszlo—being oppositional seemed to be a reflex with him—objected. "His prior testimony is public record, Your Honor. I don't see how he can object at this late date to talking about it."

The judge decided to compromise. "I don't see any need to seal this witness's testimony, but perhaps we should clear the courtroom. Everyone not associated with this case is instructed to wait in the hall until you are called. Thank you." The scattering of people in the audience filed out; I could see Niedermeier relax a little.

Mike began by asking Niedermeier about the reason he had found himself in jail with Scanlon.

"I was charged with attempted murder and some other things."

He had met Scanlon while he was in jail; and he had also met Howard Henley. For a while, they were on the same yard.

"Did you ever talk with Howard Henley?"

"Sort of."

"How is that?" Mike asked.

"He wasn't really someone you talk with, if you know what I mean. He was pretty strange, kind of off-putting. Generally, he pretty much kept to himself. But he must have decided he liked me for some reason. Sometimes he'd come over and talk to me—talk at me, really—about some of his weird ideas."

"What kinds of weird ideas?"

Laszlo objected, and the judge sustained it.

"Did he ever talk to you about his case?"

"Once or twice."

"What did he say?"

"Just that they were saying he killed some guy, but he was innocent."

"Did he say anything else?"

"It's been a long time, and, you know, a lot of the time I couldn't follow what Henley was saying, but I remember he was kind of hyped up about a conspiracy of some sort. A lot of conspiracies, he was really big on conspiracies." At the memory, he cracked a faint smile. He said Scanlon had come to him because he saw Niedermeier appeared to be friendly with Henley. "He wanted to know if Henley was mad at him. I asked him, 'Why would Henley be mad at you?' I didn't know there was any connection between them."

"Did he say why?" asked Mike. Laszlo objected. "Not offered for its truth," Mike said, "and statement against interest."

"I'll allow it, subject to a motion to strike," said the judge.

Niedermeier looked at Mike. "You can answer," Mike said.

"He told me he and Henley were both charged with killing some guy, but Henley was innocent."

Laszlo objected to the second half of the statement as hearsay. Mike argued it was admissible for the limited purpose of explaining Scanlon's statement and Niedermeier's subsequent actions. The judge agreed.

"Did Scanlon say anything about why he killed the man?" Another hearsay objection, overruled.

"Yeah. He said he killed him for the Aryan Brotherhood."

"How did he act when he said that?"

"Kind of proud. He liked telling people he was with the AB. I guess it made him kind of a big shot in the jail."

"Did Scanlon ask you to do anything for him regarding Henley?" Mike asked.

"He asked me to tell Henley he was sorry."

"Some time after that, you told the police about what Scanlon said to you, right?"

"Actually I told a jail deputy, and then a detective came to see me."

"Okay. Why did you decide to tell them about it?"

Niedermeier hedged. "Couple of reasons. I felt bad about Henley—like, he shouldn't have to go to prison if he was innocent."

"But that wasn't the only reason."

"No." Niedermeier sighed and glanced down at his hands. "I was scared for myself. I was looking at a lot of prison time, and I was hoping for a deal."

"Did you get one?"

"After I testified at Scanlon's trial, yeah. I got to plead to assault with a deadly weapon and no enhancements. But it didn't work out well for me."

"Why not?"

"Well, I went to prison with a snitch jacket, and I was greenlighted by the AB. I got stabbed on the yard, almost killed. Ended up getting moved to Nevada 'cause they couldn't protect me here."

"Let me ask you," Mike said, "you were interviewed by Mr. Willard here and an investigator a few weeks ago, right?"

Niedermeier gave Willard a glance before answering. "Yeah, they came by."

"What happened?"

"They came to my house one morning and wanted to ask me questions."

"You told them you didn't remember anything about the case, right?"

He paused. "Yeah."

"Was that true?"

"No, it wasn't."

"Why did you tell them that?"

"They came to my house without any warning and wouldn't go away. I have liver disease, and I take medication, and I was feeling pretty bad. I didn't want to be reminded of that whole part of my life. I still have PTSD from it."

"Were you drunk that morning?"

"Hell, no—sorry, Your Honor—absolutely not. I've been in AA for four years. I've got liver disease, and I'm on a transplant list. No way am I drinking."

Over Mike's objection, Willard was allowed to take Niedermeier through the sordid details of the crime he'd been jailed for, an attempt to run over an ex-girlfriend and her current lover with his car. Then he exploited Niedermeier's denial of any recollection of Scanlon's admissions. "So you lied when you told us that."

"Yes, I did."

"But you say you told the truth about Scanlon's confession."

"Yes."

"You lied to us just to get rid of us, right?"

"Yes."

"And when you told the detective that Scanlon had confessed to you, you had a much more compelling reason to lie, right?"

"I'm not sure what you mean."

"What I mean is, you were facing life in prison, and you were trying to get a deal."

"Yeah."

Mike's redirect was short.

"Mr. Niedermeier, you testified at Steve Scanlon's trial, didn't you?"

"Yes."

"Who called you to testify?"

"The district attorney."

And so the day ended.

Dot and Lillian were alone on the benches in the hallway; even Josh Schaeffer, the reporter, had left. They stood, and Dot walked over and spoke briefly with Mike, as I said a general goodbye and made my way to the restroom. When I emerged, Dot and Lillian were gone. As we fell into step together, he said, "Dot just gave me a check for five thousand dollars."

"That's great!"

"Did you say something to her?"

"Yes. I told her the court wasn't paying us for our expenses, and you were paying them yourself."

"Thanks," Mike said. "I don't think I could have asked. I'll definitely be able to use it. I have some more work for Dan, and this will help pay for it."

"Glad to be of help," I said.

"So—back to the hotel? Got a big day tomorrow with our friend Steve."

34

The ceremonies the next morning began at nine o'clock sharp. The judge took the bench, the bailiff called us all to order, and a moment later two uniformed deputies brought Scanlon into the courtroom. He was dressed in a red jumpsuit, hands cuffed closely to a chain at his waist, and chains around his ankles; and a hood had been placed over his head, so he could not see ahead or to his sides. He stumbled once, and again, as the guards led him up to the witness stand, released the handcuffs from the waist chain, used them to fasten his left wrist to the chair, and released his right arm. They took off the hood, but left his ankle chains fastened.

"Jesus Christ," I whispered to Mike. "What is this about?"

Mike walked over to the courtroom bailiff, who was watching the procession intently from his desk at the side of the courtroom. They spoke briefly, and Mike came back. "Extra security," he said, "because he's got a history of attempted escape and assaulting a guard. Still seems like overkill, though."

Scanlon was surveying the room, frowning, his free hand clenched into a fist. He caught sight of Mike and called over, "Hey, Mr. Barry, can you ask these guys to do something about this handcuff? They've been too tight all morning, and my hand is numb."

"I'll call the deputies," the bailiff said. He returned a minute later with two sheriff's deputies. One of them inspected Scanlon's arm. "It looks fine to me," he said.

"That's b.s., man," Scanlon said, his voice tense. "My wrist hurts like hell, and I can't feel the rest of my hand."

Mike got up, and one of the deputies motioned him back, but not before he saw Scanlon's wrist. Scanlon called out to the judge. "Your Honor, would you please tell these guys to loosen my handcuff? I'm in pain here."

Judge Redd turned his head toward him, irritated at being addressed so rudely by a witness, and Mike spoke up. "Your Honor, he's right. His wrist is raw, and his hand is turning white. They'd better do something, or the jail will have a lawsuit on its hands."

One of the deputies weighed in. "Your Honor, Mr. Scanlon here is a security risk. We have to take precautions."

The judge's eyes moved from him to Mike. "This is my witness," Mike said. "I need him to be able to testify without being distracted by pain."

Almost reluctantly, the judge turned to the deputies and

said, "Can you loosen the handcuff a little?"

The deputies, with an attitude that as much as said they would not consider themselves responsible for the consequences, bent over Scanlon in a show of force while one of them unlocked the handcuff, made an adjustment to it, and locked it again. They backed away, and Scanlon moved the fingers on his handcuffed hand with a grimace of pain.

"Is that better?" Mike asked.

He nodded. "Yes. Thank you."

Mike began his direct examination by asking Scanlon about his criminal history. Scanlon answered in a level voice, starting with his juvenile record and moving through his history in prison. "I started out in fire camp," he said, "but I kept getting into fights—stupid things, I was just hard-headed back then—and I got sent to Soledad and then to Folsom, got out, and then ended up back in again."

Mike then asked Scanlon to explain how he had become involved with the Aryan Brotherhood inmates who ran the yards.

"I was young and didn't know any better. These guys seemed like stars, leaders of men. If they like you, they kind of mentor you. One of them takes you under their wing, teaches you the ropes, how to get along in prison."

"Did someone mentor you in Soledad?"

A shadow of sadness crossed Scanlon's face before he answered. "Yeah, Mack Gentry. He ran the yard there."

"At some point, were you required to give something back to them?"

"Well, they sort of seduce you into believing what they believe. And then after a while they start testing your loyalty, your courage, by giving you assignments."

"What kind of assignments?"

"Lot of them involved beating someone up or stabbing them." In his debriefing report he had confessed to several stabbings on the yard, and he described them briefly, without emotion.

"At some point you transferred to Folsom, right?"

"Yeah."

"Did you find Aryan Brotherhood members there?"

"Yeah; there were a lot of AB there. I knew some better than others. Corker Bensinger, for example."

"Tell me about Bensinger."

"He was a big man in the AB, a shot-caller. One of those guys, you spend five minutes with him, you're willing to go out and die for him."

"Who else did you meet?"

"Let's see—well, Cal McGaw, of course. Bensinger was a big man in the AB, McGaw was kind of a shot-caller, too, but lower in the pecking order, the kind of guy who runs a yard."

The judge interrupted to ask Mike what the point of so much background was, and Mike answered, "This is leading up to the Lindahl murder. And I'm taking Mr. Scanlon through his criminal history because if I don't, Mr. Willard certainly will."

"You're probably right," the judge agreed, wearily.

Mike asked Scanlon if he knew Jared Lindahl.

"Yes, I did."

"How did you know him?"

"I killed him."

Mike paused for a second before going on. "Was that an assignment you were given?" he asked.

"Yeah. There was a hit on the man for selling drugs in the prison without paying tax—that's the percentage the AB gets when any white guy sells drugs there. I knew he was in the hat, though I'd never met him. He paroled before they could do anything about him. He paroled to Wheaton. McGaw knew that's where I was from and that I was about to parole soon myself. So I guess the word came down, and McGaw told me I'd been requested to take this guy out. I thought, 'Sure, I'll do it if that's how it has to be.' I didn't know any better at the time."

"Did you feel like you had a choice?" Mike asked.

"I didn't even care. I didn't really understand what I was doing. I mean, it's hard to believe you could be involved in so much violence and really not understand what you're really doing and the effects that's caused from your actions. It's hard to believe somebody would be that ignorant. But that's how I was."

"Did you kill Lindahl right away?"

"Nah. I kept putting it off. They told me before I left Folsom where Lindahl was living, but I paroled late in the year, and what with spending time with my family and the Christmas season and all… I just didn't get around to it. It was kind of a jolt, actually, getting that letter from Cal."

"So what did you do?"

"Well, like I said, they'd told me where Lindahl was living—kind of a stroke of luck because I knew that trailer park. A cousin of mine that I was pretty close to was living there, so I had a perfect excuse to be around. I figured Lindahl knew he was in the hat, and he might be leery of strangers coming to his place. I didn't want to get shot at sneaking up on him. So once I decided it was time to go ahead with this thing I spent a couple days kind of cultivating him."

"How did you do that?"

"That park is a bad place, full of lowlifes, drug users and small dealers. I knew a few of them from being around there seeing my cousin. I sort of made friends with a couple of them, and one of them—Freddy Gomez—introduced me to Lindahl. Freddy was kind of an AB hanger-on; nothing in the gang, but a little hero-worship going on. He helped me get a gun, too, from a guy he knew who sold 'em."

"That was the man named Indio, right?"

"Yep."

"So what happened then?"

"It wasn't too hard to get close to Lindahl, as it turned out. Guy wasn't too bright, believed that if I was a friend of

Freddy's I was safe. Anyway we had enough in common. We were both ex-cons, in need of money to live on. I'd got hold of a gun, and he had one already, so I invited him to come along on a robbery, and then we were good buddies. You already know how I killed him."

Mike asked him to explain.

"We went out to the back of his place to shoot at cans. I bought a six-pack of beer and asked Freddy to come with us, to kind of give Lindahl a sense of security. We just shot some cans, drank beers, hung out for a while. Then I sent Freddy to the corner store for some more beer—to get him out of the way, really. I kept my gun by my side ready, and right after Freddy left, when Lindahl turned away, I just took aim and plugged him. He went down right away, but I went over and shot him couple more times just to make sure. Then I grabbed all the beer cans because of fingerprints and split before Freddy came back. Took a watch the guy was wearing and a police scanner he had in his pocket. I thought about waiting for Freddy to get back and then getting rid of him, too, but I just lost heart or something. All I wanted to do was get out of there. I just hoped Freddy'd be too afraid to say anything. I heard he took Lindahl's gun and sold it."

Laszlo objected to the last sentence as beyond Scanlon's personal knowledge, and threw in a second objection that his testimony was turning into a narrative. The judge ordered the last sentence stricken and told Mike to move on.

"Did you get any money or drugs from Howard Henley for shooting Lindahl?"

"Hell, no—pardon my language. No, I never got nothin' from him."

"Did Howard Henley ask you to kill Lindahl?"

"No."

"Did he offer you money or drugs or anything else to kill Lindahl?"

"No, never."

"Did you meet Howard Henley at the trailer park?"

"Yeah, I met him there. Hard not to."

"In what way?"

"He was someone who'd get in your face. Everyone hated him because he was so crazy. I didn't mind him much. He had strong views, that's all, and he seemed kind of lonely for someone to talk to about his crazy ideas."

"Was he dealing drugs?"

"Not in any regular way. Mostly he just smoked weed himself."

"Did he have a lot of money?"

"Nah, man; no one there did. Anyone who could afford it would have moved out of that place."

"So Howard never hired you to kill Lindahl."

"No. After he got beat up he bitched a little, said he'd like to kill the guy himself, that's all. But he got over it. I told him, 'Hey, you win some, you lose some; you just have to do what everyone else does, and stay out of his way.' I have to say I felt sorry for those guys at the trailer park. Felt I was doing something like a public service in getting rid of Lindahl. But that was secondary. I did him on an assignment from the AB, and that's all."

Mike showed Scanlon the letter from McGaw and asked him if it was a copy of the one he received.

"Like I told you, yes."

"Have you read the letter?"

"Yes. Back when I got it and again when you showed it to me before."

"Were you surprised to get it?"

"Yeah."

"Why was that?"

"Well, it was kind of out of the blue."

"What do you mean?"

"I hadn't heard anything from anyone, and suddenly here's this letter."

"McGaw knew where you were living?"

"No, but he had my parents' address. I'd given him that as a way to contact me."

"What did it mean to you, to get that letter?"

"That somebody wasn't happy I wasn't getting the job done."

"Is it in some kind of code?"

Laszlo jumped in with a barrage of objections. The letter was hearsay, no one had established that it was code or that Scanlon was capable of recognizing that it was.

"May I lay a foundation?" Mike asked.

"You can try," said the judge.

Mike tried, but all Scanlon could say was that he knew from experience that the letter was meant as a reminder, a push to get the job done. He said the reference to whether he was still working probably meant "why aren't you taking care of business," the question about "homies" meant Lindahl, and the reference to Christmas may have meant that they knew where his family lived, but he couldn't say why he believed that. "It's just how they communicate, man. The fact that he sent the letter was a message in itself."

In the end, the judge sustained Laszlo's objection and ruled that we hadn't proven, at least yet, that the letter was actually a directive.

Mike moved on with his questioning. "What did you do after shooting Lindahl?"

"Decided to get out of town for a while, in case there was any heat. Sold the gun back to Indio for a few bucks and a .22, and took off. Figured I'd go to El Dorado, visit my cousin Keith. Thought I could stay up there with him until things cooled down or I at least knew where I stood down here, but I started getting a weird vibe from him, so I borrowed some money from him and took off. Good thing, too, because he turned me in."

"Then what did you do?"

"I just drove east, got across the state line to Nevada before the cops were onto me. Did a couple of robberies for cash to get my car painted at a shop, stole some Nevada plates and swapped them for mine. Ended up in Utah for some reason. Did a couple more robberies near Salt Lake. Then I began feeling paranoid there, and felt I'd be better off where I knew the territory, so to speak, so I started back home. I got busted in a motel outside Wheaton; those Nevada plates did me in."

"Was the letter from McGaw in your car when you were arrested?"

"Yeah, I guess. I just forgot to get rid of it."

"Had McGaw ever sent you a letter before, during the time since you left prison?"

"No—that was the only one."

"Had you written to him since you were out?"

"No, I'm not the letter-writing type."

"Eventually you dropped out of the gang. Why was that?"

A brief frown. "They asked me to do something I wasn't prepared to do."

"What was that?"

"It's pretty much all in my debriefing statement."

"Can you explain it for us anyway?"

He sighed. "Okay, sure. I was in segregation up in Pelican Bay because of that stupid escape attempt and because the prison's gang unit had validated me as AB. I was in some trouble with the AB higher-ups because of what I'd done; I'd brought a lot of bad stuff down on everyone. They decided to give me one last chance. I was told to kill my cellmate, some young guy who'd gotten on their bad side for some reason. But I got to know him, got to know his story, and decided it just wasn't fair, and I wasn't going to do it. At that point, I was toast. I'd caused them trouble and disobeyed orders. So they got someone else celled with me. Someone I trusted; we'd been cellies in Folsom. He got the jump on me, almost killed me. I lost so much blood they thought I wasn't going to live. When they brought me back to the prison hospital, I called a guard over and told him I wanted to see Ida Rader and debrief."

"How did you feel about the Aryan Brotherhood at that point?" Mike asked.

"Betrayed, angry. Hell, I'd killed a man for them. But if they were done with me, I was done with them."

Mike asked to have Scanlon's debriefing statement marked for identification, then showed it to him. Scanlon acknowledged that it was the one he had written. To the best of his recollection at the time, everything in it was true.

Mike asked him, "Do you believe you're getting any benefit from testifying here about all this?"

"Not at all. Nothing but a headache, and a sore hand."

"And by testifying here, you're actually putting yourself at greater risk inside prison?"

"Absolutely."

Then it was Willard's turn to cross-examine.

Willard began by confronting him. "Mr. Scanlon, what is your purpose in being here today?"

Scanlon replied in the same level voice he had answered Mike's questions. "I didn't just walk in; I was brought from a prison."

"But you are cooperating with Mr. Henley's legal team, aren't you?"

"Yeah."

"And what is your purpose for that?"

"I don't need one. But if you want to know, it's to right a wrong, because Howard Henley is sitting in prison for a crime I know he had nothing to do with."

"You're sure you aren't hoping for a chance to escape?"

"I'm always hoping for a chance to escape."

"You said more or less the same thing to the officers after your arrest in the prison escape, didn't you?"

"I don't remember, but I'll take your word for it."

"Didn't you tell one of them, 'A caged animal will take a chance to get free if he can get it'?"

"I don't know, but it sounds like something I might have said."

"If a chance to escape had come up during your trip here, would you have taken it?"

"Of course, man; anyone would."

"If you escaped before coming here to testify, you wouldn't have been here to right the wrong against Mr. Henley, then."

"Get real," Scanlon said. "You and I both know there wasn't a chance in hell I'd get away coming here."

Willard took him through his criminal past again,

with a few more flourishes. "You have convictions not just for robbery, but for armed home invasions and armed kidnapping, don't you?"

"I guess I may have kidnapped people to rob them once or twice."

"You went to trial on the home invasions, three counts, right?"

"I believe so."

"You were tried on them and the Lindahl murder at the same time."

"Yes."

"And you testified at that trial."

"Yes."

"And denied you'd done any of them, is that right?"

"Of course."

"Now, when you denied murdering Lindahl, were you telling the truth?"

"No, I was lying. I'm sure you've lied about a lot of things in your life."

"You were testifying under penalty of perjury when you lied in your trial, then."

"Yes."

"And you're under penalty of perjury now."

"Guess so."

"Why should we believe you're telling the truth to us now?"

"Because back then I was fighting for my life, and I did

what I had to. If I'd testified and told the truth I'd probably be on death row, just like Henley."

"So you actually met Corker Bensinger in Folsom."

"Yes."

"And he was an AB shot-caller?"

"Yes—'was.'"

"Is that because he's dropped out?"

"That's what I understand."

"Did he ever talk with you about the hit on Lindahl?"

"I'd rather not say."

"Why not?"

"He can come and say for himself whether he did. I'm not going to rat anyone out."

"You were okay with saying McGaw gave you instructions."

"Yeah, but he's dead."

"Do you know who actually ordered the hit?"

"As far as I know, yes."

"And you're not willing to say who that is?"

"No."

"Why not?"

"Because it wouldn't be right."

"But you're here to see that justice is done for Mr. Henley, right?"

"Yes."

"Is protecting this other friend of yours more important than that?"

"No. I already told the court what I did. What this other guy did doesn't seem relevant."

"You don't get to judge what's relevant here."

"Well whoo-ee!" Scanlon said scornfully.

Willard went on. "But you're saying it was the Aryan Brotherhood that ordered you. Who in that group gave the order?"

"You'll have to let him tell you."

"Will he be testifying at this hearing?"

"Possibly."

"But you're not willing to say who he is."

"I can't, no. You're asking me to name someone when it could end them up on death row."

"But don't we already know who you're talking about?"

"So what?"

"So do you have anything to lose by answering my question?"

"I definitely do."

"What?"

"Well, if that reporter in the audience says in the newspaper that I named names, and that gets back to anyone, I'm in danger in the penitentiary because then I'm a snitch."

Willard asked the judge to order Scanlon to answer the question; Mike objected that it was beyond the scope of direct and that Bensinger would be in court at the next hearing to answer it himself. The judge ordered Scanlon to answer.

"Your Honor, I can't."

"You're aware there may be consequences for refusing," the judge said.

Scanlon made a show of looking at the chains on his wrist and ankles and back up at the judge. "What can you do to me, Your Honor?" he asked quietly. "I'm already in hell."

3 5

For a moment, we all held our breath, wondering how the judge would react. Then he turned from Scanlon to Willard. "Just move on," he said.

Willard moved on—to Scanlon's debriefing statement, which, Scanlon admitted, did not include several of his AB-related crimes, and to the escape attempt in which Scanlon had stabbed a guard in a struggle for his keys.

"Do you consider yourself a violent person?" he asked.

"I was in the past. Now I try not to be. I try to leave other people alone and hope they'll do the same for me. But if I have to, I'll defend myself."

Willard needled him some more about his refusal to name the man who had ordered the Lindahl hit. "Do you think you can come in here, be sworn to tell the truth, and just answer the questions you want to?" Mike objected, and the judge told Willard, again, to move on.

"You're serving two life terms right now, isn't that right?" he asked.

"Yes. I've been told I'm not eligible to be considered for parole until I'm sixty-eight. And I don't think I have a chance in hell of getting paroled given my history."

"So basically, you don't have any realistic hope of getting out."

"Yes. I've given up that fantasy."

"So you have nothing to lose by coming in now and telling a court that Howard Henley didn't have anything to do with the murder of Jared Lindahl."

"Come on, you know better than that. And I didn't just come in now, if that's what you're suggesting. I've been telling you people for years that Henley's innocent, but none of you have been interested."

Willard changed the subject. "Do you think you're an honest person?" he asked.

"Well, I'm in prison," he said. "Honesty isn't everybody's best policy, but I try to be honest because lying in prison is a dangerous game."

"If you wanted something, and you had to lie to get it, would you be willing to lie?"

"Well, now, I'm a criminal. You already know the answer to that."

"Yes, I believe I do," Willard said.

Willard ended by asking the judge to strike all of Scanlon's testimony for his refusal to name the man who ordered the killing. Mike was standing up to argue, but the judge said, "That seems like an extreme remedy for refusing to answer one question. Denied." I wondered if I was sensing a change in Judge Redd's attitude.

On redirect, Mike began by asking Scanlon how many people he'd told that Howard was innocent.

"You told Keith Sunderland, right? What did you tell him?"

"That I killed Lindahl on order from the Aryan Brotherhood, and another guy was in jail who had nothing to do with it. And that I had a letter from a shot-caller to prove it."

"And that was just a few days after the homicide, right?"

"Right."

"Before you were arrested."

"Yep."

"And Keith went to the police with that information, right?" Laszlo's hearsay objection was sustained.

"He testified at your trial that you confessed the crime to him, didn't he?"

"He did, the son of a bitch."

"And he said you told him you did it for the AB."

"Yes."

"And when you were in jail, you told another guy, Christian Niedermeier?"

"Yes."

"What did you tell him?"

"That I did the crime on orders from the AB, and I asked him to apologize to Henley for me, tell him I was sorry he was in jail for something he didn't do."

"And Niedermeier also testified to that at your trial."

"The confession, but not the apology part."

"And do you remember talking to Gordon Marshall, Howard's first habeas lawyer?"

"Yeah. He came to see me with an investigator—long time ago now, when I was in Pelican Bay."

"Were you open with him at first?"

"No. I was debriefing, and I was still in a dangerous environment. I didn't want to make it worse by talking to anyone else."

"But later, after you were transferred to a different prison, you wrote to him, right?"

"Yeah."

"You asked him to come see you because you wanted to set the record straight about Henley, didn't you?"

"Yes."

"And did he come see you again?"

"Yes, when I was at Calipatria."

"And did you tell him then about Howard's innocence?"

"I did."

"And you signed a declaration saying what?"

"That the killing was ordered by the AB, and Howard had nothing to do with it."

Mike had a document marked for identification, and gave it to Scanlon.

"Is that a copy of the declaration you signed?"

Scanlon held it up to his face with his free hand and inspected the first page. Awkwardly, using his free and chained hands he turned and read each page. "Yes, that's the declaration and my signature."

Mike thanked him. "Now a couple of months before you were brought here, you had a visit from Mr. Willard and an investigator, no?"

"I did."

"What happened at that visit?"

"They come up to see me to question me about this case, and I told them I don't want to talk to them. But they kept on nagging me to speak with them. And there was a guard lieutenant there, so I said, all right, five minutes. So we go in an attorney interview room, and he starts asking me questions. And I tell him I'd rather wait, because I kept feeling like he was trying to trip me up and get me to say something I don't mean. So he says, 'Okay, I guess you don't want to talk,' and goes up to hit the buzzer at the door to let the guard know we're through. And while he's up there, the investigator starts insinuating threats towards me."

"Threats like what?"

"'Well, you know, if you come back to court to testify'— I can't remember verbatim exactly what was said, but it was, like, 'We can see to it that you go back to general population in Pelican Bay, and don't you have problems with the Aryan Brotherhood right now?' He didn't outright just say, 'Hey, you know, if you don't do what we tell you to do, we're going to put you in a life-or-death situation,' but he implied it where there's no mistaking."

"Now Mr. Willard suggested that you don't have anything to lose by testifying here about Howard's innocence."

"I do recall he said that."

"Now that isn't exactly true, is it?"

"Not if they can do what they threatened to."

Willard did a short re-cross, more to blunt the effect of Mike's redirect testimony than for any real purpose; and Scanlon was handcuffed and hooded and led out of the courtroom. Even the judge seemed uneasy as we all watched it happen.

After Scanlon had left, we discussed the remaining testimony. We had two more witnesses who needed to be brought from prisons outside California. "Will that be it, then?" the judge asked—a little pointedly, I thought.

"I think so," Mike said. "We're trying to locate one more witness; we'll let everyone know if we decide to call him."

The judge had a trial set to start the following Monday that he thought might run as much as three weeks. "And then we'll be in the middle of the holidays." We found a two-day stretch in the second week of January that worked for everyone, to resume the hearing, and Judge Redd made orders that it be so, then stood up and left the bench.

"I'll try to see Scanlon when we leave, to say so long," Mike said, as we gathered laptops and papers, "and we can get dinner afterward, if you don't mind." I said that would be fine. Then we squared our shoulders, burdened as they were with briefcases and shoulder bags, and left the courtroom to meet the questioning faces of Dot Henley, Lillian, and Josh Schaeffer. They all looked a little taken aback by the spectacle of Scanlon and his testimony.

"So that was Steve Scanlon," Dot said. "I've never seen him before."

"He gave me chills," Lillian said.

"What do you think the judge thought of him?" Dot asked.

"I can't tell," Mike said. "I thought Scanlon did pretty well, all things considered. But," he added with a small sigh, "I don't think we've really got the judge on board with us."

Dot nodded. "That's what I thought, too."

"Those two prosecutors," Lillian said. "They were pretty rude, don't you think?"

"It's just courtroom tactics," Mike said.

We exchanged good wishes for the holidays and the usual jokes about "see you next year," and the two of them left for home. "Man," I said to Mike, "Dot and Lillian look younger than I feel right now."

Josh Schaeffer, as usual, had a few questions about what had just happened, which we tried to answer. His stories about the hearing had continued to be fair, and even a little sympathetic now and then, and we were feeling more comfortable talking with him than we had at first. "I've gotten to know Mrs. Henley pretty well, coming here," he said. "Nice lady."

We agreed.

"Strange for someone like her to find herself here," he mused, with a movement of his head and eyes that took in the hallway and the courtroom door. "In the best of families, huh?"

36

At some point in middle age I stopped liking the holidays. Even before Terry died, they were a confusion of layered images, happy and sad, which my mind replayed involuntarily every year; and every year it became more difficult to show a brave and festive face to my family and the world.

The happy Christmas memories—with my mother and father and sisters, cross-country skiing in the state park on a crystalline day, white with snow; the trees we cut every year at the tree farm outside Anchorage—melt together with the last Christmas Terry and I spent with the two of them, before my father's heart attack, and the Christmas at my sister Candace's house after my mother's cancer diagnosis.

Christmases with Terry and Gavin, which live in my memory as an idealized dream of trees, lights, presents, and cookies, happened on the other side of the chasm that is Terry's suicide; on this side are seasons when, with Gavin at school halfway around the world and not coming home, I numbed myself with obsessive work during the day and eggnog spiked with rum in the evenings, and fought the urge to break down in tears whenever I saw a Christmas tree in someone's window.

I've thought sometimes of taking the month and traveling someplace, if such a place exists, where no one knows about Christmas. A little like Paul Bunyan, I'd put on a Santa hat and carry a sprig of holly and a candy cane, and where someone asked me why the silly hat and striped pencil, there I'd settle until after the first of the year.

This year, I did the next best thing: I flew to Australia, where it was early summer, and went to a wedding, which made it all feel much more like June than December. It was the best possible reunion with Gavin, sunlit and busy with plans for the ceremony and the reception. I was delighted to meet Rita, his fiancée, and her family, and grateful to be there as Gavin's clan. I cried, of course, during the service, and drank just enough at the reception; I was proud and happy and not (I hope) too maudlin when it came my turn to speak.

After the long flight back, I decked my house with colored lights to ease the pain of separation and cheer the dark days around the solstice; wrote and mailed Christmas cards to a dozen clients and former clients on the Row; baked cookies and foisted them off on Ed or traded them with Harriet for hers; and shopped with Harriet for presents and gift bags to wrap them in. Ed and I bottled our cider and tried a little; it tasted flat and sour to me, but when we took some to Vlad for a professional opinion he declared it a success and said it would be better once it had acquired some carbonation in the bottles.

Almost as soon as I arrived home, I paid another visit to Walt Klum; it was my relay in the race to keep him alive until—we hoped—he felt well enough to sign the form requesting new counsel. Walt didn't seem much different, at least at first, but he stayed for the whole visit, ate a peppermint ice cream sandwich from the machines, and cracked a small smile when I said the company must have stocked them just for Christmas.

Inmates are allowed to receive one package each quarter of nonperishable food and personal items like shampoo and toothpaste from friends or family outside. Abby had sent Walt the largest quarterly package the prison allowed, and he was well supplied with crackers, processed cheese, beef jerky, dried soups, cookies, instant coffee, and so forth. Between that and the money we'd put on his books for supplies from the prison canteen, he didn't have to go hungry when he became afraid of prison food. He said he felt better having that to go to. And when he told her about his fears of the guards, she had reassured him. "She says I did the right thing, telling you and her and the doctors. She says that may stop them from doing anything if they're thinking of it. And if anything happens, you'll all know why, and Ms. Stanhope says she'll help me if they give me a disciplinary write-up."

I told a couple of funny stories about Charlie and talked about my trip to Australia. He was surprised Gavin was married. "Hard to believe—he was in high school, wasn't he, when you were working on my appeal?"

He spoke fondly of Melanie, the young investigator Abby had mentioned to me. He said she'd spent a lot of time on his case, traveling to his hometown outside Oroville and to Missouri and Oklahoma, where his mother's and father's parents had come from. "She learned a lot about my family. She's a hard worker—dedicated." I said it sounded as though she'd placed a lot of importance on building a case for saving him from the death penalty, and he nodded. I didn't go on to say it, but I hoped it would occur to him at some point that she would be heartbroken to see her efforts wasted. As we separated outside the cage, Walt wished me a merry Christmas.

For a couple of weeks I allowed myself to forget about Howard, except for the calls I accepted from him, during which he ranted on about the hypocrisy of Christmas, the conspiracy marshaled to keep him on death row, and the lack of effort Mike and I were making to free him. But then one afternoon Mike called to tell me Dan Connelly was pretty sure he'd located Dwayne Forbush. "He's in Indio—surprise, eh? Dan is checking flights down there."

"Indio—home of date milkshakes."

"I've heard of those—never tried one," Mike said.

"I have. Had to go to Indio once on a case. It's in the middle of the desert, and they grow a lot of dates. Date shakes are a thing there—too sweet, though, even for me. Wish Dan good luck for me. I'll keep my fingers crossed."

A couple of days later, Mike called. "Merry Christmas, Janny. Guess what?"

"You seem full of holiday spirit. What's up?"

"Really good news. I just heard from Dan."

"And?"

"He found Dwayne Forbush and got a really good interview. Forbush remembered the Henley case and was sure he never met Henley till he saw him in the jail. Said the detectives showed him a photo of Henley after he was arrested, but he'd lawyered up and wouldn't talk to them. The DA approached his lawyer, apparently, offering him a deal if he'd testify that he sold a gun to Henley, but he turned it down, because he wasn't willing to lie. He remembers selling a gun to Scanlon and buying it back, because it was unusual; most people bought guns and kept them. He may still have the gun. Said he stored guns he thought might be hot in a footlocker in the attic of his brother's house. He recalls he had some idea of maybe changing out the barrel and reselling it, but he got busted before he could get around to it. He says his brother died a few years ago, but his sister-in-law still lives in the same house, as far as he knows. He figures the footlocker was still there when his brother passed away, because he would have asked Dwayne before doing anything with it."

Mike was so excited, I could hardly get a word in. "That's amazing!" I finally managed. "Can we get to the gun, if it's there?"

Mike calmed down a little. "Dan and I are working on that. Forbush is in a wheelchair—hurt his back working construction some years ago—and he lives with his mother. He's willing to come to Wheaton to testify, and he has a niece living down there—actually his brother John's daughter—who would be willing to go with him as a companion, so she can visit her mom, but he needs to find someone to take care of his mother. He can help us identify the gun, if it's there. Dan gave him a subpoena, and I'm going to be working on getting his travel expenses covered by the court. Thank Dot for that five thousand bucks; it's already been damned handy."

"Merry Christmas to you, too," I said.

"It's merrier already," Mike replied.

37

On Christmas Eve, Gavin and Rita made their usual holiday Skype call. It was Christmas Day and summer there, and they were planning to spend the day at the beach. Gavin told me he had decided to apply for professorships at several Australian universities.

"So you're really settling there," I said. I felt sad, but somehow not surprised. When I'd seen them at their wedding, Gavin had seemed very at home, and Rita's family had been welcoming and surprisingly large. She had two brothers and a sister, and we had been surrounded by an ever-changing and cheerful crowd of parents, aunts, uncles, cousins, nieces, and nephews. I had thought at the time that Gavin seemed in his element among all his new relatives.

I was still feeling a little bereft as I made the drive to Wheaton a week and a half later. The post-holiday blues had hit me, and another visit with Walt Klum, struggling with his own loss, hadn't done anything to raise my spirits. It was getting close to the time of year when Terry had killed himself. He had died in early February, and for several years afterward I'd felt anxious and depressed in the late winter. The feeling had subsided recently, but this year it was back.

I'd been dreaming more than usual. Once it had been a nightmare involving the case I'd worked on out of Indio, a life-without-parole murder. The crime had been particularly bizarre and gruesome: my client had stabbed and strangled his ex-girlfriend, then gouged out her eyes and cut off her breasts. Psychiatrists from both sides had testified he was mentally ill, but they couldn't agree on a diagnosis; one had said he was schizophrenic, the other a sexual psychopath.

I had gone to see him in the prison system's mental hospital in Vacaville, where they had taken him after he attempted suicide in prison. Strangely passive from the medications they had him on, and barely tethered to reality, he moved like a shadow and spoke to me in a faraway voice about how tired he was all the time.

In my dream, I found myself somehow in the victim's apartment, as it appeared in the crime-scene photos—a scene of butchery, with blood on the walls and smeared and pooled on the floor and bed. The woman's body lay in front of me, her injuries hardly visible under the enveloping, varied reds of the blood that covered her face and body. I knew my ex-client was somewhere nearby, but I didn't know where, or how to get out of the building without being ambushed by him. In the dream I stood, paralyzed with terror, waiting for whatever was going to happen, until my fear woke me, and I sat up in bed, shivering, until morning.

The night before I left for Wheaton, I had another dream, but one I couldn't quite remember on waking. All that was left of it was the wistful memory of a pale blue stoneware coffee mug I had bought somewhere with Terry—how many years ago? Awake, I wondered what had happened to the cup, and realized I no longer remembered. I thought perhaps it had lost its handle and served some time as a pen holder on Terry's desk until it had been tossed in some housecleaning or during the move. The atmosphere of the dream, its sense of things lost, stayed with me through much of the drive, as a sort of floating melancholy. I felt old and tired.

Mike had asked me to come down a couple of days before the hearing, to be a witness in case we found the guns where Dwayne Forbush said he had hidden them. He had driven down the day before, to meet Forbush and his niece.

"Well, they got here fine," he said in a call the evening before I left. "They're staying with Karen, Dwayne's sister-in-law. That's where he had the footlocker—in an attic crawl space. Karen says she never goes up there, has no idea what might be in it. I'm going out tomorrow and buying a ladder and a pair of bolt cutters, so we'll be ready when you get here."

When I got to Wheaton, I didn't stop at the hotel, but went directly to Karen Forbush's house. It was a small white bungalow on a tree-shaded side street—not a new house, but well cared-for, with a Japanese maple in the front yard and a border of roses, pruned for the winter, along the driveway.

Karen Forbush's daughter answered the door. She was a few inches taller than me, a little heavy, but pretty, with a rose-petal complexion and glossy dark-brown hair. Behind her I saw Mike with a middle-aged man in a wheelchair and a woman about the same age, who I assumed was Karen. The young woman introduced herself as Katelyn. "This is my Uncle Dwayne," she said, gesturing toward the man as she led me inside, "and that's my mom, Karen." I said hello to Karen, a gentle-looking woman with faded dark hair and sad eyes, and shook hands with Dwayne, who was light-haired, with muscular arms and shoulders from navigating in a wheelchair.

Katelyn seemed excited about the purpose of our visit. I gathered she had asked Mike a lot of questions; she seemed to know a fair amount about the Henley case and what we were hoping to find. She offered to get me a cup of coffee, but I declined; I'd already had too much on the drive down.

"Well, I guess we're all here," Mike said, after we'd spent a few minutes making small talk about our trips. "Shall we see what's up there?"

Mike set the ladder up in the hallway off the living room, climbed it, and slid aside the loose board that covered the opening to the crawl space, then clambered in. I followed. "Watch yourself," he said. "There's some plywood, but it doesn't cover everything; the rest is only two by fours."

I climbed clumsily over the top and sat on the plywood area. Katelyn surprised me by coming up after me. "I'm curious," she said, standing on the ladder and taking in the dim expanse of beams and roof. "Hope you don't mind."

"Of course not," Mike said. "It's your house, after all." I moved carefully aside to give her a spot to sit next to me.

The attic space was dark except for the daylight that filtered dimly through the soffits. Mike slowly scanned the beam of his flashlight through the gloom and stopped at a place near the end, where a couple more pieces of plywood had been set over the beams. A path of plywood pieces led from it to the piece we were sitting on. On the makeshift floor at the end we could see a few hand tools, scattered and dusty, and a small footlocker. Mike crawled over on hands and knees, and we followed.

We all kneeled and watched as Mike took the bolt cutters and cut through the stem of a padlock on the front of the footlocker. He lifted the dust-covered lid and shined his flashlight into the box. "Hah," he said, almost involuntarily.

"Oh?" I asked.

"It's guns," he said, almost in a whisper. He motioned me over. "Take some pictures of this on your phone," he said, and he held the flashlight while I took a series of photos of the contents of the box. There were five that I saw: a couple of revolvers, a smallish semiautomatic, something that might have been a Glock, and a .22 rifle with a folding stock. The box smelled musty, but everything in it appeared dry and well preserved. When I was finished, Mike closed the lid.

"Now what?" Katelyn asked.

"Now we show your uncle the photos and call the police," Mike said. "We're all witnesses that we haven't touched or disturbed the contents of the box."

Back in Karen's living room, Dwayne Forbush studied each of the photos before pronouncing judgment. "It's been a long time," he said. "I'll have a better idea when I can see the actual guns. But one of those revolvers seems to be a Smith & Wesson .38. I used to have logs of purchases and sales—they were in code, in a notebook. But that's long gone; the police got the notebook when they searched my apartment, and I never saw it again."

The patrolman who arrived ten minutes after Mike's call to the station seemed baffled about why he had been dispatched to us. After taking him up into the crawl space and showing him the footlocker and its contents, Mike tried to explain. "You see," he said, "one of those guns may be evidence in a hearing we're having, and I want to make sure there's no problem with the chain of custody, so I don't want to touch them myself. Can you get a criminalist out here to take pictures and take custody of them?"

It took a while, but eventually the patrolman was joined by a detective and a criminalist. The detective interviewed each of us and took notes; and as Mike watched from the ladder, the criminalist took photos and carefully bagged the guns.

When the criminalist came back downstairs, Mike asked him to show the two revolvers to Dwayne. One, Dwayne rejected out of hand—"That's a Taurus, I remember it had something wrong with it"—but the other he studied for a minute or two as the criminalist held it suspended on a ruler, before him. Eventually, he nodded his head and looked up. "It's been a while," he said, apologetically, "but it's definitely the kind of gun I sold him. I remember he was real pleased when I said I had a Smith & Wesson, and the color of the metal and stock seem right. Beyond that, I couldn't swear to you that it's the gun."

"That's okay," Mike said. "They'll be testing it anyway, assuming it can still be operated."

By the time the police were gone, and we'd closed up the crawl-space opening, everyone was tired from the excitement of the day. Karen, Katelyn, and Dwayne seemed anxious to get on with their evening. Mike went over to Dwayne and spoke quietly with him for a couple of minutes. As we were leaving, Mike asked Karen if she wanted the ladder, and she said she could probably find someone to give it to.

I was exhausted from the drive and all that had followed, but hungry, too, and the Mexican restaurant near the hotel seemed like just what I wanted. As we walked in, the server who came up to seat us said, "Welcome back," and I realized we were becoming regulars there; it might be the only place I'd actually miss after our trips to Wheaton were over.

After a beer and a dinner that started with guacamole and ended with a comforting flan, I felt hardly awake enough to carry my bags into my room. Within ten minutes of getting into bed, I was asleep, too tired, for once, to dream.

38

Judge Redd's court, even after over a month away, seemed depressingly familiar. The still air smelling faintly of polished wood and old paper brought back a succession of memories of witnesses and arguments, of small victories and disappointments. One difference now was that Mike and I were clinging to a new and tentative hope that Forbush's testimony and the gun might be evidence the judge could not discount or ignore.

Mike had emailed Willard a copy of Dan's report of his interview with Forbush, and in the minutes before the hearing started, he told Willard about finding the gun. "I've asked the detective and the criminalist to come to court today; I don't know if they're going to be here."

Willard said, "Obviously, we're going to want to run tests to see if the gun matches the bullets from the victim's body."

"Of course," Mike said.

Laszlo had another inspiration. "Before we do that, we should do touch DNA testing. You said you didn't think the gun was disturbed from the time Mr. Forbush put it in the locker. We should see whose DNA is on it."

Mike and I shrugged. "Worth a try," he said. "But we'll want a say in who does the testing, and the method."

When Judge Redd took the bench, we explained the new developments to him. "All right," he said. "But this hearing has gone on for a very long time, and I'd like to see some prospect of it finishing."

Mike began by calling Dwayne Forbush, who rolled up the aisle in his wheelchair.

Mike asked Forbush where he was living in 1998 and 1999. "Over in Hanover," Forbush replied.

"Did you own some guns then?"

"Yes."

"Were you buying and selling them?"

"Buy, sell, repair—yes."

"Did you ever sell a gun to a man named Steve Scanlon?"

"Yes, I did."

"When was that?"

Forbush thought for a moment. "Early 1999, I'd say, or maybe end of 1998."

Mike had a mug shot of Scanlon marked for identification and gave it to Forbush. "Is this the man you remember as Mr. Scanlon?"

"It's been a long time, but I believe yes."

"Did you ever sell a gun to a man named Howard Henley?"

"No."

Mike had another photo, a mug shot of Howard, marked. He gave the photo to Forbush. "Do you recall ever selling a gun to this man?"

He looked at it and handed it back. "No. I've never met the man."

"But you told me you'd seen that mug shot before, right?"

"Yes."

"Where?"

"Detective showed it to me after I was arrested, asked me then if I knew him."

"What did you tell him?"

"I didn't tell him anything except that I wanted to talk to a lawyer."

"Do you remember the detective's name?"

Forbush shook his head. "Not anymore—sorry."

"Were you asked to testify in Howard Henley's case?"

"Yes."

"Who asked you?"

"My lawyer told me the district attorney had offered me a deal if I would testify that I sold a gun to Mr. Henley."

Laszlo's mind must have been wandering, because he let Forbush finish his sentence before interrupting with an indignant hearsay objection and motion to strike. The judge granted both. Mike thanked him and went on.

"But you never sold a gun to Mr. Henley, though?"

"Objection, asked and answered," Laszlo yelped.

"Correct," Forbush said, before the judge managed to rule.

"Do you remember what kind of gun you sold to Steve Scanlon?" Mike asked.

"It was a revolver, Smith & Wesson .38."

"Is there any particular reason you remember it?"

"I remember we talked a little. I happened to have that Smith & Wesson, and he liked the idea of getting a decent gun, not some Saturday-night special."

"Is there any reason this transaction sticks in your mind?"

He nodded and looked a bit rueful. "Yeah, 'cause I bought the gun back from him a few days later."

"How did that happen?"

"He called me, said he needed money, wanted to sell the gun back to me, get a cheaper one. So we met, and I bought the gun back and sold him a .22."

"Did he tell you he'd used the gun to kill someone?"

"No. I should have known better than to take it back from him—but no."

"Did you find out later that he was wanted for murder?"

"Yes."

"How?"

"Saw something in the paper or on the TV news, if I recall."

"Did you do something about the .38 you'd sold him because of that?"

"Yes."

"What?"

"I put it away in a safe place."

"Where was that?"

"A footlocker I had in the crawl space above my brother's house."

"Why was that?"

"Well, I was worried that the guy might have used it. Thought I might be able to modify it in some way, change the barrel and firing pin, maybe, but in the meantime I just wanted to hide it."

"Did you ever move it out of that footlocker?"

"No."

"Was there a reason?"

"Yeah. I got arrested, went to prison."

"When was that?"

"April of 1999."

"What was the arrest for?"

"Receiving stolen property, gun trafficking."

"And were you convicted?"

"Yes."

"How long were you in prison?"

"Six years."

"And when you got out, what did you do?"

"I paroled back to my hometown, Indio. Been there ever since."

"You're in a wheelchair, I see. Were you injured at some point?"

"Yes."

"How?"

"I was doing roofing work, lost my footing and fell. Injured my spinal cord, and I can't walk anymore."

"How long is it since you've been to Wheaton?"

"Before two days ago, ten, eleven years."

"So you haven't been back since you got out of prison."

"That's right."

"Yesterday, you were at your sister-in-law's house when the footlocker in the crawl space was opened, right?"

"Yes."

Laszlo, who had been quiescent to this point, objected that unless Forbush had managed to get into the crawl space he didn't have personal knowledge of what had happened there. The judge sustained his objection and struck Forbush's answer.

"Okay," Mike said. "Let's put it this way. Yesterday, a police detective and a criminalist came to your sister's house, right?"

"Yes."

"And the police criminalist showed you a couple of guns?"

"Yes, he did."

"Did one of them look like the gun you sold and bought from Scanlon?"

"One was a Smith & Wesson .38, so it could have been, yes."

Mike marked another photo and gave it to him. "Is this a

photo of the gun the man showed you?"

"Yes."

"You had a few other guns in that locker, didn't you?"

"Yes."

"And you saw photos of the guns that were found in it yesterday, didn't you?"

"Objection," Laszlo said. "Lack of personal knowledge."

"Okay," Mike said. "Well, you saw some photos yesterday on an iPhone?"

Forbush seemed almost amused. "Yes, I did."

During dinner the night before, I had sent the photos I'd taken to Mike; and after I'd gone to my room, he had gone out and made color copies at a 24-hour copy shop. Mike had a half-dozen marked for identification and showed them to Willard and Laszlo and showed one to Forbush.

"Does the footlocker in that photo appear to be the one you kept in your brother's crawl space?"

"Definitely."

"And does this photo look like the guns that were there the last time you went into the locker?"

"It's been a long time, but as far as I can remember, yes."

"Are there any guns in the picture that you hadn't put there?"

"Again, it's been a long time, but I don't think so."

"Your brother was John Forbush, right?"

"Yes. He's passed away."

"The house we were at yesterday is the house where he

was living in 1999, and where you left the footlocker, right?"

He nodded. "That's right."

"John's wife, Karen, still lives in that house?"

"Yes."

"Was John a gun collector?"

"Not really—he had a few, like a lot of people, but that's about it."

"Is there any reason he might have gone into your footlocker up in the attic?"

"No—he didn't have a key to the padlock."

"And your sister-in-law?"

"She didn't even know it was up there until the other day."

Laszlo made a hearsay objection. When Mike offered to bring Karen Forbush in to testify, the judge overruled it.

"So anything in that locker would have been something you placed there."

"I guess so."

Laszlo was waiting to pounce.

"Mr. Forbush, you were a fence, weren't you?"

"I wouldn't say so."

"You were convicted of receiving stolen property, isn't that so?"

"Yes."

"You pled guilty to that charge, didn't you?"

"Yes."

"Aren't the guns in your footlocker stolen?"

"The Smith & Wesson, no. I don't specifically recall about the others."

"You knew the Smith & Wesson had been used in a murder, didn't you?"

Mike's objection that Forbush would have no personal knowledge of that fact was sustained.

"Well, you admitted you had good reason to think that was the case, didn't you?"

"Probably—after I saw the article in the paper."

"That's why you hid the gun, wasn't it?"

"Yes."

"Were you involved with the Aryan Brotherhood?"

"No, I never was."

"Did you associate with members of that gang?"

"Not socially. I did business with a few along the way."

"And one of them was Mr. Scanlon, isn't that true?"

"That's what I heard."

"You said you don't remember the name of the detective who showed you the photo of Howard Henley?"

"Not any more."

"Was it Detective Springer?"

Forbush thought for a moment, then said, "I wouldn't rule that out, but after all this time I couldn't really tell you."

"Are you aware that two of the guns in your footlocker were reported as stolen?"

"I was not."

"But you knew they were, didn't you?"

"Like I told you, this many years later I don't know. I doubt it."

"But part of your business was buying and selling stolen guns, wasn't it? Isn't that what you pled guilty to?"

"I pled guilty to receiving stolen property. But it was really a setup. Some pressure was put on me to buy the guns they arrested me for."

"Like what?"

"Like I was told by someone I thought was a friend that the guys trying to sell them were gang members, and they'd make things tough for him and me if I didn't take the guns."

"You were aware early in 1999 that you had a gun that Steve Scanlon might have used in a murder, weren't you?"

"I suppose you could say that."

"But you didn't tell the police."

"No."

"And you didn't say anything about it after you were arrested."

"No."

On redirect, Mike asked Forbush about the setup that led to his arrest. Forbush said, "This guy Freddy Gomez came to me, scared. He'd said he'd gotten himself in deep with some Mexican gang folks, owed them money or something, and they were trying to use him to move some guns. I'd known Freddy for a while. I didn't think much of him, but his brother worked with me, and Freddy sometimes brought me business. And he, as he told it, was in fear for his life.

So I told him I'd check out the guns. Freddy brought them to me, and I agreed to buy some of them, and next thing I know I'm surrounded by cops."

"You didn't take the gun you got from Scanlon to the police."

"No, I didn't."

"Was there a reason you didn't?"

"Couple of reasons," Forbush said. "First, I try not to get too involved with the police in general. And second, the guy was Aryan Brotherhood."

Laszlo objected that Forbush hadn't explained how he knew this.

"Okay," Mike said. "How did you know?"

"Gomez told me. The guy himself told me. And after I was busted, I heard around the jail that he was."

"Why would knowing that make you reluctant to give up the gun?"

"Well, I figured if the cops knew I'd sold him a gun, they'd use that information somehow, maybe want me to testify against him. I hadn't been to prison before, but I've been in the world long enough to know that if you snitch on one of those guys, you're a dead man."

After Forbush was excused, we broke for the midmorning recess. The detective who had taken statements from us and the criminalist who'd come to the scene were both in the hallway. When we resumed, Mike called the criminalist to testify about the state of the footlocker when they saw it and our statements about the circumstances of finding the guns.

The detective didn't have much to say. He listed who was in the living room when he arrived, and said he'd taken statements from those of us who said we had been in the crawl space when the guns were found, and had incorporated those statements into a report.

The criminalist testified that he had taken photographs of the attic, the footlocker, and the guns inside it; the photos were marked for identification. He had then carefully collected all five guns from the footlocker and put each into a separate evidence bag. He had worn gloves the entire time and had picked up the revolvers by their trigger guards using a dowel.

He had shown the two revolvers to Dwayne Forbush, whom he identified in the courtroom. "Mr. Forbush," he said, "made a visual inspection of the two guns. I did not allow him to touch them."

He also testified that he had later run the serial numbers of all the guns and that two of them, but not the Smith & Wesson, had been reported stolen in the 1990s.

"What do you want to do about testing the guns?" Judge Redd asked Willard and Mike, after the witnesses had left.

"We want the testing to be done by independent experts, for sure," Mike said. "Especially the DNA, since it isn't clear there will be more than one chance to test it."

Willard said he'd be satisfied with having it done by the Taft County sheriff's laboratory.

The judge apparently knew something about the Taft County lab, because he agreed with us that independent experts would be a good idea. "Try to find people you can agree on within the next week, and let me know."

Mike asked how the fees of the experts would be paid, and the judge said, "I'll see to it that it's taken care of." Something was changing, I thought.

39

We had two witnesses for the afternoon, Walter "Corker" Bensinger and Scotty Maclendon, two former AB shot-callers whose names Mike and Dan had come across earlier in their investigation. Both had been brought from prisons outside California, one in Oregon, the other in Nevada. Mike and Dan had interviewed them months ago, and Mike had touched base with them at the jail before meeting me at Karen Forbush's house. Over lunch he checked in again with Bensinger, while I introduced myself to Maclendon and went over once more what we'd be asking him.

Maclendon was the image of the photos of old AB guys I'd seen on the Internet when I was first researching Howard's case—another grizzled dude, with shaved head and a luxuriant gray mustache. The dark blue edges of tattoos showed above the collar of his orange jail jumpsuit, and the parts of his forearms I could see were a mass of blue designs.

We were assigned a bathroom off the holding cell, the

only private space available, the deputy claimed, for our interview. Maclendon, in ankle chains and with handcuffs fastened to a chain around his waist, was given the seat on the toilet, and the guard brought in a plastic chair for me. The deputy said the door had to be kept open, but he stood a few feet away, at what he apparently considered a discreet distance from us.

It wasn't an arrangement conducive to making either of us feel at ease, but as soon as the guard withdrew, Maclendon said, in a rough-edged baritone, with mock formality, "Nice to meet you. I hope you'll excuse the accommodations."

Maclendon's purpose as a witness was largely to explain the way the Aryan Brotherhood hierarchy operated when it ordered hits and communicated its orders to members and associates in the prisons. His role in the Lindahl episode was fairly minor; he said he had been part of the circle from which the order to greenlight Lindahl issued, but the actual decision had come from others. I showed him McGaw's letter to Scanlon—"May he rest in peace," he said; "McGaw was a good man"—and he said it almost undoubtedly contained a coded message more or less asking Scanlon why he hadn't done the job yet, but he couldn't articulate his reasons for thinking so. Not that useful, I thought; I could practically recite Laszlo's objections word for word.

I didn't gain much from the interview, but Maclendon and I left the room with a backward glance and a laugh—the intimacy forged by meeting in embarrassing circumstances.

On my way back to the courthouse I picked up a packaged tuna sandwich and a sticky-sweet, weirdly flavored coffee that was supposed to be French vanilla. I managed to eat half the sandwich and gulped down the coffee, reminding myself that it was better than falling asleep in the middle of the hearing.

Maclendon was our first witness. On direct examination, I took him through his long history with the Aryan Brotherhood. It had started, Maclendon said, with growing up in a family of Hell's Angels. When he'd been imprisoned at the age of eighteen, he walked into an immediate support system of older prison-gang members. "They looked after me," he said, "and I tried to show them I was worth it. I worshiped those dudes; they showed me how to live in prison, not just survive." Dave Leverett, one of the highest-ranking members of the Brand, sponsored him for membership when he was twenty-three.

I asked questions and listened, struggling to follow, as he explained the Byzantine and ever-evolving hierarchy of the Aryan Brotherhood: the chains of command, the manner in which moves against members and non-members were decided and voted on, the overlapping cells of members and associates given information on a need-to-know basis, the multitudinous ways in which information was covertly passed between prisoners and prisons. Notes were left in the law library, pushed under the bars of cells or passed by guards and lawyers; word was sent to inmates elsewhere through friends and family outside, by phone calls and innocuous-seeming letters containing coded messages, or by verbal messages memorized and passed along from inmate to inmate. It was, by his account, pretty efficient.

Maclendon said, as he'd told me, that he had been part of the circle that made the decision to greenlight Lindahl, but he hadn't been personally involved in making the decision.

"I heard the actual order to put the guy in the hat came from Bensinger, but I didn't pay much attention to it. I heard that the guy paroled and that someone from his hometown had been sent to take care of him." He'd heard Scanlon's name before then, "but I didn't know he was the guy, at the time. I didn't even know until later that it happened—we ordered a lot of hits back then."

"I got to know Steve around 2006 or 2007; we were neighbors for a while in Pelican Bay. Steve talked with me sometimes, through the pipes. Couple times he talked about the Lindahl hit. Told me how he did it; he seemed pretty proud of it."

"Did he ever mention that anyone else was involved in it with him?" I asked.

"Other than the AB, no."

"Did he ever mention someone named Howard Henley?"

"No. Until your investigator came to see me, I'd never heard of the guy."

I showed Maclendon the letter from McGaw.

"We showed you this letter before; do you remember it?"

"I do."

"You testified earlier that you have some familiarity with how the AB gets messages to its members in and out of prison. Does this letter appear to be communicating a message in some kind of code?"

"Yes."

"Can you explain what the coded message is?"

"Well, it's hard, not knowing the context."

"Okay, suppose Mr. McGaw was writing the letter to an associate outside who had been assigned to kill someone who was in the hat."

"Well, some parts of it could relate to that."

"What parts?"

"'Are you still working?' That could mean he's wondering whether the guy on the outside is getting the job done. Other stuff, like the martial arts and the guy's letters being delayed could mean something, but I don't know what."

Laszlo's objection was inevitable. "Your Honor, the witness is clearly speculating about what the letter means." His objection was sustained, and, with an inward sigh, I moved on.

"I understand that you are no longer involved with the Aryan Brotherhood."

"That's right."

"You left the organization and debriefed?"

"Yes, in 2010."

"Was there a reason or reasons why you chose to leave?"

Laszlo objected that Maclendon's reasons were irrelevant, but the judge let him testify, subject to a motion to strike.

"I began debriefing in 2010, after I was charged in a racketeering case. The Feds were coming down hard on the organization, and I'd been thinking for a while that the leadership was getting greedy and corrupt. There were all these factions and power struggles, and men were being killed for supporting the wrong set. Trust is everything to me, knowing that your friends have your back and your leaders won't steer you wrong, and I was losing that. I couldn't see spending the rest of my life in an underground supermax prison for the sake of the Brand as it is."

"Do you have anything to do with the Aryan Brotherhood anymore?"

"Nothing at all."

"You're in prison out of California for a reason, no?"

"Yes. I dropped out, and I'm cooperating with the authorities, so I'm marked for death. I'm not safe in the California prison system."

"Do you have anything to gain by coming here and testifying for Howard Henley?"

"No."

"In fact, being brought back here puts you in danger, doesn't it?"

"Yes, it does."

"How is that?"

"Any AB who crosses my path has orders to kill me if they can."

Walter Bensinger, our next witness, was a stouter version of Maclendon, except that his head appeared to be naturally bald, and his mustache was white. His history with the Aryan Brotherhood was less colorful, though the attraction of the gang was the same; he had fallen in with them because they seemed like real men, competent and disciplined, in contrast to the average run of prison inmates. He had risen through the ranks by the usual process of carrying out orders, and had eventually been made a member, though he was lower in rank than, say, Maclendon or Dave Leverett.

"Were you in Folsom Prison in 1998?"

"Yes, I was."

"Were you involved in ordering that Jared Lindahl be greenlighted?"

"I guess so. I brought it to the attention of the council that the guy was selling drugs on one of the yards and blowing us off about paying the tax."

"And he was greenlighted for that?"

"Yes. We put the word out that he was in the hat, but he paroled before anyone could get at him."

"Did you know Steve Scanlon at that time?"

"I did."

"How did you know him?"

"He was in my yard, and so was Cal McGaw."

"What was your impression of Steve?"

"That he was a good kid. Bit of a hothead, but willing, up for any kind of assignment."

"Did you become aware at some point that Steve was going to be paroling to the same town as Lindahl?"

"Yes. I think Cal McGaw told me."

"What did you do when you learned that?"

"Suggested to McGaw that he approach Steve about doing the job."

"And did he?"

Hearsay, Laszlo said, and the judge sustained his objection.

"Did you learn at some point that Lindahl had been killed?"

"Yeah. I was a little sorry to hear that Steve got popped for the killing, but I guess he wasn't as smart as he could have been in how he went about it."

Mike showed him the letter and asked him if he could see a coded message in it.

"Knowing Cal, he wouldn't write something like that just to say hello. He would have meant business. Looks to me like he was getting on Steve's case about it; maybe he was dicking around, not getting the job done. Cal may have thought he was getting cold feet."

Laszlo was on it, and the judge sustained his objection that Bensinger, like Maclendon, was just speculating about the meaning of the letter.

"At some point, was Steve Scanlon himself in the hat?"

"Yes, he was."

"How did that come about?"

"Well, he was in Pelican Bay, and so was I, for that matter. Steve made some half-assed attempt to escape and injured a guard pretty badly. Prison came down hard on the Brand for that, and a lot of us ended up in the SHU or even solitary confinement, as validated AB members. It was kind of a last straw, as far as Steve was concerned. He was starting to be seen as a loose cannon. We gave him one last chance to redeem himself by killing his cellie, but he wouldn't do it. So the order was made—I wasn't one of the folks who made it, in case you're interested."

"What came of it, if you know?"

"He was hit, stabbed by his cellmate, as I recall, but he survived, and he debriefed and dropped out."

"You dropped out at some point, too, didn't you?"

"Yeah. The powers that be greenlighted someone I knew, and I felt it was b.s. and said so. The way things were going, I figured it wouldn't be long before I'd have a target on my back, too. So I left and debriefed."

Like Maclendon, Bensinger didn't know Howard Henley; he'd never heard of him before Mike and his investigator came to talk to him. He, too, had nothing to gain from testifying at this hearing. "Being back in California puts me in danger. But if the guy's really innocent, I hope he gets justice."

Laszlo's cross-examination of both men went the same way: a catalog of the assaults and homicides they had committed in prison for the Aryan Brotherhood, and the fact that they had each left some of their crimes out of their debriefing statements. Maclendon had not included any reference to the Lindahl killing, even though he knew about it. "I couldn't remember everything," he had said. "I mean, the Brand ordered a lot of people hit, and frankly this Lindahl thing was no big deal."

Willard and Laszlo closed by recalling Detective Springer, who testified that he had no recollection of meeting Forbush or showing him any photos.

"My God, it's almost over," Mike said over a celebratory dinner at Wheaton's best Italian restaurant, with a bottle of pretty good Cabernet. "Now we go home and wait for the test results."

"How do you think the hearing went?" I asked.

"Great! Of course we'll win," he said. "Shit—I wish I could believe it. It's hard to fathom why we're here with a client on death row when the real killer has been telling everyone who would listen for, what, seventeen, eighteen years that our guy is innocent. What is up with that?"

I had no answer. "Have another glass of wine," I said. "I'll drive us back to the hotel."

40

At home again, while Mike worked out the hiring of experts with Willard, I caught up on my other cases and saw Walt Klum again.

Late in January, as I was preparing to make another visit to Walt, Abby called me. "Great news—Walt signed his attorney request this morning."

"Wow, whew, congratulations!" I said.

"Yes—Melanie is driving to Sacramento with it right now, so we don't lose any more time; we feel like every day counts. And we want it on file in case he gets wobbly," she added.

"Wow," I said again; I felt as relieved as Abby sounded. "What made him change his mind?"

"I owe it to Melanie," Abby said. "She went to talk to Edna's daughter Audrey, up in Grants Pass, and persuaded her to visit, got it all set up, and then made another trip up there, drove her down and back, and went to the visit with her, so she'd feel more comfortable. Audrey had gone with Edna once or twice to visit Walt and was on his list of approved visitors, but she hadn't thought of seeing him once her mother became too ill. She's a lovely woman, just like Edna, and seeing her seemed to turn Walt around. It was like a miracle. I mean he's still awfully fragile, but at least he's clinging to life, so to speak."

Caught up in Howard's case, I hadn't realized how heavily Walt's situation had been weighing on me. Unable to concentrate on work, I went outside, thinking I might do some winter pruning on my apple and pear trees. The day was fine and clear, with a chill, damp breeze from the ocean. Instead of going to the shed where my pruners were, I walked around my little acre, inspecting the scaffolding of branches and twigs on the small bare trees of the orchard, the raised beds with their dark earth and stands of chard, broccoli, and bok choy, the hoop house hiding its bed of greens, the ground everywhere covered in the soft new grass and tiny flowering plants of Mediterranean winter. Redwood and tanoak trees made a forest beyond the deer fence, and the sky floated, a tentative eggshell blue, above it all. I was filled with relief and gratitude. The world was a wonderful place, I thought, and I wanted to shout something, but I didn't know what.

Charlie had followed me, and was alternately sniffing at some intriguing smell in the ground and looking up at me expectantly. I stooped and ruffled the hair around his ears. "Let's go for a walk," I said. He gave an answering bark, and we headed purposefully down the driveway.

41

When I went to see Walt the next week, he could talk about nothing else but Audrey's visit. "She's so much like her mother," he said. "Just a great girl. We talked a lot about Edna; we both miss her so much. Audrey's married, has a couple of grown kids. Hard to imagine that I have great-nephews, and young men at that."

His heavy face brightened into something almost like a smile. "It's been good seeing you, too. And Melanie—Ms. Stanhope's investigator—is the best. She's worked on a couple of other guys' cases here; guys I know say I'm lucky she's on mine."

As I left, I said I'd like to come see him now and then, to say hi, if that was okay. "I think I'd like that," he said.

After Walt, I paid a visit to Howard. Like most meetings with Howard, it was unproductive except as a chance to see him in action. I tried to explain what had happened at the last hearing. He had never heard of Forbush, Maclendon, or Bensinger, and he asked why we had bothered to call a bunch of witnesses who had nothing to do with his case. When I told him Forbush had said he'd sold a gun directly to Scanlon, and we'd found the gun, he said, "See, I never gave a gun to Steve; it was all a lie, like everything else." He wondered, for the umpteenth time, why we hadn't put on evidence that he was in jail the day of the murder and why we hadn't proved that he had been prosecuted to silence him for speaking out against the corruption of the city government in Ventura. This moved into a complex, mumbling discussion of the significance of various numbers in his life and case and how they related to one another, and then a complaint that his doctors refused to make a medical order for him to get a vegetarian diet. It left little for me to do but sip at my Diet Pepsi, nod and say "uh huh" at strategic intervals. As the visit ended and the guard was walking him out of the cubicle, he called back over his shoulder, "You do understand what I'm saying, don't you?"

"I'm trying," I answered.

"Think about it," he said.

I came home that evening to a voicemail from Mike, asking me to call. It was past office hours, so I had to wait until morning. I dropped some groceries off at Ed's, made myself some dinner, accompanied by a bottle of our cider, which was, as Vlad had said, better once it had produced some carbonation, though still sour. After that, too tired to work or think, I spent the evening watching an old Wallander mystery on PBS.

Mike was in court when I called the next morning, but I heard from him before noon. "What's up?" I asked.

"Not too much. A little news. Willard called yesterday and said the DNA testing on the gun had come back, and the lab said it was uninterpretable. If I understand what he was saying, the gun spent too many Wheaton summers up in that crawl space, and the DNA is badly degraded."

"I don't know whether to feel good or bad," I said.

"Me neither. But they aren't letting go. There's another test they can do on the sample, called Y-STR. I looked it up online, and apparently it's a test that identifies just the DNA on the Y chromosome, so it only picks up males, but that works for us. And it has potential to work on samples like this one, where the DNA is old."

"Okay," I said. "I guess they'll do what they have to do."

"Yeah," Mike said. "Willard says they're holding up the firearms testing until after the DNA is done because they want to keep the gun untouched in case they need to try to get another sample from it."

"We'll get there when we get there, eh? Howard doesn't understand much of what we're doing, anyway." I described my visit with him.

"Pretty much what I've been going through. Did you see Walt Klum?"

"I did."

"Good news that he's decided to go ahead with his case."

"Definitely a weight off my mind."

"Mine, too."

"How long before we hear about the Y-STR testing result?"

"A week or two," he said.

So more waiting. But at least the news so far wasn't bad.

42

Life went on while we waited on the forensics. I planted apple, pear, and plum trees I'd grafted the previous year, including the one on which I cut my hand the day Mike first called about Howard. It was an Arkansas Black, and bigger than any of the others; apparently a little blood in its diet was a good thing. Then, taking my life into my hands, I grafted another generation of the little beasts, fitting scion wood into slices on rootstocks.

It was a calm period in my life, relatively speaking: Walt was saved, Gavin and Rita were safe and happy, and the anniversary of Terry's death came and went with a minimum of emotional fanfare. It was easy to absorb myself in the work of making fruit trees and concentrate on slicing the wood with that razor-sharp knife. I managed, for once, to complete the year's labor and produce a row of little potted stick trees, their small trunks bandaged with wax film and blue painter's tape and each festively labeled with its variety printed on orange ribbon, all without any loss of blood.

Death penalty work has its own seasonal cycle: February was the time of a major annual conference devoted completely to defending capital cases. This year, as usual, it was happening in Monterey. Mike and his wife were going, and so was I, with Charlie; they'd be staying at a cute B and B, and we'd be at our frayed-around-the-edges dog-friendly motel.

The conference was a three-day marathon of lectures and workshops about capital case defense at every stage from trial through federal appeals and the hopeless last-ditch hearings seeking clemency from the governor. It was the big event of the year, the gathering of the clans; when Terry was alive, we had never missed it.

Terry had been one of the darlings of the conference; he was always invited to speak at a workshop and a panel or two. Among the elite of this crowd I was a person of no importance, except for the fact of being Terry's wife. Some of the insinuations that I had been too clueless to see that Terry was in trouble had come from colleagues of ours I'd known through the conference. The veiled accusations—never said to me directly—had more than a little to do with my quitting the whole business and fleeing to the woods.

After taking up Andy Hardy's case I had steeled my courage and made an appearance at that year's conference. Many of the faces there were new and a lot younger than mine, but I'd met a dozen or so people I'd known from before, some of whom asked where I'd been. Like me, they were all a little grayer, a bit stouter, a little more weathered in the face than before.

The notoriety of Terry's death had completely died away, and I'd sat in sessions and workshops, walked with Charlie on the trail along the waterfront, explored tide pools, eaten some lunches and dinners alone and others with old acquaintances, and generally had a pretty good weekend. There had been some difficult moments, when I saw a bookstore or a restaurant that had been a favorite of ours, or noticed that a place we once liked was gone. But the feelings had passed quickly, and I was actually looking forward to going back this year.

I made it to Monterey early enough this time to register at my hotel and hit the bar and the finger-food table at the Friday evening reception. The crowd around the table put me a little on edge. *I really have been living too long in the backwoods,* I thought, *if I get claustrophobic in the scrum around an hors-d'oeuvre buffet.*

As I was balancing a paper plate of cheese and crackers and grapes and heading for the table where I'd left my beer, I saw Mike coming over from across the room. "Janny," he said, as he reached me, "I heard from Willard today about the Y-STR testing. I called you, but I guess you'd already left."

I wasn't sure I wanted to know, but I asked anyway. "What was the result?"

"Couldn't be better: apparently a faint but readable profile consistent with Scanlon, a minor contributor, unknown, and Howard was excluded."

"All right!" A cracker slipped from my plate onto the carpet.

"It's good. Of course, Willard said they'll argue that the absence of a profile for Howard doesn't mean he didn't have the gun at some point. But given the result, combined with Forbush's testimony, that'll be pretty weak. And now they can release the gun for test-firing."

"Whatever happens, you've improved my weekend."

By coincidence, or synchronicity, one of the workshops that weekend happened to be about DNA typing. Dutifully, I made my way there. The speakers, a molecular biologist and DNA expert, and a public defender experienced in trying DNA cases, mentioned Y-STR typing, but didn't go into detail about it. After the workshop ended, I stood in the little huddle that had formed around them, listening impatiently as other lawyers sought answers to what seemed like interminable questions about their cases. Eventually I reached the front of the crowd, and blurted out, "I have a habeas case where we just got a Y-STR result that excludes our client, and now I have to do a direct examination of the expert, and I don't know what to ask him."

Allan, the public defender answered first. "Can't take yes for an answer?" he joked. "Seriously, congratulations. I don't think I can help you, though; I haven't had a Y-STR case myself."

The scientist, whose name I'd lost track of, weighed in. "I've worked on some. Why don't you give me a call when you're back in your office?" He handed me his business card, and I thanked him profusely and retired in clumsy and grateful confusion, dropping my iPad and trying to avoid swearing at it as I picked it up.

43

One of the first things I did once I was home was ask Mike to forward me the DNA report he had received by email from Willard. After trying to read it, I called the scientist from the DNA lecture. His name was Drew Thornton, and he was a professor at UC Irvine. When we talked, after a couple of rounds of phone tag, I followed up our conversation by sending him the report, too.

He called back the next day. "Wow," he said. "This is all good news."

"Thank you. I just want to make sure I don't mess it up in some way."

"I think you'll be all right. DNA Analytics is a reputable lab, and Dr. Panetti is honest. I agree with her call that the autosomal profile is uninterpretable, but there are forensic scientists who might try to see a peak or two in it that corresponds to your client. Fortunately for you, she isn't one of them.

"The Y-STR profile is very clear. The testing detected

only two haplotypes—that means a group of genes inherited from only one parent. The DNA on a Y chromosome is, collectively, a haplotype because the chromosome is inherited intact, as a unit, from a boy's father. The testing in your case detected Y chromosome DNA haplotypes from two individuals, a fairly clear major contributor and a partial haplotype of a minor contributor. Neither of the haplotypes is Mr. Henley's. So he's excluded.

"Something else you need to understand about Y-STR typing is that Y chromosomes aren't unique. They're carried intact through the male line, meaning a man has the same Y haplotype as his brothers, father, paternal uncles and grandfather, and so forth, along the male line. This could be important, since it appears from the report that one of the haplotypes found matches a person of interest in your case."

"Right."

"Your opponent could argue, legitimately, that the DNA could have come from any one of a number of male relatives. Dr. Panetti has included in her report an estimate of how frequently that haplotype is likely to occur in the general male population, based on databases of known Y-STR haplotypes; it seems to be about 1 in 9,000. But of course it's different if, say, you're in a small community where a lot of people are related to one another."

"That shouldn't be a problem for us," I said. "In our case, the man whose DNA is on there has confessed repeatedly that he killed the victim using the gun it was found on."

"That's pretty extraordinary," Dr. Thornton said. "I'd say you're in great shape with this result. Did I answer your questions?"

"I can't think of anything else."

"Well, if you do, please feel free to call me. Best of luck with your case."

"Thank you so much," I said, hoping I'd understood enough of what he'd told me that I'd be prepared if Laszlo or Willard or the expert tried to play fast and loose with the findings.

Two weeks later, Willard emailed the report on the comparison of the gun from Forbush's locker with the bullets from the scene. The report went on for three single-spaced pages, plus some diagrams, explaining how the examiner, Ken Olsen, had determined the particular model and manufacture date of the gun; how the gun was cleaned and oiled after seventeen years in storage (it was not encouraging that he got the number wrong) and then test-fired; and how the bullets from the test-firing were compared with the bullets found in Lindahl's body, using a comparison microscope. The bottom line, though expressed with caution, was that the bullets recovered from Lindahl were consistent at every point he examined with those test-fired from the gun. Lands and groove matched, class characteristics and individual characteristics matched.

With those loose ends tied up, Willard notified Judge Redd's clerk, and the case was set for two more days of hearings in late March. The hearing was in its home stretch, and I tried to feel prepared for whatever was going to happen. But as I thought that we might finally be finished with presenting our evidence, I kept coming back to the letter. Laszlo had successfully objected to all our attempts to explain its meaning, to establish that it was exculpatory evidence for Howard and that the police and district attorney should have known it was. What we needed was an indisputable expert to interpret it, if that was possible.

Hoping Mike wouldn't mind me striking out on my own a bit, I put in a call to Ida Rader. When she called me back, I explained our plight. "Are there any such experts?" I asked.

"I know someone," she said. "There's a man from, if I recall, the Los Angeles area, a former federal agent, who made a career studying encoded messages sent by gang members. He speaks at seminars for correctional officers. I've heard him, and he knows what he's talking about. I'll hunt down his contact information and email it to you."

Her message came a half-hour later. The man's name was Matt Boyarsky. I found his website and a good deal of other information about him on the Internet, including articles he had written. He had been a cryptographer in the military and after leaving the Army had gone into the federal corrections system, where he had become one of their experts on decoding gang communications. His articles suggested that many intra-gang kites and letters were actually ciphers of one sort or another, substituting symbols for letters or words. But McGaw's letter, with its apparent transparency and innocuous subject matter, was a bit different: a letter that the writer knew would be read by the prison's mailroom staff and intercepted and kept if it appeared suspicious. I hoped Boyarsky could help us with it.

I gave him a call and left a voicemail. When he phoned back, I described the letter to him and explained we were in a hearing on a habeas corpus case. He said he might be able to help us, and told me his fees for reviewing documents and testifying. Then I called Mike.

"We still have some of Dot Henley's money left, so let's go ahead and ask him to examine the letter."

To get Boyarsky the best copy I could, I overnighted one to him. He called me back a couple of days later. "Sorry for the delay," he said. "I was testifying in a case yesterday. Anyhow, I've looked at the letter. It's not really that much of a code, more like the kinds of letters inmates and their families use to communicate things they don't want the prison to know. They use simple things like word substitutions, swapping past tense for present, name changes, and such, to hide what they're really saying. It's all pretty uncomplicated, and also sometimes depends on shared knowledge to make it difficult for an outsider to interpret. There is definitely something secret being passed on in this letter, though, and I can make a fairly good guess at some of it. You said it was sent by an

Aryan Brotherhood member in prison to this Steve Scanlon about a hit he was supposed to do. There seems to be a fair amount about that in there. 'How are your homies there?' and 'Are you still working?' The reference to having had a nice Christmas with his family and wishing him a great '99 looks like a question whether he's going to do the job and a reminder that time is passing and he should be getting on with it—maybe with a veiled threat thrown in about consequences to his family. His 'homie,' in context, would be the intended victim, since they're both living in the same town. The stool pigeon thing is a pretty clear threat, kind of reminding him he'd better stay strong and with the program. The martial arts reference is a bit suspect, too, may have something to do with how he might be planning to kill the guy, though there are too many illegible words in the copy for me to read much into it.

"Funny thing, though, is I've seen this letter before. I wasn't sure at first, it just looked vaguely familiar, and I had to check my old files. I keep a database of encoded gang material I receive, for research purposes. A detective sent this one to me in 1999, and I gave him a verbal report about it. He didn't follow up; I thought the case must have been resolved."

My heart skipped a beat, and I struggled for words, finally managing to stumble through something along the lines of "Oh—really—wow—uh, I don't know how that happened, but we haven't had the case for very long." I said I was pretty sure my lead counsel would want him to testify and told him when the next hearings had been set; he said he was available. I thanked him, hung up, and called Mike.

Mike, instead of being breathless like me, was indignant. "Those sons of bitches," he said. "Springer had the letter, Blaine had the letter in her file. Springer, at least, knew it was just what Scanlon said it was; he consulted a fucking expert! I can't imagine he didn't tell Blaine. And the two of them decided to bury the letter because they didn't need it to convict Scanlon, and they knew it would help Henley. Jesus—we've got to put him on whether the court approves his fees or not."

"I'm just baffled," I said. "Why do you think they would do this just to get Howard?"

"I think," Mike answered, "it was what Springer said in his testimony. He honestly believes Howard is a dangerous guy who needed to be taken off the streets. I don't know whether it's bias against the mentally ill or just against Howard. But he convinced himself and, I guess, Blaine, that Howard was a killer, and after that all he focused on was the evidence that supported his theory. He's a true believer. The letter would just confuse people, so he buried it."

"That's a pretty charitable analysis," I said. "I think what he did was criminal."

"It's psychology," Mike said. "These guys get so convinced they know what the truth is that they find reasons not to believe any evidence to the contrary."

I called Boyarsky to let him know we would be retaining him. To make sure we met the thirty-day requirement for discovery, even though the judge had been happy to ignore it when Willard and Laszlo dumped documents on us at the last minute, we served and filed a notice that we would be presenting his testimony, with a précis of what we expected him to say. "They'll be prepared for him, unfortunately," Mike said, "but I guess it's better than having him excluded."

44

I had now seen all four seasons on the road to Wheaton. It was spring now, with a fuzzy halo of new green leaves on the almond and peach trees, and the political signs blaming Democrats for the shrinking San Joaquin Aquifer another year more worn and faded. With any luck, I thought, I won't have to make this drive again.

The judge had a new clerk, who wasn't familiar with the Henley hearing and needed to be brought up to speed a bit. But Dot and Lillian were there, and Josh Schaeffer had showed up from the *Gazette*. The greetings in the hall had the feeling of a reunion.

Two other people I didn't recognize were also waiting in the hall. Mike said he thought they were the expert witnesses, and I tested his hypothesis by introducing myself to one of them. Her name was Susan Panetti, the lab supervisor whom Dr. Thornton had praised as an honest examiner. She had supervised the testing of our sample at DNA Analytics, the testing laboratory, and had written the report on the results. She was slender and dark-haired and matter-of-fact. Mike had asked me to do her direct examination, and I had talked with her by phone about the testimony she would be giving. There wasn't much for me to do but answer a couple of questions she had about the nature of the hearing we were in. "It's a post-conviction hearing seeking a new trial, with new evidence," I said. "We—the defendant's lawyers—will be doing your direct examination because we have the burden of proof. Kind of a reversal of our usual role."

The other possible expert was talking with Willard and Laszlo, and Mike joined the conversation briefly before we were all called into the courtroom.

Susan Panetti was our first witness. She testified that the DNA on the gun appeared to be from a mix of an unknown number of individuals, male and female. "It always surprises me," she said, "how often we find female DNA on guns."

Panetti's testimony followed what she had written in her report, as Dr. Thornton had interpreted it for me. The DNA on the gun was too degraded for standard testing, but they were able to get Y-chromosome profiles that included Scanlon and excluded Henley.

Willard's cross-examination stressed the fact that Y-STR profiles are not unique and that Scanlon's profile could be expected to occur in about 1 in 9,000 men, and that the absence of a profile matching Henley didn't mean he hadn't handled the gun, just that there might not be a testable quantity of his DNA left on it. It was the type of cross-examination the defense usually does, and I listened to it with a feeling of irony that our positions were reversed.

Ken Olsen, the firearms examiner, testified next. Mike had agreed to retaining him as a neutral expert because he had a reputation for being skilled and impartial, but like most forensics experts, his background was in law enforcement and prosecution-linked laboratories, and he appeared to struggle with the fact that his result in this case favored the defense.

The gun's manufacture date, according to its serial number, was 1985, so it fit with the account he had of its being used in a homicide in 1999 and stored after that. It was in good condition, considering that it had spent over a decade and a half in an attic crawl space in the summer heat of the Central Valley. He had had to clean it and oil it to make it operable without damaging it, but once that was done, he was able to test-fire it using cartridges as similar in type as he could find to those that were likely used in the shooting of Lindahl. Two of the three slugs recovered from Lindahl's body were not very distorted; the third was flattened and broken into several fragments.

Olsen had compared the two relatively intact bullets with the test-fired ones, matching the markings made by their contact with the inside of the gun barrel as they passed through it: lands and grooves, class characteristics present from the manufacture of the gun barrel, and individual characteristics instilled in the gun barrel from use over time.

The subject bullets, he said, were consistent with the test-fired bullets in every respect; there was no dissimilarity that would preclude their having been fired from the same gun. Farther than that he would not go. He declined to indicate how unlikely it was to find two sets of bullets fired from different guns that matched so closely, beyond saying that he had never personally seen such a close match in bullets not fired from the same gun. And, citing forensic best practices, he would not go so far as to opine that the bullets from Lindahl had been fired from the recovered gun to the exclusion of any other.

Having read trial transcripts in which firearms examiners had no problem with opining "with reasonable scientific certainty" that a bullet had been fired by a particular gun, I wasn't impressed with his caution when it came to calling a match for the defense. On the other hand, it left Laszlo with nothing to object to and little to cross-examine about.

Matt Boyarsky had driven up from Los Angeles to testify in the afternoon, and when we broke for lunch, he was waiting for us in the hall. He was a fit-looking man in his mid-fifties, with salt-and-pepper hair, square tortoiseshell glasses, and a pair of lines on his forehead over his nose that suggested years of poring over hard-to-read letters. And an attractive man—I noticed the wedding ring on his finger and gave a small inward sigh.

We discussed his testimony over lunch at the Chinese

buffet, which had become our lunchtime spot for chatting with witnesses. Boyarsky had brought a copy of the letter from his database and the notes that had accompanied his first review of it. "The detective's name was Springer," he said. "With the Wheaton PD." (I liked his voice, too. Damn.) His news was what we'd suspected, but I saw Mike's eyes narrow.

In court that afternoon, Willard and Laszlo looked a little uncomfortable as Mike called Boyarsky to the stand. As Mike questioned him, I felt a subtle change in his tone and manner, a heightened intensity. Remembering Laszlo's many objections, Mike took Boyarsky through his qualifications in great detail: his military career as a trained cryptographer, his long experience studying and decoding the missives of street and prison gangs, the articles he'd written, the classes he'd taught to law enforcement and correctional officers. Laszlo objected anyway, but Judge Redd—who'd certainly qualified many a police officer as a gang expert based on little more than a three-day training class—overruled him.

Boyarsky then went through what was legible of the letter and explained, as he had to me, the manner in which inmates conceal meaningful statements in letters by changes of character and tense and the use of a word to mean something else. He explained the language in the same way he had to me over the phone. When he started to say that the reference to martial arts might be a suggestion about how to go about killing the victim, Laszlo objected to the last sentence as speculation; and the judge sustained the objection. "This letter conveys a message—'What are you doing out there, and why isn't the job done?'—with a threat of consequences."

Then Mike asked Boyarsky, "Have you seen this letter before?"

"Yes," he said.

"When?"

"In 1999." I saw the judge turn his head at that.

"Can you explain the circumstances under which you previously saw it?"

"A Detective Springer, of the Wheaton Police Department, called me and asked me if I would review it and let him know whether it contained a coded message. He sent me a copy by Federal Express, and I examined it and told him pretty much what I've told you today about what I saw as its meaning."

"Did you hear from him again?"

"No. I sent him an invoice and, if I recall, eventually received a check from the city for the consult, but that was all."

"How is it that you know this is the letter Detective Springer sent you?"

"Well, I keep a database of coded communications for purposes of my research. I included a copy of that letter in it. When I received the copy you sent, it rang a bell; I knew

I'd seen something very similar before. So I consulted my database and found the earlier one, with my notes of where it came from."

Laszlo spent his cross-examination sowing doubt about Boyarsky's ability to read what he had into the bland and often illegible phrases of the letter, questioning how he could tell, except by rank speculation, that the letter said anything beyond what it said on the surface. Boyarsky referred again to his experience studying coded communications and deciphering them, and pointed out that I'd told him that Scanlon had said this was the only communication he'd had received from McGaw since leaving prison.

"In light of that, his question whether Scanlon was still working stands out, because there's nothing in the context that suggests he would have known Scanlon had a job. Also, McGaw wasn't actually in a position to know that Scanlon had spent time with his family over Christmas. Of course, in addition to the sort of 'nice family you've got there' kind of threat, he may have been warning Scanlon that the AB had people on the outside watching him. It's also a significant fact that Scanlon himself immediately understood the letter for what it was."

After Boyarsky was excused, Laszlo asked the judge for permission to recall Springer the next morning as a rebuttal witness. The judge granted his request, adding, "I'd like to hear from him."

Mike had been working on his closing argument for a

week, and that evening I helped him make some final tweaks, listened to him recite it, and pronounced it good.

When we arrived in court the next morning, Springer was there, and Sandra Blaine was with him.

The case was called, and Laszlo called Springer to the stand.

"Detective Springer," the judge said.

"Your Honor."

Willard asked him if he remembered consulting an expert about the McGaw letter.

"I do not. It's been almost twenty years since the Lindahl murder, and I've worked on a lot of cases since then."

He'd heard about the inmates who had testified at the habeas hearing that Scanlon was an Aryan Brotherhood associate and had been ordered to kill Lindahl. "I don't tend to believe them. They're a gang of violent criminals, and they have their own agendas. Besides, even if Scanlon wasn't lying about the AB, in my mind it never ruled out that he took money and drugs from Henley, too."

Willard summarized what Boyarsky had said about the meaning of the letter. Springer was dismissive. "I don't see how you can read that much into it," he said. "And besides, it doesn't add anything; Scanlon already said the AB was involved."

"Even if the letter was evidence that the Aryan

Brotherhood wanted Scanlon to kill Lindahl, would you have considered it exculpatory evidence?" Willard asked.

"No," Springer said. "We had enough evidence from witnesses that Henley wanted Lindahl killed and hired Scanlon with the proceeds of his drug dealing. Henley was guilty whether or not the Aryan Brotherhood also wanted the man dead."

On cross, Mike got Springer to admit that he wasn't disputing Boyarsky's testimony that the consult had taken place or that he had received information from Boyarsky that the letter did at least appear to be what Scanlon had told Sunderland it was.

"I just don't remember any of it," he said.

"Then you don't remember whether you thought the letter might be exculpatory?"

"No. But I can't imagine that I did."

"And you don't recall whether you gave the letter to Ms. Blaine?"

"True."

"Or whether you discussed your consult with Mr. Boyarsky with her?"

"No."

"Do you remember why you thought the letter was worth asking an expert about?"

"I do not."

During the brief recess that followed, I said to Mike, "Well, that was pretty bald-faced."

Mike nodded. "I just wanted to ask him, 'You know you're lying, don't you?' I almost wish I had."

Sandra Blaine wanted to testify again, Willard said when we reconvened. Mike pointed out that she had already testified that she had not seen the letter or been aware that it had been recovered until last fall, and asked for an offer of proof of what she intended to say now. Willard said, "She wants to be clear that Springer did not talk with her about the letter or his consultation with Mr. Boyarsky. She is anxious to clear her name in all this."

"She's already denied ever seeing the letter," Mike objected. "I don't see what having her say the same thing again would accomplish at this point."

Judge Redd agreed. "I have heard from Ms. Blaine previously. I don't think further testimony about her unawareness of the letter would add to the evidence already presented. There has been a lot of testimony presented here, and some of it has been pretty repetitive. Unless Ms. Blaine has something new to say, I'm sustaining the objection."

And so it was over, except for the final arguments. The exhibits marked for identification were offered and accepted into evidence with remarkably few objections from Laszlo, and Mike began his argument, summarizing the evidence Henley had presented, both in the pleadings in his habeas corpus case and at the hearing, and explaining why the evidence of his innocence and of the concealment of exculpatory evidence by the prosecution required that he be granted a new trial.

I could tell Mike was still angry about the cover-up as he went through the evidence of Howard's innocence that was known before his trial—but he channeled his feelings into an effective speech. "We have heard that Steve Scanlon confessed repeatedly to committing the murder of Lindahl for the Aryan Brotherhood. He told at least two people that Henley had nothing to do with it. He said he had a letter from an AB shot-caller that confirmed his assignment— the same letter had already been found and given to the police and apparently the district attorney, and its meaning as a warning and reminder to Scanlon was affirmed by an expert. None of this was presented to the jury at Howard Henley's trial.

"And new evidence has come to light, which we have heard in this court. Several former members of the Aryan Brotherhood have confirmed that Lindahl was greenlighted by the gang, and that Scanlon was assigned to kill him. Dwayne Forbush has testified that he sold a gun to Steve Scanlon and did not sell one to Howard, contradicting Freddy Gomez's pretrial statements that he directed Howard to Indio when Howard asked where he could buy a gun, and that he'd seen Howard hand a revolver to Scanlon. The gun itself has been found and matched to the bullets that killed Lindahl. DNA testing found Scanlon's profile on the gun, but not Howard's. There is, at this point, a mountain of evidence that Howard Henley did not solicit the murder of Jared Lindahl; and all the government has are unreliable and refuted statements of an informant looking for a deal. The government's misconduct in this case was egregious; it has left a man who is almost certainly innocent on death row for eighteen years. That and the sheer amount of exculpatory evidence not only warrants, but requires, that Howard Henley be given a new trial," Mike ended, his eyes flashing in anger.

Willard summed up for the prosecution, pointing out the evidence that showed Henley had hired Scanlon, how much of the evidence in Henley's favor had in fact been known before his trial, the time that had passed, and the lack of credibility of the inmate witnesses, including Scanlon, who had testified at the hearing. The new evidence, he said, was merely cumulative; it confirmed Scanlon's confession that he had killed Lindahl and that the killing had an Aryan Brotherhood connection, but it did not preclude the possibility that Scanlon had taken money or drugs from Henley to do the same hit.

Mike summed up with a brief, intense rebuttal, pointing out that Forbush's testimony and the DNA testing showed that Freddy Gomez had lied about Howard buying a gun from Forbush and giving it to Scanlon and made it that much more likely that Gomez had lied in his further statement that Henley had paid Scanlon to do the killing. "Howard Henley has been on death row for eighteen years," he reminded the judge, "while evidence that could have freed him was ignored or deliberately concealed from his defense."

The arguments complete, the judge pronounced the matter submitted, and we thanked him and stood as he rose from the bench and left the courtroom.

"*Ite, missa est,*" Mike said under his breath, as we turned to leave. The smart-ass reply I thought of making stuck in my throat.

4 5

We were all tired. After goodbyes in the hallway to Dot and Lillian and reassurances that we thought it had gone pretty well in the end, Mike and I both went straight home without lingering in Wheaton.

Defense attorneys tend to get the blame for the slow progress of death-penalty cases, but the judicial system moves at its own pace. After the hearing, Mike and I, and the attorneys general, filed post-hearing briefs arguing what the proven facts were and how the law applied to them. Mike and I argued, of course, that the evidence required the granting of a new trial, and Willard and Laszlo disagreed. Then we waited.

I went back to my routine of work and calls from Howard and other clients, current and former, exercise classes, gardening, and occasional musical evenings at Vlad's and trips with Harriet to nurseries and garden club meetings. Once, I had to travel to San Francisco for an oral argument and stayed an extra night to make welfare calls on

Howard, Walt Klum and Arturo Villegas at San Quentin. But mostly I stayed near home, and I wanted nothing else. The judge's report would happen when it happened, and aside from occasional stabs of anxiety, I surprised myself by how philosophical I felt about it.

But Mike's call, when it came, brought with it a jolt of panic. "Is it the report?" I asked him in a faint voice.

"Yes and no," he said. "I just got a phone call from Josh Schaeffer, the kid at the *Gazette*. Judge Redd is recommending that Henley get a new trial. Josh isn't a lawyer, needless to say, so he didn't follow the reasoning that well, but he was reading bits and pieces of the report to me over the phone. He's scanning the report to email it to me; I'll forward it to you. I guess it'll be a couple of days before we get it in the mail."

"Oh my God," was about all I could say, as I slumped back in my chair. "We actually won?"

"Yeah," Mike said, and I could hear the relief in his voice. "I don't know if I could have taken losing this one."

I read the report as soon as Mike emailed it. Judge Redd had outdone himself; his conversion from the trial judge who had no doubt of Howard's guilt to a fact finder convinced that a terrible wrong had been done to a possibly innocent man was hardly short of miraculous.

He began with the facts of the murder and the evidence found in the initial investigation, noting that Scanlon had confessed to the murder and spoken of the Aryan

Brotherhood's involvement days after it happened, and that he had never varied from that account. He wrote that at the time of his trial Howard, though obviously mentally ill, had the right to fire his attorney and go it alone because the United States Supreme Court had held that anyone mentally competent to stand trial at all could not be denied his constitutional right to represent himself. He defended his rulings at Howard's trial, excluding the testimony of Sunderland and Niedermeier, on the grounds on which the state Supreme Court had upheld them: that Howard had failed to lay an adequate foundation for their admission and that the part of Scanlon's statements to the two men implicating the Aryan Brotherhood was not admissible evidence under any exception to the hearsay rule.

His recommendation that the state Supreme Court grant Howard a new trial was based on two findings. The first was that the letter from McGaw was, as it turned out, known to, and in the possession of, Detective Springer before Howard's trial. While Springer might have been justified in believing, just from the text of the letter, that it was not relevant to Howard's case, he had more than that: Scanlon's statement that the letter was a directive from the Aryan Brotherhood, his own confirmation that McGaw was an AB associate, and the opinion of his expert, Matt Boyarsky. At that point, the judge said, the prosecution had an obligation to turn the letter, and the information they had obtained about it, over to Howard and his advisory counsel. The question whether

Sandra Blaine knew of its existence did not need to be answered, because the prosecution's obligation to turn over exculpatory evidence applied to law enforcement agencies as well as the district attorney.

The judge found that Dwayne Forbush's testimonial evidence was not available at the time of Howard's trial, because Forbush, awaiting his own trial, would have exercised his Fifth Amendment privilege not to testify at Howard's.

Scanlon's testimony and that of the other inmates about the Aryan Brotherhood and the Lindahl killing also fell into the category of newly available evidence, since all of them were active AB members and associates at the time of Howard's trial, and it was very unlikely that any of them would have testified to what they said at the hearing. So was the evidence of the gun, including the firearms comparison and DNA testing, because Forbush would not have revealed the existence and location of the gun before Howard's trial.

The standard for ordering a new trial based on newly discovered evidence of innocence is a difficult one to meet: the evidence has to be credible and material and of such force and value that it would have more than likely changed the outcome of the trial. It was difficult, given the way in which Henley had conducted his defense, to assess what might have changed the outcome. However, the judge doubted that either the newly available testimony or the physical evidence alone would have been sufficient. But the sum total of all of it, combined with the evidence of the letter known before trial and concealed, met the burden, in his view. His conclusion was that a new trial was warranted, both because of misconduct by the police before Howard's trial and new evidence discovered afterward.

Ed was in the Napa Valley making cabinetry for a winery, but I invited Harriet and Bill to join me for drinks and dinner at Vlad's that evening. The place was busy—tourist season was starting, and a local old-time group was playing—but we found a table and drank pints of IPA and porter and ate our fill of garlic fries, mini-tacos, and small plates of mac and cheese, tapping our feet to the music. Somewhere after the second pint I decided that someday I wanted to learn to play mandolin and got sentimental when the band played an old Scots fiddle tune. In the end, Bill, who had stayed pretty sober, drove us home in my car, with Harriet and me laughing in the back seat and promising to pick up his truck for him first thing in the morning. "Oh, you'll be sorry you said that," he said, "when the two of you wake up tomorrow."

Judge Redd's report was not the end of the game, though. The judge's mandate from the state Supreme Court had been to act as what the court called a referee, to take evidence, make factual findings, and make a recommendation. The state Supreme Court would review Judge Redd's findings and recommendation and decide whether it agreed with him that Howard should get a new trial. First there would be another round of briefing, in which the losing side made objections to the referee's findings and the winning side defended them, and then more waiting while the Supreme Court weighed everything before it and decided how it should rule.

So we filed our defense of Judge Redd's ruling and waited some more. Mike presented our claim for fees and expenses to the state Supreme Court, saying, "Maybe they'll be inclined to be generous since we won," and divided the money when the check arrived. They weren't as generous as they might have been, but it was enough to allow me to dream briefly of a trip to Paris before I consigned most of it toward a new roof for my house.

46

Mike visited Howard soon after Judge Redd issued his report, to give him the good news. He told me afterward that Howard seemed somewhat pleased, but concerned that he'd be retried and sent back to the Row. "I told him I really doubted it," Mike said. "They have the gun and the DNA and Forbush's testimony, and Scanlon and the other AB guys who testified at the hearing would testify at a retrial. And they have to deal with the embarrassing facts about their concealment of the letter. I doubt that this case will be tried again. I'm not sure how he took that; you know how he is. He seemed to listen and then went off on some other topic."

But with the prospect of exoneration and release from prison before him, Howard changed. He still called, but only every couple of weeks, to rant about why the court was taking so long to issue a decision and why we didn't do anything to hurry it along. He spoke of suing the lot of them—the prison, Sandra Blaine, the judge, the mayor of

Wheaton, the governor. He complained about the prison— the guards, the food, the absence of air conditioning. But the urgency and focus of his anger was missing.

It isn't unusual for men faced with the prospect of leaving prison to be anxious or even depressed about what the future might hold for them. When I traveled to San Quentin to visit Walt Klum, I saw Howard also. He looked older and tired, but when I asked him how his health was, he said he felt okay. He seemed a little more connected with reality: in between descriptions of the multitudinous conspiracies against him and flights into strange realms of religion or space travel, he sometimes talked about getting out and seeing his mother, of eating home cooking and learning about computers and the Internet. Often he worried that the state and his family would make him see doctors, put him on medication, or try to lock him up in a mental hospital. I tried to keep him focused on the positive side of his freedom, and he seemed a little easier when the visits ended.

Once he talked about the parable of the prodigal son. "My father was like his father; he thought I was dead, and then I came back. And," he said, with something like satisfaction, "my brothers were angry like his brothers." He stared intently at me across the table. "Now my father's dead."

"I know," I said.

"Yes," he said again, impatiently. "He's dead, and so am I. How do I come back if he isn't there?"

"But you're not dead," I said lamely.

"I'm dead," he said. "I was dead the last time, too, but they didn't know."

One day I had a letter from him in my mail. I waited until I was back home to open it; Howard's letters, though less frequent, never included anything but long rants and drawings. This one was a single folded sheet of paper with the words, "John 8:23" hand printed in the center.

I looked up the verse online. There were many versions, from different editions of the Bible, but the King James, which was generally Howard's choice for quoting, read, "And he said unto them, Ye are from beneath; I am from above: ye are of this world; I am not of this world." It seemed of a piece with what he had been saying in his visits and phone calls; I figured I'd mention it to Mike, the next time we talked.

In October, wildfires burned through Sonoma County. All of us, it seemed, knew someone who had lost everything as the fires burned past the woods and into the town itself. Mike's home and office were okay, but some friends of his who had lost their home were staying at his house. Harriet and Bill were also hosting refugees. I didn't have room for guests, but I was playing foster mom to a couple of dogs while their families found someplace to live.

On a hazy October morning, after I had spent an hour walking Charlie and his foster sisters in the smoky air and was bringing a basket of apples into the kitchen, I heard my office phone ring. I left the basket on the counter and hurried to pick it up. It was Mike.

"I just heard from the prison," he said. "Howard passed away last night."

I felt as though the floor had dropped away under my feet.

"Oh, no," I said.

"Yeah." He sounded as stunned as I was.

"What happened? Do they know?"

"Not much yet. What the woman from the prison said was that guards found him in his bed and unresponsive. He apparently died in his sleep. I just called Dot; she'd already heard from them."

"How is she taking it?"

"Pretty well. I asked her if she'd be okay—not that there was much I could do, I guess—and she said she was and that she'd called Lillian and her sons, and they were coming over. I offered to work with the prison on funeral arrangements, but she says they'll take care of it.

"When I get the death certificate," he said, "I'll notify the court. They'll probably let the case drop as moot, but I'm going to file a motion asking them to write an opinion because the misconduct here was so egregious, it needs to be called out in some way."

I said I'd help him with it.

I went through the rest of the day feeling lost and unfocused. I couldn't stay at my desk, so I set up the apple peeler and made applesauce, then took the dogs for another walk. There was an exercise class that afternoon, and I decided I really should go. When I met Harriet at her house, I told her, "Howard Henley died last night."

"Oh, no, you mean the man whose case you just won?"

"Yeah."

"Oh, I'm sorry. All that work you did—and he was innocent, too. And now he'll never get to be free—that's really terrible."

"It really is," I said. "You know, I've known him for probably fifteen years. He used to phone our office and ask for me, then spend the whole call ranting. Why I should miss that, I don't know. But he didn't deserve to be there."

Getting winded and sweaty was good therapy, though my heart wasn't in it. When I came back to the house I fed my menagerie of cats and dogs and made myself a dinner of scrambled eggs and toast and applesauce and ate it without really tasting it. The evening opened out before me oddly empty. I couldn't shake the feeling of floating that had followed me through the day.

I turned on the television, then turned it off. I tried to think of something to read or some music to play that would calm the bitterness I felt and the resurrected sense of loss. I felt, for once, very alone, with no one to talk to, to help me think through the tangle of thoughts and emotions that seemed to tighten around my chest. It occurred to me that in all the time I'd been acquainted with him, I'd never really learned who Howard was. He was a cause, an innocent man wrongly on death row, but on a personal level, he was a stranger, difficult and incomprehensible. I saw of him, at different times, a constant minor irritant, a collection of exasperating demands and delusions, a man in self-inflicted torment from his paranoia, the unlucky possessor of a damaged mind. If there was any solid ground beneath his shifting mental state, I never found it. His life had seemingly been nothing but a twisting path downhill, a succession of self-inflicted wounds culminating in a farcical trial and a wrongful conviction of murder. And he had died in prison for no good reason.

"I'm dead," he had told me in my last visit. "I was dead the last time, too, but they didn't know." But in a way we did know. We knew that there was no way we could save Howard because whatever there was to save was gone. We had fought to keep him from being killed by the state and to free him from prison, for the principle that innocence should be vindicated. We had satisfied our own need that justice should be done. But Howard the man was beyond saving, a man no one wanted, who couldn't exist in the world, who had nowhere to go because he had lost the ability to be free.

I wondered how it must feel to be a parent and watch your child turn into someone like Howard, alien, hostile, frightening. I thought of Lyle Henley's endless patience and Dot's vigil at the courthouse, the unconditionality of their love for the solemn boy in the old photos and the crazed, ruined man that had both been their child. Of Howard and Steve Scanlon, each in their separate hells, and of Springer and Blaine, unshaken in their belief that they had done what was right.

In the end, we had won—but won what? There was a poem by Wilfred Owen I'd learned in school, about a soldier killed in World War I; I looked it up online and read it again.

Move him into the sun—
Gently its touch awokc him once,
At home, whispering of fields half-sown.
Always it woke him, even in France,
Until this morning and this snow.
If anything might rouse him now
The kind old sun will know.

Think how it wakes the seeds—
Woke once the clays of a cold star.
Are limbs, so dear-achieved, are sides
Full-nerved, still warm, too hard to stir?
Was it for this the clay grew tall?
—O what made fatuous sunbeams toil
To break earth's sleep at all?

And finally the floating feeling ended, and I sank to earth. *Goddammit, Howard,* I thought, *I can't even cry for you.* I walked into the kitchen and poured myself a glass of brandy.

47

Dot Henley invited Mike and me to a memorial for Howard, to be held at her house on the Saturday of Veteran's Day weekend. "It's nothing formal, just a get-together for our family and friends. I'm hoping the weather holds, and we can have a barbecue," she said, "but if not, we'll just have it inside."

Mike and I decided to save the planet by driving down together from his house, leaving early in the morning to get there by two or three in the afternoon.

There had been rain a few days earlier, but the day of the memorial was dry and the sky a wintry blue dotted with white clouds. A dozen or more cars were parked in the roundabout and driveway in front of Dot's house, and a few more on the road in front.

Hearing voices from behind the house, we walked around it and found a sizeable group of people socializing or picking from the food tables. Bob and Kevin and a couple of other men were cooking hamburgers and hot dogs on a fancy gas barbecue. It was Kevin who first noticed us and waved us over.

"Ms. Moodie, Mr. Barry! Good to see you—come on in and have a beer and some food, and say hi to Mom." He smiled, his face flushed from the heat of the grill. "We've got burgers, hot dogs, beans, potato salad, lot of other things, and drinks with and without alcohol. My buddy Zach here is cooking tri-tips, and those'll be up pretty soon. Help yourself; and Mom's over there." He gestured toward somewhere in the middle of the tables and chairs scattered on the lawn.

We walked in the direction he had pointed until I spotted Dot sitting in an Adirondack chair, with several people around her. I recognized her friend Lillian, but no one else.

Dot was wearing a dark blue dress and a black cardigan. She seemed a little tired, but cheerful. She smiled when she saw us. "I hope you don't mind my not getting up," she said, "but once I sit in one of these chairs, it takes a lot of effort to get out."

"I know that feeling," I said.

Someone found chairs for Mike and me, and we sat with the group around Dot. Lillian said hello and introduced her husband Ed, a solid man in jeans and a madras shirt. Dot pointed out the people gathered around: a cousin, a couple of tall, athletic grandchildren, and her daughter, Howard's younger sister, Corinne. "Corinne came down here from Ashland, Oregon. She works in the costume department at the Shakespeare Festival, and she's an—honey, I can never pronounce it…"

"Ayurvedic practitioner."

"Right."

Corinne was a faded bohemian, with long, graying hair bound in a single braid at her back by a crocheted piece of blue yarn. She wore a long dress in Indian cotton, a brown paisley print shawl, and an array of necklaces and rings. She gave me a vague smile and said, "I'm glad you tried to help Howard. I didn't stay close to him. I had to let go of a lot of anger."

"What was the problem?" I asked.

"Really nothing anymore," she said. "Just that I was here, in high school, when he started acting weird and getting into trouble. It was awful to go through all that as a teenager. You can imagine what it was like, how the other kids talked about him, and me. I was always different anyway, and I'd get called Crazy Corinne because I was Howard's sister. It took me a long time to stop blaming him for my problems."

"I'm sorry," I said. "I know he could be difficult."

"Corinne," said Dot from her chair, "let Ms. Moodie settle down and get something to eat."

"Oh, yes," Corinne said, "I forgot. You should do that. There's an awful lot of meat here today, but I made sure Mom and Bob got some vegetables."

Mike had made his way to the food, and I joined him. We filled our plates, got bottles of beer, and found places at one of the tables on the lawn, where we introduced ourselves to a few more family members and friends.

After I'd eaten, I made my way to another table I'd spotted. It was set up on the patio, like a shrine, with memorabilia and candles and an urn. There were a couple of school award certificates, a class ring, and behind the urn a poster collage of photos of Howard. Most were from his childhood: baby pictures of Howard in Dot's arms, as a toddler holding Lyle's hand, Christmases under the tree, family photos from trips, Howard with a dog, Howard and his brothers and Corinne at Disneyland, the photo I'd seen in Dot's album of Howard in his Boy Scout uniform. His high-school graduation photo was there; in his robe and mortarboard he was unsmiling, already a little distant. This was the age, I remembered from my reading, when young people often experience the first terrifying delusions and hallucinations that foreshadow the psychosis that will later overwhelm them. There was one of him as a very young man, on a boat. And then almost nothing—one snapshot of him and his father outside a building, Lyle smiling, Howard thin and unkempt.

Dot came over, walking gingerly across the lawn with her cane, and stood with me. "Lillian and Bob's daughter Megan made the collage for me. He was a good-looking kid, wasn't he? And so nice. He loved that dog, and he cried so when she got hit by a car and had to be put down."

"How have you been?" I asked.

"All right," she said. "My hip surgery is scheduled for right after New Year's."

"Congratulations," I said. "Hope it goes really well."

She thanked me. "I'm a little worried, needless to say. But the doctor says I'll be fine."

"Did the prison ever tell you what the cause of Howard's death was?" I asked.

"Heart failure, they said. Apparently he'd had heart disease for a while, but he was too out of touch with reality to understand what his symptoms were and tell anyone."

"This must be hard," I said. "It sort of upends the order of things to have your child die before you."

She hesitated a moment before answering. "You know, after I heard Howard had passed away, I realized that in some way he died for me a long time ago. After he disappeared that time, to Florida or wherever, he came back a stranger, and I just didn't know him. And then he went to prison, and I never saw him after the first couple of times we visited; he hardly seemed to care that I was there. I did what I could for him—we all did—but when he actually passed away, I realized I'd done my grieving for him years ago—he'd been gone for that long. So it wasn't that bad.

"Lyle, on the other hand—Lyle never gave up on him, never stopped loving him and feeling pain for his condition. Howard was his firstborn, and he had a special place in Lyle's heart. It hurt him to see Howard become so angry and hostile to us, and it broke his heart when Howard was convicted and sent to death row. I went to the hearings for Lyle's sake, really, as much as Howard's. I hope that up in heaven he's able to see that you proved Howard's innocence."

"I hope so, too."

Bob joined us. "The tri-tips are ready. Mom, you should let me get you some." He glanced at the table shrine and said to me, "You know, maybe some good came from all your work after all. You probably don't know this, since it's local news, but after Judge Redd came out with his report, the *Gazette* published a big story and an editorial about Howard's case and how he ended up on death row even though he was probably innocent—the evidence they hid, the way they relied on that drug addict Gomez to make their case, the fact that they didn't do anything to find out if Scanlon was telling the truth, and the way they kept the testimony about Scanlon's confession out of the trial."

"That young reporter, Josh, wrote it, the one who came to the hearings," Dot interjected.

"That's right," Bob said. "Springer retired not long after that. Sandra Blaine was running for reelection this year, and she lost to some up-and-coming DA from her office. I don't think Howard's case made all the difference—Wheaton isn't the kind of place to turn on a DA for occasionally convicting someone who's innocent. But some of the shine was taken off her record, and people saw her a bit differently."

He glanced again at the urn. "It's funny. Kevin and I said we'd go out tomorrow and scatter Howard's ashes somewhere. But we're at a loss where. Howard was here, but not here, if you know what I mean."

I nodded.

"Yeah. There isn't any place we can think of that meant anything to him, or that you could say was someplace he'd have belonged."

"What about Sandra Blaine's lawn?" I joked.

Bob laughed. "I like that."

"I was just kidding," I said, in sudden panic.

"No, seriously, I think that's what we should do. I'll talk to Kevin, and we'll go there really late tonight. Come on, Mom, let's go find Kevin and get you and Ms. Moodie a slice of that tri-tip."

When I woke the next morning at our favorite hotel in Wheaton, there was a text on my phone from Kevin. It was ten seconds of video of a shadowy, bent figure moving backward while pouring something from a jar. "Did it!" he wrote. "Got out just ahead of the cops."

I don't know what Howard would have thought about it.

4 8

There is sort of an epilogue to Howard's story. A few months after we notified the state Supreme Court of Howard's death and filed our motion, the court issued an order. It wasn't long, but it said:

The Court has considered the record in this case and the findings of the referee on the order to show cause issued on January 11, 2016. Because of the death of the petitioner, there is little to be gained by issuing an opinion in this case. However, because the evidence in the record suggests that the petitioner may have been wrongly convicted, the court is reluctant to declare it moot. Therefore, the petition for writ of habeas corpus is granted, and the judgment in Taft County Superior Court case No. 22976 is vacated. This court having received and filed a certified copy of a certificate evidencing the death of petitioner Howard Henley during the pendency of these proceedings, the superior court is directed to enter an order to the effect that all proceedings in the cause have permanently abated.

What the order meant was that the court had told the superior court to set aside Howard's conviction and all the proceedings against him. The law requires this when someone dies while he is appealing his conviction; in essence, it is a legal act of compassion that places the deceased defendant, in the eyes of the law, back where he was before he was convicted. It doesn't necessarily apply to someone like Howard, whose appeal had finished. Had the court simply dismissed Howard's habeas petition as moot because of his death, he would have died a convicted felon.

By its ruling, the court did at last what the legal system had failed to do while Howard was alive: it gave him back his innocence.

ACKNOWLEDGEMENTS

Madman Walking was inspired by a real case; the defendant, like Howard Henley, died on death row some years ago. The problem illustrated in this book, of mentally ill defendants in the criminal justice system, persists into the present; and too many men and women with serious mental illnesses are still unfairly tried and imprisoned.

My thanks to Scott Kauffman and Bicka Barlow, the dedicated and resourceful attorneys for the man in the actual case, for their help in providing me transcripts and other case materials, and to Dr. Christie Davis and Jennifer Friedman for instructing me on the science of forensic DNA typing of aged samples.

My editors, Miranda Jewess and Sam Matthews, not only made the book better than the manuscript I gave them, but were unfailingly encouraging and patient with my anxieties.

Finally, I thank my life partner, Michael Kurland, a wonderful writer himself, for coaxing me into pursuing my dream of writing fiction, mentoring me, reading my efforts, and giving me valuable feedback. It was his faith in me, through all my doubts about myself, that brought about my becoming, rather late in life, a published author.

ABOUT THE AUTHOR

L.F. Robertson is a practicing defense attorney who for the last two decades has handled only death penalty appeals. Until recently she worked for the California Appellate Project, which oversees almost all the individual attorneys assigned to capital cases in California. She has written articles for the CACJ (California Attorneys For Criminal Justice) Forum, as well as op-ed pieces and feature articles for the *San Francisco Chronicle* and other papers. Linda is the co-author of *The Complete Idiot's Guide to Unsolved Mysteries*, and a contributor to the forensic handbooks *How to Try a Murder* and *Irrefutable Evidence*, and has had short stories published in the anthologies *My Sherlock Holmes*, *Sherlock Holmes: The Hidden Years* and *Sherlock Holmes: The American Years*. The first Janet Moodie book, *Two Lost Boys*, was her first novel.

TWO LOST BOYS
L.F. ROBERTSON

Janet Moodie has spent years as a death row appeals attorney. Overworked and recently widowed, she's had her fill of hopeless cases, and is determined that this will be her last. Her client is Marion 'Andy' Hardy, convicted along with his brother Emory of the rape and murder of two women. But Emory received a life sentence while Andy got the death penalty, labeled the ringleader despite his low IQ and Emory's dominant personality.

Convinced that Andy's previous lawyers missed mitigating evidence that would have kept him off death row, Janet investigates Andy's past. She discovers a sordid and damaged upbringing, a series of errors on the part of his previous counsel, and most worrying of all, the possibility that there is far more to the murders than was first thought. Andy may be guilty, but does he deserve to die?

"This is a must-read"
KATE MORETTI, NEW YORK TIMES BESTSELLER

"Suspense at its finest"
GAYLE LYNDS, NEW YORK TIMES BESTSELLER

TITANBOOKS.COM

AFTER THE ECLIPSE
FRAN DORRICOTT

Two solar eclipses. Two missing girls. Sixteen years ago a little girl was abducted during the darkness of a solar eclipse while her older sister Cassie was supposed to be watching her. She was never seen again. When a local girl goes missing just before the next big eclipse, Cassie – who has returned to her home town to care for her ailing grandmother – suspects the disappearance is connected to her sister: that whoever took Olive is still out there. But she needs to find a way to prove it, and time is running out.

COMING MARCH 2019

DID YOU ENJOY THIS BOOK?

We love to hear from our readers.

Please email us at Reader Feedback or write to

Titan Books, 144 Southwark Street, London SE1 0UP

To receive advance information, news, competitions,
and exclusive offers online, please sign up for the
Titan newsletter on our website.

For more fantastic fiction, author events,
competitions, limited editions and more…

VISIT OUR WEBSITE

titanbooks.com

LIKE US ON FACEBOOK

facebook.com/titanbooks

FOLLOW US ON TWITTER

@TitanBooks

EMAIL US

readerfeedback@titanemail.com